Garland for a Dead Maiden

CRIME FICTION
The 'Carnaby' series (1967–84)
Carnaby and the hijackers
Carnaby and the gaolbreakers
Carnaby and the assassins
Carnaby and the conspirators
Carnaby and the saboteurs
Carnaby and the eliminators
Carnaby and the demonstrators
Carnaby and the infiltrators
Carnaby and the kidnappers
Carnaby and the counterfeiters
Carnaby and the campaigners
Fatal accident (1970)
Panda One on duty (1971)
Special duty (1971)
Identification parade (1972)
Panda One investigates (1973)
Major incident (1974)
The Dovingsby death (1975)
Missing from home (1977)
The MacIntyre plot (1977)
Witchcraft for Panda One (1978)
Target criminal (1978)
The Carlton plot (1980)
Siege for Panda One (1981)
Teenage cop (1982)
Robber in a mole trap (1985)
False alibi (1991)
Grave secrets (1992)

Written as Christopher Coram
A call to danger (1968)
A call to die (1969)
Death in Ptarmigan Forest (1970)
Death on the motorway (1973)
Murder by the lake (1975)
Murder beneath the trees (1979)
Prisoner on the dam (1982)
Prisoner on the run (1985)

Written as Tom Ferris
Espionage for a lady (1969)

Written as Andrew Arncliffe
Murder after the holidays (1985)

Written as Nicholas Rhea
Family ties (1994)
Suspect (1995)
Confession (1997)
Death of A Princess (1999)
The Sniper (2001)

THE 'CONSTABLE' SERIES
Constable on the hill (1979)
Constable on the prowl (1980)
Constable around the village (1981)
Constable across the moors (1982)
Constable in the dale (1983)
Constable by the sea (1985)
Constable along the lane (1986)
Constable through the meadow (1988)

Constable at the double (1988)
Constable in disguise (1989)
Constable through the heather (1990)
Constable beside the stream (1991)
Constable around the green (1993)
Constable beneath the trees (1994)
Constable in the shrubbery (1995)
Constable versus Greengrass (1995)
Constable about the parish (1996)
Constable at the gate (1997)
Constable at the dam (1997)
Constable over the Stile (1998)
Constable under the Gooseberry Bush (1999)
Constable in the Farmyard (1999)
Constable around the Houses (2000)
Constable along the Highway (2001)
Constable over the Bridge (2001)
Constable goes to market (2002)
Heartbeat Omnibus I (1992)
Heartbeat Omnibus 11(1993)
HEARTBEAT TITLES
Constable among the heather (1992)
Constable across the moors (1993)
Constable on call (1993)
Constable around the green (1994)
Constable in control (1994)
Constable along the lane (1995)
Constable versus Greengrass (1996)
Constable in the dale (1996)
Constable about the parish (1997)

THE 'MONTAGUE PLUKE' SERIES
Omens of death (1997)
Superstitious death (1998)
A well-pressed shroud (2000)

Written as James Ferguson
EMMERDALE TITLES
A friend in need (1987)
Divided loyalties (1988)
Wives and lovers (1989)
Book of country lore (1988)
Official companion (1988)
Emmerdale's Yorkshire (1990)

NON-FICTION
The Court of law (1971)
Punishment (1972)
Murders and mysteries from the North York
 Moors (1988)
Murders and mysteries from the Yorkshire
 Dales (1991)
Folk tales from the North York Moors (1990)
Folk stories from the Yorkshire Dales (1991)
Folk tales from York and the Wolds (1992)
Folk stories from the Lake District (1993)
The Story of the Police Mutual Assurance
 Society (1993)
as Nicholas Rhea
Portrait of the North York Moors (1985)
Heartbeat of Yorkshire (1993)
Yorkshire days (1995)

GARLAND
FOR A
DEAD MAIDEN

Nicholas Rhea

Constable • London

First published in Great Britain 2002
by Constable, an imprint of Constable & Robinson Ltd
3 The Lanchesters, 162 Fulham Palace Road
London W6 9ER
www.constablerobinson.com

ISBN 1–84119–483–2

Printed and bound in Great Britain

A CIP catalogue record for this book
is available from the British Library

Chapter One

Detective Inspector Montague Pluke, the officer in charge of Crickledale Sub-Division's Criminal Investigation Department, had recently been appointed Honorary Custodian of Horse Troughs for England's largest county, North Yorkshire. It was a rare honour. As probably the only such office-holder in England, he regarded this as the pinnacle of his career in troughs and wondered whether it allowed him to use the letters CHT after his name. Upon his appointment that memorable Friday, the Chief Executive of the County Council had said, 'Mr Pluke, I am delighted you have accepted this position. We need an expert on the history of horse troughs as well as someone with a thorough knowledge of the North Yorkshire terrain, in addition to the necessary administrative skills. Your task will be to trace, classify and catalogue every trough, to ensure they are correctly sited and maintained, to see they are not vandalized and that the water flows constantly without pollution. I have the greatest faith in you, Mr Pluke, and perhaps I should add that I do know your books. *The Horse Troughs of Crickledale and District since the Sixteenth Century*, fully illustrated by the author, is one of my favourites. I appreciate your new responsibilities must be undertaken in your spare time – as a busy detective your leisure time must be very limited – and I stress there is no pressure to complete this project within a specified time. I look forward to your continuing contribution to Yorkshire history and conservation.'

'I am very honoured to be offered this opportunity,' Pluke had said with due modesty.

5

'Well, that's settled. I'll make the necessary arrangements to confirm your appointment. Have you any questions?'

'Only of a minor nature. For example, if I discover a trough which has been damaged or which is not flowing freely, or which has even vanished completely, what are my responsibilities? Do I commission the repairs or replacement myself?'

'Good heavens, no, Mr Pluke. You need to notify us. You should contact my Trough Liaison Officer – TLO – and she will contact the appropriate authority – the highways department, National Park, local authority, parish council, Yorkshire Water, private owner or whoever is responsible for that particular trough or trough site. They will be expected to arrange the repairs, renovation or replacement; if they fail to do so within a specified time – two months from service of the appropriate notice – then the county council will do so and send them an invoice. The authority for this procedure is the Horse Trough (Conservation and Protection) Act, 2001, section 12, one of New Labour's many radical schemes for the countryside.'

'Good. That eases my administrative burden somewhat,' Pluke had sighed.

'It goes without saying we will provide whatever assistance you require, Mr Pluke, clerical or otherwise. Our aim is to have a county rich with horse troughs, all fully operational and conserved for posterity. We want them to become objects of interest to tourists and experts alike – and indeed to horses. The only burden I have to impose upon you, Mr Pluke, is to furnish me with a quarterly report. I require that for presentation at county council meetings – to account for any expenditure that might be incurred. I am sure you understand our funny little financial ways. My secretary will provide you with the necessary forms, especially drafted for this purpose, and you'll see they want you to list all troughs visited during each quarter, along with their precise location, their prevailing condition and any recommendations for renovation or improvement. You may discover that many are missing, no

doubt stolen by townspeople for their gardens and rock-
eries, and in such cases we shall have to decide whether or
not to replace the missing item, preferably with an exact
replica. Some might be lost in undergrowth, some may
have been moved to new locations or even built into stone
walls. We'd like you to find them all. Tough decisions may
be needed, Mr Pluke. And more than a touch of diplomacy
when troughs are discovered on private land. Postage and
other expenses will be paid at current county council rates.
With your permission, I shall ask our press officer to issue
a news release to announce your appointment. It is important that members of the public are aware of your
conservation role. With wide-ranging experience, I'm sure
you can understand why you have been chosen for this
most important of conservation tasks.'

'I will do my best,' Pluke had smiled. 'And suitable
publicity might prompt members of the public to notify
me of hitherto unknown troughs.'

And so a dazed but proud Montague Pluke had walked
out of County Hall clutching a briefcase full of specially
printed stationery and lists of names and telephone numbers of those from whom he could seek assistance or
advice.

At home, Millicent, his devoted wife, had prepared a
sumptuous celebratory meal of roast potatoes and chicken
but he merely toyed with his drumstick as he contemplated his new responsibilities. To find and record *every*
horse trough in North Yorkshire's extensive rural landscape could take years . . . It was a lifetime quest, he
realized, but it was something he could continue after
retirement from the force. And then if you added East
Yorkshire, West Yorkshire and South Yorkshire, along with
those former parts of the county now administered by
Cleveland County, Durham and Cumbria, it could develop
into an entire new career. Maybe a deputy honorary Custodian of Horse Troughs would be needed if the scheme
was extended to include the whole of Yorkshire? And a
full-time secretary? And a fully equipped Trough Custodian's office, ideally in Crickledale? And a dedicated

website – www.plukehorsetrough.co.uk perhaps? And a monthly magazine called *The Trough*? And then, perhaps, expansion throughout Great Britain and the foundation of the National Horse Trough Society – with M. Pluke CHT as President . . .

For all his expansive ideas, however, Montague realized he was rapidly growing older and that the task, however worthwhile, might become too burdensome even for a man of his undoubtedly robust constitution and fortitude. But who, among his contemporaries, possessed such dedication and such an unrivalled knowledge of troughs and their history?

As he discussed his new responsibilities and concerns with Millicent, she smiled and said, 'Montague, if they hadn't thought you were right for the job, they wouldn't have appointed you. You are Britain's leading authority on horse troughs.'

'Perhaps I am, but I did make it quite clear that the detection of crime takes precedence over any horse-trough duties,' he assured her.

'One would never have expected you to think otherwise, Montague, but I am sure your travels around the more remote parts of Yorkshire, even in the course of your detective work, will reveal unknown troughs. That is to be expected. There will surely be times when your two responsibilities create a conflict of interests but you have the strength of character to cope with that kind of moral and practical dilemma. Now, it is Friday, you have no police commitments over the weekend, it is your weekend off and you can relax. You know I will help you with your trough research, just as I like to assist with your detective work –'

'Millicent, I do value any assistance you can provide but I cannot put you at risk from savage and ruthless villains with whom I must deal as a police officer.'

'No, of course you can't, and you don't. I just like to know what's going on so I can keep my ears open for gossip at the Ladies' Club or when I'm in town. Now, eat your supper and then you must tell me everything about your interview with that gentleman from the county council.'

Having climbed from his bed that Saturday, taking care to place his right foot first upon the floor and ensuring he did not get out of bed at the wrong side, Montague decided to commence his trough duties without delay. He would begin with a ramble around Thordale, one of the smallest and more remote dales within the North York Moors.

During his work in and around the moors, Pluke had gained a little knowledge about the area's lore and legend. For example, he knew that two reputed witches had lived there – Aud Lizzie and Aud Jemima; even today, a rowan witchpost survived in a farmhouse. On a more rational level, there had been a drowning in the gill and the alleged murder of a young man, also by drowning in the same gill. Both had happened in bygone times. For all its sombre reputation, however, the dale was picturesque in its isolated setting yet it was away from the more popular of the tourist trails and inhabited only by a handful of sturdy moorfolk.

Its rugged and heather-clad surroundings provided Thordale with a bleak and harsh beauty for it comprised little more than a picturesque gill which tumbled through a steep and narrow gorge before flowing along the floor of the small and fertile dale below. There was only one house and four farms in that short dale, the house being near the head and two farms occupying sites at either side of the gill's lower reaches, albeit separated by open fields. Thordale extended only four miles and there was no village or focal point such as a shop or inn. Its human population was small but it did boast several hundred blackfaced moorland sheep who spent their lives on the heather-clad moors, as well as dairy cows, pigs and poultry who lived on farms in the dale. At the lower end of Thordale, however, was the village of Gunnerthwaite which boasted a shop, while a few more villages with pubs, shops and garages lay within a five- or six-mile

radius. For Pluke, however, Thordale had one very important feature: the solitary house at the dalehead, something
Pluke had spotted by chance while examining a local
map.

It was this opportune sighting which had prompted him
to dedicate this weekend to an exploration of Thordale.
The house was called Trough House so where better to
begin his duties as Custodian of Troughs? Clearly, Trough
House was of sufficient stature to justify inclusion on a
map. Because he'd never explored Thordale – nor learned
anything of Trough House – he had decided to ask
Millicent to accompany him. It would be a pleasant outing
and they could take a picnic, an ideal start to his new role
as Montague Pluke, CHT.

'You'll need your notebook and camera, Montague.'
Millicent was most enthusiastic and was bustling about the
house while Pluke checked his route. 'And your walking
boots, a spare pair of socks, a spare sweater and your
waterproofs. Just in case. And your mobile phone. I don't
want you breaking a leg and being marooned on those
moors . . .'

Within the hour, and with Pluke making sure his rabbit's
foot was in his pocket for good luck, they were heading
north from Crickledale. Millicent was at the controls of
their Vauxhall Astra because Montague was considered too
inept at the wheel. As a shaken police driving instructor
had once observed, 'The minute he gets hold of a steering
wheel, Pluke becomes a danger to all road users and
I recommend that he never be allowed to drive police
vehicles – or any other vehicle.' At work, therefore, Pluke
was driven by his deputy, Detective Sergeant Wayne Wain,
but at home Millicent acted as family driver.

They drove towards the distant and mysterious North
York Moors, with the treeless heather-clad landscape rising
ahead and the White Horse of Kilburn shining brightly
below the summit of Roulston Scar. Pluke was acting as
map-reader, guiding Millicent through the picturesque
lanes in their gorgeous autumn colours and taking a scenic
route rather than the more direct major roads as he rea-

soned he was more likely to discover hidden or unknown horse troughs in the verges of the minor roads. Eventually, without finding any noteworthy troughs, they reached a lofty point high on the bleak Rockdale Moor, where they came to the end of the metalled carriageway. Beyond lay a remote, windswept plateau and they had to make use of an unsurfaced track.

Grouse butts had been constructed along one side and they provided some shelter for moorland sheep which, even in the depths of winter, grazed on these open, treeless and inhospitable heights. A grouse protested as it clattered from the thick heather, shouting, 'Go-back, go-back, go-back,' but there were no other signs of life, the only indication that man had once worked on these moors being the distant peat bogs, now disused and full of water which glistened in the sunlight. There was little evidence of their former role. With the passage of time and the effect of nature, they looked like a dozen or so natural but very symmetrical ponds although the earth along their eastern edges appeared to have been ravaged very recently. It was almost as if a giant earth-digger had run amok, while the heather above and behind them, a blanket of pure purple during August and early September, was now reverting to its winter shade of reddish-brown.

A few patches of brilliant purple did remain, however, and the total effect was one of a picturesque and dramatic setting. After driving along the track, they reached a small wooden signpost which announced 'Thordale 2', then added beneath, 'Steep Hill Ahead, 1-in-3. 33%. Narrow road. Unsuitable for caravans, coaches and heavy goods vehicles.'

'Are you sure this is the right way?' Millicent had shown the first signs of uncertainty. The ground seemed to fall away suddenly, almost as if they were about to drive off the edge of the world – beyond, though, were extensive views with the North Sea in the far distance and Thordale in the foreground. It was almost like an aerial view with Thordale's four farms clearly visible. Gunnerdale, famed for the collection of maidens' garlands in its parish church, lay in the far distance, a clutch of dark stone houses sheltering in a cleft in the windswept moors.

'Yes, down here,' Pluke reassured her. 'It's very steep but according to my map, Trough House is not far ahead. This track takes us down into the head of the dale where it joins a surfaced road – the gill will be on our right. It's more civilized down there and Trough House is about half-way down on the left. It's clearly shown on my map.'

Bumping and bouncing, their little car coped admirably with the steep and narrow track as heather brushed its sides and loose stones rattled beneath. Even with the gill so close, the track bore signs of becoming a secondary watercourse in heavy rain. Their route was pitted with deep ruts which had been gouged from the earth to reveal rocks and boulders.

Pluke realized that the moors above, being covered with peat, marshland and acres of sphagnum moss, would gather rainfall like a huge sponge. The peat bogs could accommodate only so much and any surplus water would make its way down this gill, the only watercourse leading from these heights. Tough hawthorns and rowans grew among the rocks which formed its upper banks, finding security for their roots well above the waterline; birds would nest here too, but there was always a risk from floodwater. There would be times, in conditions of melting snow or heavy rainfall, when the powerful flow would be swollen with excess water rushing from the heights and it would be more than the narrow gill could cope with. The surplus would roar down this lane or find some other convenient route where it would uproot plants, shift rocks and create deep ruts in the lane or surrounding landscape. The pitted surface of their route gave testimony to those ruthless floods and to the power of nature; it seemed there had been some heavy rain very recently because the gill's bed and the adjacent landscape bore signs of being ravaged by untamed forces. This was wild country indeed – little wonder Thordale had such an awesome reputation.

Millicent displayed her skills as she guided the bouncing vehicle ever more steeply into the head of the dale and soon they had descended to a level where deciduous trees flourished and green fields patterned the more gentle landscape. It was a dramatic contrast to the heathery windswept heights only a short distance above while the peat-coloured waters of Thordale Gill rippled and dashed nearby, leaving traces of white froth as they tumbled down the rock-strewn course.

Towards the bottom of the hill were mountain ashes in their brilliant red and gold autumn colours, their branches laden with luscious rowan berries; there were silver birches whose trunks looked like shining white metal against the grim backcloth of moorland granite, and dark alders which thrived along the water's edge. Stout oaks stood firm beside the beck too, their gnarled old boughs looking as if they'd been there for centuries. Surely they had. And all around was a vast acreage of maturing heather, remote and mysterious. But Pluke, concentrating on his map, seemed oblivious to his surroundings. As Millicent coaxed the Astra down the final yards of the descent, he was still trying to determine the precise location of Trough House.

'It should be somewhere here,' he muttered. 'On our left hereabouts, behind that wall, among those trees.'

'Maybe it's just a ruin,' she suggested. 'Some maps don't distinguish between ruins and existing farms.'

'You could be right,' he had to agree. 'But surely there would be something left? A pile of stones, some evidence of a dwelling? Perhaps you could pull in at the first available place and park? Then I can get out and have a look.'

'There's nowhere to park on the hill,' she snapped. 'It's far too narrow.'

'At the bottom then?' he suggested. 'We're nearly there.'

She continued with great care, still bouncing over the rocks and sometimes catching the exhaust on the ground or brushing against protruding heather or hawthorn shrubs. But as the ground levelled out, she found a suitable stretch of flat grassland. It overlooked the gill and seemed firm enough to take the weight of their car, so she eased its wheels on to the grass, turned it around to face outwards, then parked.

'There,' she said. 'Now you can go and find Trough House while I have a walk near the stream. This is a really pretty place, nice and sheltered.'

'You're not coming with me?' he asked her with some surprise.

'If there's just a pile of stones, it's not likely to be very interesting.' She smiled sweetly. 'I'd rather walk beside this gill, it will be nice and relaxing after driving down that hill!'

'But suppose I find a hitherto unknown horse trough? Wouldn't you want to share that moment with me?'

'Montague, you are the horse-trough expert, that kind of discovery is for you and for you alone. If you do find something fascinating, come and tell me and I'll have a look. Now off you go, and don't forget your camera and notebook. You have a key for the car. If you get back before me, let yourself in. The picnic things are in the boot so if you finish early shall we look for somewhere with a nice view? The hills above Gunnerthwaite maybe?'

'If that's what you want. So where will you go while I'm searching Trough House?'

'I'll be right here on the banks of this beck. I can just see a lovely pool among those trees, it looks delightful, a quiet place where I might see dippers and minnows, kingfishers even. Don't worry about me. Now, off you go and good luck.'

'Well, just as you wish, my dear.'

She had never shown any great enthusiasm for his horse-trough experiences – tolerance was a more apt word – even though she was proud of his achievements. She left the car and as he watched her diminutive, grey-haired, bespectacled and sensibly shod figure in her bright red coat depart towards the banks of the gill, he reflected that Millicent might even have become a poet. She did have a very romantic turn of mind.

As he locked the car, he felt a sudden chill, almost as if

14

an icy wind had swept from the moors to produce goose-pimples all over his body. Shivering briefly, he dismissed it as a mere atmospheric feature of this area's mini-climate, and continued his mission. Equipped with his trough-hunting accoutrements, Montague Pluke embarked on the short climb part-way back up the hill towards the supposed site of Trough House. He was a distinctive sight in his ancient, threadbare yellow Burberry check coaching coat with its shoulder cape and black check markings, his slightly too-small panama hat with its sky blue band, his sky blue bow tie (blue being his lucky colour), his half-mast trousers which matched his overcoat, to say nothing of his beige spats, pink socks and brown brogues.

His strong characterful face with heavy dark-rimmed spectacles and good strong teeth was topped by a thatch of thick dark hair which had a habit of always protruding from beneath his hat at every angle. Had anyone seen the clothing beneath his top coat, they would have discovered a matching jacket rich with hanging pockets fastened with buttoned flaps. And beneath that, he wore a chestnut waistcoat complete with silver pocket watch and chain. Montague never claimed to be tidy or well dressed, but he was comfortable and he was distinctive. Once seen, never forgotten.

Today, though, he felt sure he would be lucky – after all, he had his rabbit foot in his pocket and those rowans were considered an omen of good fortune, although they did sometimes flourish near old burial places. He did not think this area was an old burial place – that kind of thing was more likely to be situated on the heights from which he had just descended. Now, though, his destination was a patch of oaks, sycamores, birches and hawthorns which flourished in a field on the hillside. Their presence, along with the briars and nettles which formed a dense covering of undergrowth, did suggest the place had formerly been used for human habitation. A check on his map reassured him that he was approaching the site of the former Trough House. That belief was supported by evidence of stone walls, now derelict, but apparently built originally in the form of oblongs and squares. The remains of a small house or an outbuilding? Or a shelter for livestock? Very few dressed stones remained, certainly not enough to have formed a farmhouse or even an outbuilding. So who had removed them? Rockery builders from the towns, no doubt.

There were no signs saying it was private or that tres-passers would be prosecuted, and an old wooden gate led into the field which contained those walls. As there seemed to be no prohibition against entry, he pushed open the gate, but at that instant the air was filled with the terrifying screams of a very distressed woman.

'Millicent?' he shouted.

Chapter Two

Montague's immediate reaction was to run towards the scream but his police training took over as he remembered the words of his old training sergeant: 'Never run into trouble. Walk slowly, take your time, look serious. Remember the decorum of your profession and uniform, don't lose your dignity and make sure you've got plenty of time to work out what you're going to do before you get there. And don't panic. The public doesn't like police officers who panic.' And so he reduced his gallop to a rapid walk.

'Montague?' He heard her voice again, no longer a scream but still carrying a note of urgency. 'Montague, can you hear me?'

It *was* Millicent. Not just any woman screaming. It was his Millicent! Forgetting decorum, Pluke broke into an ungainly lolloping sort of gallop with coat tails flying and one hand holding his panama on to his head. Everything bobbed up and down as he ran – camera, hat, mobile telephone, loaded pockets . . .

'Millicent?' He began to feel breathless as his brogues thudded down the hill and hammered across the flat stretch of ground where the car was parked. He shouted anew: 'Millicent? Where are you?'

'Here, Montague.' Her voice came from downstream. 'On the bank near the pool. You must come quickly.'

The immediacy seemed to have evaporated but he did not slacken his pace as he hurtled towards her.

'What is it?' he was shouting as he found a footpath beside the water.

At this point, the rush of the gill had slowed to a gentle flow and it had broadened to form a deep and placid pool as it meandered along the more level ground. He could see the water was a beautiful transparent brown colour, rather like cold tea he thought, the result of passing through peat on the moors above. Racing beneath the canopy of dense alders, gnarled oaks and graceful rowans, he saw Millicent ahead. Her bright red coat made her instantly visible on the bankside as she stared across the water, apparently rooted to the spot. She didn't even look at him as he approached and, from the expression on her face, he realized she was concentrating upon something unpleasant.

'Millicent?' he panted. 'What is it?'

'Look,' and she pointed to the far side of the stream, to the high bank which overhung the deep and almost circular pool. The water's constant flow had carved this tranquil place, a quiet retreat at the foot of the moors. The water seemed quite deep for it was dark, calm and smooth with just the hint of a gentle flow through the central area. It was like a massive vat of new beer in a brewery – then Pluke shivered again, involuntarily, as he noted a tangle of alder roots at the far side. Those long tough fingers of wood helped retain the earth and secure the rocks which were buried in the bankside. Behind the roots the ground had been scooped away by the relentless force of the water. The roots, gnarled and darkened, had no earth into which to secure themselves and so they stretched down from the top of the bank and their tips disappeared into the edge of the water. The result was a shallow cavern-like hollow with the roots looking like the widely spaced bars of a prison window or a monster's colossal ugly fingers or even a mangrove swamp. The cavern, much of it in shadow, was some three feet high by nine feet long, and something – someone – was lying partially inside it and partially in the water. In the subdued light, it was very difficult to see but as he concentrated upon the object he thought it looked like a bundle of dark and soggy clothes.

'I think it's a woman,' whispered Millicent.

'What makes you think that, Millicent?' He peered across the water, trying to identify the object in the dark cave. 'It looks like a bundle of old wet clothes to me. It's not a dead sheep or a cow or a dog or anything like that, is it? Some animal that's been swept into that cavity?'

'If you go further that way, just a yard or two, and look back, you can see her head and hair. I'm sure it's a woman and not an animal, Montague. I screamed, it was such a shock, then I shouted but she didn't respond. I haven't been across, the pool's too deep anyway, but I didn't want to touch her, I couldn't. I didn't know what to do.'

'Leave this to me, Millicent.'

Pluke could discern what looked like a head of light brown hair near one end and what seemed to be a pair of bare feet at the other. It could indeed be a human body but most of it was wedged deep in the cavern behind those bar-like roots; it seemed to be almost entirely covered by a long dark brown garment of some kind.

He said, 'You could be right, Millicent. I'll have to check. Wait here and guide me when I get to the other side. I'll have to find a way across, this pool's too deep.'

'Do be careful, Montague, I don't want you falling in and drowning.'

'It's just a moorland stream, Millicent, there'll be plenty of shallow crossing places higher up,' he informed her with confidence.

'She might have fallen in, she might have drowned.'

'I am in no danger of drowning, I can assure you. And we do not know with any certainly that this is a deceased female person. One must never jump to conclusions, Millicent. It could be anything. An animal. A tailor's dummy left here here as a joke, a sackful of turnips fallen off a tractor, a discarded scarecrow. First, a careful examination must be made followed by a professional assessment of the circumstances. That is my immediate duty.'

Millicent remained as Montague ventured upstream to find a crossing place, ideally a natural dam of large stones. Although there could be other deep pools, some with underground caverns, most of the paths of such moorland streams were very shallow and their beds were littered with large stones. Even the biggest boulder could be dislodged by floodwater, however, and come to rest against others to form whole or partial dams. These created very convenient crossing places for pedestrians. As Pluke clambered up the bed of the gill, there was more evidence that it had recently been in flood; the scouring of the banks was plain to see and it was probably associated with the ravages on the moor near the peat ponds, the sign of a recent cloudburst.

Soon he found a suitable crossing place about fifty yards upstream and paddled across the natural barrier with arms outstretched like a tightrope walker, regaining the far side without even dipping his toes in the water. His crossing accomplished, he was able to progress downstream along the opposite bank.

'I can't look underneath the bank from here, the overhang's too great,' he shouted to Millicent as he hove into view. 'Can you guide me to the alleged body?'

'Just another few yards,' she called as he pottered along. 'Towards me . . . below those big alders and oaks . . . yes, just there. Now look under the bank, directly beneath your feet, Montague. You're standing right on top of that cave.'

Stooping almost double while hanging on to the branch of an alder for safety, he was still unable to peer beneath the overhang although he could see what appeared to be bare feet so he decided to jump down to the water's edge. There was a narrow band of sandy earth beside the flow, as well as the inevitable stones and rocks, but now he had no qualms about getting his feet wet. Such were the demands of his duty that a couple of wet feet were of little consequence. He found a suitable launching point, leapt from his perch – a height of three or four feet – and found himself on the edge of the water. And still without wetting his feet. It was the work of a moment to reach the object of his quest; and what had first appeared to be little more than a lifeless dirty wet heap did now appear to have human form.

The clothing was an all-embracing earth-coloured dress with long sleeves but the bare toes of a pair of feet were touching the edge of the water. The dress came down to the ankles, effectively covering the rest of the body. The hands were delicate, he noted, and well manicured with remnants of clear varnish on the nails, and the feet looked cared for. He halted to study the scene before making the final approach, knowing he must physically examine the discovery to establish exactly what it was. He did call once or twice, saying inane things like 'Hello' and 'Are you all right?', wondering perhaps if the person was asleep. Had she been exploring the banks of the gill for otter holts or fox earths, he wondered, and met with an accident? But when no reply was forthcoming he manoeuvred himself through the shallow water on convenient rocks so as to bypass the remains and gain a better view. Now, there was no doubt. These were the remains of a woman.

It was clear she had been dead for some time. That was evident both from the stench which wafted towards him and from the fact that her head had very little flesh left upon it. One ear had survived – he noted it had been pierced but there was no ear-ring. In fact, there was no jewellery of any kind. Her teeth looked sound. The flesh that was visible – on her lower arms, feet and neck – was a dark brown colour, the colour of peat. She'd been very well hidden, the colour of her skin and clothing lending to her concealment. Millicent had been extremely observant; most people would never have noticed her, or never realized it was the sad remains of a human being.

'You are right, my dear,' he called from his vantage point. 'It is a very deceased female person who has been here for some time. Now, I must not contaminate the scene, just in case we are dealing with a murder. I'll come back to you soon.'

'Oh, Montague, this is dreadful, that poor woman . . . I'll go back to the car, I can't bear to stay here a moment longer . . .' and so she hurried away.

Not wishing to subject Millicent to any further unpleasantries, Pluke allowed her to leave and then made a careful examination of his surroundings, jotting down reminders in the notebook he carried for his trough records. He noted the colour of the water, the route of the gill, the body's proximity to his car-parking place, the remoteness of the locality, the absence of buildings and people, the state of the body and the odd resting place behind those widely spaced, but natural bars. It was a brief but efficient assessment which would be transferred to his police notebook at the first opportunity. Currently he was off duty but when an off-duty police officer – especially a senior detective – discovers a body in suspicious circumstances, then he becomes immediately on duty. And so it was with Montague Pluke. No longer was he the Honorary Custodian of Horse Troughs for North Yorkshire – now he was Detective Inspector Montague Pluke, head of Crickledale Criminal Investigation Department. He felt sure this moorland gill did not lie within his jurisdiction but such formalities were now of secondary importance. His examination of Trough House now abandoned, he returned to the car to find Millicent in the driving seat. She looked pale, miserable and forlorn.

'Let's go,' she said. 'I must get out of here, I can't bear to stay a minute longer, Montague . . . that poor woman.'

'I cannot leave until the local police arrive,' he told her with all the firmness of his rank. 'I must direct the investigating team to the scene.'

'Oh, dear, you're on duty now, aren't you? But this is a long way from Crickledale, it's not your responsibility, surely?'

'On such occasions, boundaries become irrelevant, Millicent.' He now sounded very professional. 'I am a police officer and I must do my duty.'

'You must do whatever you have to do, Montague. But can I go?'

'You can, but you will have to be interviewed because you discovered the body. Now, where's my mobile telephone?'

'It's on your trousers belt, in its pouch,' she said gently. 'So what if I leave? I mean, I don't have to stay, do I? I can go and find a nice place to have my picnic, then I could return to collect you. And I can be interviewed at home, can't I?'

'I see no reason why not,' he consented. 'I don't want you to remain in these harrowing circumstances.'

'So how long shall I give you?'

'A couple of hours should be adequate. I should be able to summon the local police and get them to the scene well within that time.'

'And then you'll be free to come home? It is your week-end off.'

'Yes, of course.'

'I don't want you involved in a murder enquiry on your weekend off, Montague, especially if it is not within your sub-division.'

'It might not be murder, Millicent. She might have died accidentally, drowned perhaps, or died from exposure on these moors, or she might have committed suicide. It could even be a natural death, a heart attack perhaps.'

'All right. I'll go but I'll leave your share of the picnic and I'll collect you in a couple of hours or so.'

Looking distinctly unhappy, Millicent started the engine and drove away down the dale. Montague hung his picnic knapsack on the branch of a convenient tree, then loosened the catch and ferreted inside for the salt cellar. Millicent always included salt on their picnics and, sure enough, he found the small pot wrapped in a plastic bag, a simple device to catch stray particles. Carefully, he extracted the pot, took it to the edge of the stream and poured a good measure into the water.

This was to fulfil an ancient superstition. Many rivers had a reputation for claiming human life and although some could be temporarily placated by a single death, others were known to claim more. The Trent, for example, was said to claim three lives per year as was the Dee, while the Dart and Tweed took only one each. Some were content with just one human life every seven years. And this was surely the gill which had claimed previous lives in this dale. If that was the case, it seemed no one had placated the water at that time. Now Pluke had poured in a generous measure of salt. That should prevent any future drownings, he told himself.

Satisfied that he had achieved a vital piece of work, he activated his mobile telephone and called Crickledale police station. His call was answered by Sergeant Cockfield pronounced Cofield, the officer in charge of the tiny control room.

'Good morning, Sergeant, this is Detective Inspector Pluke speaking,' he began.

'Ah, good morning, sir. You're not in the office today, then?'

'No, it's my weekend off, Sergeant, or to be precise, it was my weekend off. I am reporting the discovery of a female body,' and Pluke then provided details of Millicent's discovery, along with a map reference.

Sergeant Cockfield pronounced Cofield listened carefully then checked his own map of territorial boundaries and said, 'Well, sir, Thordale lies just outside Crickledale Sub-Division but only this morning we received notice that Detective Inspector Pankin, in whose area it does lie, has been taken into hospital with suspected appendicitis. Headquarters have directed that our sub-division takes temporary responsibility for all matters of criminal investigation during his absence.'

'So the case is mine after all?'

'I'm afraid so, sir. So do you want a full call-out? Or is this death from natural causes?'

'We shall not know for some time, Sergeant, so yes, implement the usual call-out procedures but limit the number of detectives to a dozen – I don't think a full complement is justified unless the death is suspicious. I shall remain until the arrival of my teams and will be in charge of the enquiries.'

'I shall make the necessary arrangements, sir, and will notify the coroner. Now, your deputy, Detective Sergeant Wayne Wain – you'd like him to attend?'

'I would and I shall remain until they arrive, my mobile telephone will be switched on. This is not an emergency, Sergeant, she has been dead for some time.'

'Understood, sir, no flashing blue lights and all that.'

24

The routine procedures were swiftly put into operation, even though it was a Saturday morning. Knowing approximately how long it would take to muster the necessary experts, and fully aware that the body would not go away, and that it was highly unlikely anyone else would venture into that particular place in the meantime, Pluke decided he could usefully occupy himself by returning to Trough House. It was only a minute or two's walk away and he might have an uninterrupted, if brief, search among those trees and ruins.

With another bodily shiver, Pluke plodded up the rough, steep hill towards Trough House. From this angle, he had a fairly good view. The site contained a clump of trees, a mixture of deciduous and coniferous, and among them he noted elderberry shrubs and rowans, both species being planted close to dwellings in times past to ward off evil spirits and thwart the machinations of witches. The taller trees would have been grown to provide shelter from the ever-present wind, while the ground-covering of briars and nettles was evidence of the bygone presence of human beings. As he passed through the fieldgate, he gained a clearer view of the former buildings, now little more than a collection of exposed foundations surrounded by the remains of stone walls. There were no roofs, floors or windows and each derelict building was in a tumbledown condition with very few remaining stones. As he pottered among the ruins, he found clear indications of a former dwelling-house and its surrounding outbuildings but every portion had now been overtaken by the wilderness. None of the former walls was more than knee high, there was no furniture, no woodwork at all, no windows, no staircases leading up or down. Nothing but the scant remains of a bygone farm. And – it was evident – no horse trough.

He spent a little time trying to clear some tangled undergrowth in the hope it might reveal a trough or two, but without the necessary tools it was very difficult and he found nothing. He did feel, however, that a farm of this size would have had a trough or even several, and that their supplies would have come from water abstracted from the moor, probably from the same moor-top source as the gill which flowed nearby. Unless the farmer and his family, along with his animals, took their water directly from that gill? That was very possible, even if it was some distance away. So when did the house fall into this dreadful decay? And why?

He realized how little he knew about the history and topography of Thordale – it was one of those secluded and unknown parts of the moors. As he struggled to recall something of its mysterious past, he heard a tractor chugging along the lane. It went up the hill and continued until its noise disappeared; he did not see it, for the the bushes and high walls of the lane concealed it from view. Absorbed in his self-imposed task, Pluke lost track of time but he was reminded of his crime detection role when he heard a car ease to a halt not far away. Quickly, he abandoned his search and hurried back to the side of the gill. Wayne Wain's car was parked on the grass earlier used by Millicent, and emerging from it was the detective sergeant, more than six feet tall with dark curly hair, exceedingly handsome, very well-dressed and smiling with pure white teeth.

When he noticed Pluke's rapid approach, he said, 'My goodness, sir, we can't let you go anywhere without finding trouble, can we? So what have we this time?'

'A deceased female person, Wayne,' said Pluke. 'Lying on the edge of the gill not far away from where we are standing.' Pluke, who never addressed subordinates by their forenames, felt he could call his sergeant 'Wayne' because it sounded exactly like his surname.

'Suspicious, according to Control?' added Wayne Wain in the form of a question.

'"Cause of death undetermined" is perhaps a better phrase at this stage, Wayne. It could be from natural causes but I must treat it as suspicious due to the circumstances. I did not examine the corpse other than to establish she was not alive. It is not the most pleasant of objects and is lying in a most curious place, hence my suspicions. But follow me.'

With coat tails flying and his panama threatening to

bounce from his head, Pluke hurriedly led his sergeant towards the bank from which Millicent had made her grim discovery.

'You got here in good time, Wayne,' complimented Pluke. 'Well ahead of the rest.'

'I was already part of the way here, sir, I'd been to a reported burglary on this side of Crickledale, so I had a head start on the others. You'll be in charge, will you, if it's a murder?'

'Indeed I shall, Wayne. Millicent will be far from pleased, she was looking forward to a pleasant weekend hunting troughs on the moors, here in this very dale. She found the body, you know.'

'Did she? So where is she now, sir?'

'She wanted to get away from the scene, she's gone down the dale. It is all rather harrowing for her, you understand, not being a police officer. Coping with dead bodies is not part of her daily routine.'

'I'll have to interview her, sir, in considerable detail, about finding the body. You do appreciate that the finder of the body is an immediate suspect if the case does turn out to be a murder?'

'I am very aware of that, Wayne, and Millicent does know she will be subjected to an interview, but I assure you she is innocent. She had no idea the body was here.'

'But she did find it in a very remote and almost inaccessible place, sir. Some murderers do hide bodies in remote places, and then pretend to "find" them.'

'Wayne, you are being highly officious and I hope you do not make such allegations when you interview my wife. Millicent is not guilty, I know that and you know that. This is the first time either of us have been to this place. Now, let me show you this body although it will be advisable to await the arrival of the forensic teams before you go right in and contaminate the scene.'

'I am not in the habit of contaminating scenes of crime, sir!'

'The fewer of us trampling around the far bank, the better,' Pluke stated with an air of finality. 'Now, this is

27

where Millicent was standing when she noticed the bodily remains.'

By now, they were standing on the bank as the deep pool spread before them and Pluke pointed out the long-rooted alder below which the corpse lay in its cavity of earth, rock and tree roots.

'That's a woman?' asked Wayne Wain in some disbelief.

'It is what is left of one, but she has – er, had – light brown hair,' Pluke told him. 'If you venture a little further to your left, you will see her head, severely injured. Her feet are touching the water's edge and they are bare. You can see her hands too, well manicured with varnish on the nails – damaged varnish, I might add. Much of her exposed flesh has decomposed and there are signs of a battering, a savage one, I'd say. She's wearing a long dark brown dress and the exposed parts of her flesh are covered with mud or sediment. There is earth and sediment in her dress too, quite a substantial amount. Her skin is dark brown, Wayne, so she is well disguised, not at all easy to see in those shadows. Peat stains, I think. I did wonder if she had been buried, what with all that damage, earth deposits and discolouring.'

'She's not easy to see. Mrs Pluke did very well to spot her, sir.'

'Indeed she did, and it does make me wonder how many other people have been here before us and not noticed her. She has been there some time, I am sure. The upper part of her dress is dry, although the part upon which she is lying is wet.'

'It's a very odd place to lie, sir, in that cavity behind those exposed roots.'

'These moorland streams are subjected to regular flooding, Wayne. This one has recently flooded, the signs are readily visible. The water roars down from the heights, the result of melting snow, cloudbursts, heavy rain and so forth, and the force of it can wash objects like dead sheep, tree trunks and other very weighty things, into all manner of peculiar places, even over natural dams formed by rocks and stones. In severe cases, even huge rocks can be rolled downstream. The fact that this woman appears to have been dead for some time, and that we have had several severe rain storms during recent months, does suggest she might have been swept into that space by the sheer power of the water. I believe that is more likely than her being placed there by a killer wishing to hide the body. It would be most difficult for anyone to manoeuvre a dead body into that cavity but a powerful rush of water could do so, especially if aided by subsequent floods. I would not be surprised if she had been drowned upstream in a severe storm and washed down to this point. She might have fallen into a deep pool upstream and drowned, her body thrust to the surface by a surge of new water. Or she might have suffered another form of death on the moors, natural causes, in other words, and been carried here. Or she might be a victim of crime, Wayne, and have been buried somewhere within the watershed of this gill. Her remains could have been unearthed by the power of the floodwater. But all that will be revealed during our investigations, I am sure.'

'So this might not be the scene of her death, sir?'

'It is most probably not, Wayne. Our scene of crime – if it is a crime – could be a considerable distance away. This gill rises high on those moors, deep among the peat and heather, and it tumbles steeply for a long way before it reaches this point. It is more than a mile from here to the summit of this road on Rockdale Moor. And when the gill is in spate, it will be a most powerful and rather terrifying sight. My theory is supported by the fact there were severe storms during the recent summer, Wayne – they received wide publicity. It is hardly likely she drowned in the gill, most of it is far too shallow, although she could have drowned in that pool where she was found – and there may be others just as deep upstream. Judging by the state of the body and her clothing, I think she has been swept for quite a long way over rocks, and so I feel her death must be thoroughly investigated.'

'Message understood, sir,' said Wayne. 'So you don't want me to go over to the other side just now?'

'I think not, there is no reason to do so,' Pluke said, then,

29

hearing the sound of an approaching car, added, 'Ah, I think I hear Millicent returning.'

But it wasn't Millicent. It was a large Volvo estate car which parked next to Wayne's vehicle and from which climbed a young ginger-haired man who said, 'I'm Dr Martin Ingram, I've been sent to look at a body.'

'Ah, good. I am Detective Inspector Pluke of Crickledale CID, and this is my deputy, Detective Sergeant Wain. So where are you based, doctor?'

'There's a group practice at Gunnerthwaite, I am one of the partners. This area lies within our practice, I'm on call today. We act for the local police when required, taking blood samples, visiting sudden deaths and so on. Gunnerthwaite is the village at the end of Thordale, about four miles downstream.'

'Splendid,' beamed Pluke. 'There is no doubt the woman is dead but, as you know, we need that to be certified,' and he then explained about the discovery, detailing Wayne Wain to escort the doctor via Pluke's earlier route. It would enable Wayne to inspect the corpse with the minimum of disruption of the scene. The inspection took but a few minutes after which Dr Ingram confirmed he would certify the death, adding his own view that the remains had been there for some time. His job was not to determine the cause of the death, however; that would be the task of the pathologist. Ingram went to his car and from his briefcase produced a certificate which he duly signed and passed to Pluke.

'Who is she?' he asked Pluke.

'At this stage we have no idea,' Pluke admitted. 'Identifying the remains is high priority.'

'Sorry I can't help,' the doctor smiled. 'Not that there's much of her face to look at, but I don't recognize what is left. She's not one of my patients, we've no one missing from their usual haunts. This is a very extensive rural patch, Mr Pluke, with lots of acres and sheep, but very few people. I would know if a local woman was missing.'

'I'm sure you would,' agreed Pluke.

And with that, Dr Ingram left in his heavy old Volvo,

chugging down the dale as Pluke and Wayne awaited their investigative teams. Before the teams arrived, however, Millicent returned.

'Ah, Wayne.' She smiled at the sight of the handsome detective. 'Now that you are here, perhaps Montague can leave?'

'I'm sorry, my dear,' Pluke said. 'I have been appointed officer in charge of this enquiry and must supervise examination of the scene and removal of the body. But you can go home and Detective Sergeant Wain will drive me to Crickledale in the fullness of time.'

'Oh, Montague, if you hadn't decided to come out here looking for horse troughs, this would never have happened!'

'It would, Millicent, but perhaps not today. However, had you not found the body, the killer – if indeed we are seeking a killer – might have evaded justice. The body would have disappeared completely due to the ravages of nature and in a very short time. It was fortuitous you discovered her, Millicent. Now, I suggest you make your statement to Detective Sergeant Wain and then you can leave. Have you had your lunch?'

'I couldn't eat anything but I found a most delightful parking place on a hilltop near Gunnerthwaite. It was overlooking the moors with the sea in the far distance. Most romantic, Montague. I wish you had been there with me but I did feel better afterwards. I pottered around the village too, such a nice quiet place. And I bought you a present . . .'

'A present? How thoughtful! What is it?'

'A surprise, I'll show you at home. I'll arrange a nice meal tonight and hope you won't be late.' She sighed as the prospect of a leisurely weekend evaporated. This was reinforced with the sudden arrival of a convoy of vehicles, some carrying police insignia and others without.

'I'm afraid it will be after nine, Millicent, this is where my work really starts,' and for Montague Pluke, there began another investigation into a mysterious death.

31

Chapter Three

Among the arrivals was Dr Simon Meredith, the fair-haired, slightly balding forensic pathologist. After being briefed by Pluke, he began to examine the remains. Detective Sergeant Tabler, in charge of the Scenes of Crime Department, had also arrived and so Pluke directed them both to the body's resting place while he remained with the ever-increasing contingent of police officers. They included Task Force officers who would make a meticulous search of the entire area, several detectives, Scenes of Crime Officers and a photographer and video operator, both of whom were already recording Meredith's arrival, route and subsequent examination. While Meredith and Tabler were undertaking their tasks, Pluke took the opportunity to briefly outline the situation to the gathering and by the time Meredith had concluded his examination, everyone was familiar with the basic facts. Meredith, with Tabler in close attendance, returned to Pluke.

'Mr Pluke, due to the state of the body, I can't even hazard a guess at the cause of death without a laboratory examination. She's been dead some time and I support your theory that the body has been forced into that cavity by the power of the water. Floodwater, I mean, not the normal flow. There is evidence of earlier flooding in there – there are hefty deposits of all sorts. Scraps of heather, sheep's wool, lots of broken twigs and earth, a dead rabbit, scraps of litter and assorted debris. Like you, I suspect the scene of her death is elsewhere, possibly upstream.'

'I agree,' confirmed Tabler. 'She couldn't have been

killed in such a confined space and I doubt if anyone, even with help, could get a body into that cavity.'

'Attacked up on the moor on a summer's day, caught while dipping her feet in the water?' proffered Wayne Wain. 'Left for the floods to bring her down here?'

'Quite possible,' agreed Meredith. 'There are indications of injuries to the head although that could be the result of being buffeted against rocks. I need to make a closer examination of her skull. Even from superficial examination, I'd say the body has been severely bundled about, if that's the right phrase. Battered from rock to rock, I mean, and I'm sure it happened after death. I do feel her style of dress is odd – the long, old-fashioned frock. An arty-craft type on a summer walk perhaps? So where are her shoes? Attacked near the water's edge while dipping her toes as Sergeant Wain suggests? Shoes washed away too? And how did she get here? Car? Bike? Caravan? Where's her handbag? Belongings of any kind? There's a lot of puzzles for you, Mr Pluke.'

'I may get some answers when I get her identified,' Pluke told him. 'That is my immediate priority. Can you provide a description for me to circulate?'

'I can't help with any great detail although I can confirm she is female, probably in her early thirties, about five feet nine inches, slim build, natural light brown hair cut short, eyes – they've gone. Crows probably picking them out. Fingernails and toenails cared for with flakes of varnish still on them, pierced ears – or right ear to be precise. The other's missing. Good teeth, three or four fillings. No jewellery on the body. No rings or watch. Her outer clothing consists of a dark brown full-length dress – not of modern design, I'd say. No stockings or tights, and no underwear.'

'Dressed for a warm day?' suggested Pluke.

'Very likely. She's wearing no clothes at all, apart from that old-fashioned dress which has also been ripped and torn – on rocks, I'd say, not by an attacker. It may be significant that she was not wearing hiking boots or heavy walking shoes. Her style of dress does not suggest a serious rambler – she could be a Sunday afternoon walker, although her feet are bare. She wouldn't walk in bare feet on these moors. Attacked while paddling upstream perhaps? And, of course, at this stage I can't say whether she's been sexually assaulted. It is difficult, at this stage, to suggest how long she might have been here. The action of the water, cold and pure moorland water, may have contributed to her present condition – some of her flesh is well preserved – although the abrasive action of floodwater must have accelerated her apparent decay or even stripped some of her flesh while deterring severe insect infestation. My initial instinct is that it's a fairly recent death – by that I mean within the last few weeks – but I'll get a clearer picture once I get her into the laboratory.'

'You don't think she's ancient?' asked Wayne Wain. 'Preserved in peat, say?'

'I doubt it, her teeth, pierced ears and nail varnish all suggest a modern woman,' Meredith said. 'I do know that peat will preserve a body for a remarkably long time, but I do believe she is a modern young woman.'

'From what I saw, I'd say her skin is white,' Pluke added. 'Her hair does not suggest a dark-skinned lady. The skin colouring is of the kind which might result in staining from the peat moors or even from being in peat-coloured water but I think she's been lying in peat, rather than water. It's an even all-over colouring.'

'I agree. She was lying above the water level although on wet ground,' explained Meredith. 'I doubt if she's been under water long enough to be stained from it, even if she was covered by more than one flood. These floods rise and fall very quickly. I'd favour the burial theory. The sooner I get my examination started the better.'

'We'll soon have her moved, the shell is on its way,' Wayne Wain told them.

'Meanwhile, my officers will make a most meticulous search of the entire course of the gill, Dr Meredith, with due emphasis on finding the scene of her death and her possible grave,' Pluke assured him. 'We have a very capable new inspector in charge of the Task Force and he misses nothing. Inspector Theaker is the name. Newly promoted. If there is anything to be found, he will do so.'

'How nice to find someone with such confidence in his staff. Now I must leave you. I'll arrange for a forensic test of her nail varnish and we'll take an impression of her teeth in case we have to consider identification by dental records.'

As Meredith left the scene, Pluke sought Inspector Theaker of the Task Force and outlined the pathologist's remarks, with due emphasis on the debris in the cavern and along the entire length of the gill. He also stressed the need to find a possible grave and even anything which might have been used as a murder weapon.

'Is it murder then?' asked Theaker.

'It's not confirmed, but Dr Meredith does suspect head injuries. I'm awaiting his laboratory investigation.'

'Fair enough, Montague, we'll do what we can.'

'You have a map?'

'I do, and I know the gill. I've walked these moors for years. Those peat ponds on top of Rockdale Moor feed several tributaries which all find their way down here. They're very small ones, all fast running and only inches wide. This gill has a very wide catchment area which is why it floods so dramatically, especially after any sudden downpour. I'm not sure if the smaller tributaries would carry a human corpse even in flood conditions but I do reckon a flash flood could empty a shallow grave, especially a new one. We'll consider every possiblity.'

'We need to determine the dates of any recent floods too,' Pluke reminded him.

'There was heavy rain this week and a severe storm during the recent summer,' Theaker said. 'I can't remember its precise date.'

'We'll find out. Now, how well do you know Gunnerthwaite?'

'It's the nearest village, about four miles down the dale from here.'

'True, but does it have anywhere we can use as an incident room?' Pluke asked. 'There's nothing here.'

'There's a church hall, Montague, next door to the vicarage.'

'Good, I shall ask Inspector Horsley to explore the possibility of using it if we have to mount a murder investigation.'

Pluke found Inspector Dick Horsley among the assembled detectives and despatched him to explore that feasibility even though the death had not yet been confirmed as suspicious. He suggested Horsley take the small band of detectives – they could begin enquiries immediately in the hope of identifying the dead woman and tracing her movements. As everyone departed about their specific duties, Pluke and Wayne Wain remained to supervise the removal of the woman's mortal remains, a task faithfully recorded by the Scenes of Crime team with their video camera and stills photography. Within less than an hour and a half, the body had been carefully placed in the plastic coffin shell for transportation to Meredith's laboratory. The Scenes of Crime team went to join the Task Force in their search of the gill's bed and the peat moor and suddenly, the scene was eerily deserted. Pluke shivered again.

'I need to walk the route of the gill, right up to the peat bogs,' Pluke told Wayne. 'I want to familiarize myself with every twist and turn of the water, I want to know the position of every rock and hollow, and I have to find a possible grave.'

'If you're going to do all that, shall I go to Gunnerthwaite?' Wayne suggested. 'I can be organizing house-to-house enquiries while Inspector Horsley's busy getting the incident room up and running. We have to get her identified as soon as we can.'

'Excellent suggestion, Wayne. And I shall ring Sergeant Cockfield pronounced Cofield and ask him to check neighbouring police forces to see if there is any missing woman who might be our unfortunate victim. Someone must be missing a young lady of this description.'

Montague Pluke was left alone with his thoughts and the sombre mood of the landscape around him. He stood for a long time in solitary silence, observing the last resting place of the unfortunate woman. He could hear the trickle of the water as it tumbled over rocks, birds twittering out of sight and the whisper of the gentle moorland breeze as it sighed through the trees. Somewhere beyond his ken he heard a skylark singing, and he was able to distinguish the call of a yellowhammer crying to the world from the brisk air of the surrounding moors.

In spite of its undoubted beauty, an air of sinister gloom did pervade the area and yet there was nothing here – no ruined abbey, castle or pub, nothing but four farms and the ruin of Trough House. It was a very odd place, he realized. What stories had it witnessed? Had Trough House been involved in any of those past deaths? They'd been drownings, so how dangerous was that pool? Because of the wealth of trees along each bank at this point, the pool was cast in shadows, some black and deep and others less intense. In spite of its idyllic appearance, this was not a happy place. He sensed a palpable air of foreboding – it was not the sort of secret corner where one could relax with a picnic, nor was it the sort of place Pluke would want to revisit, even on a bright and sunny afternoon.

Thoughts of picnics made him realize he had not eaten his pack-up and his haversack was still hanging on a tree. His experiences not having put him off his food, but not wishing to eat here, he slung his haversack over his shoulder and began to stride up the lane towards the summit. Although he had no wish to interfere with the work of the Task Force, he did want to inspect the entire route of the gill and its source near the peat ponds. He hurried away, keen to distance himself from this sinister place.

He crossed his fingers to ward off bad luck and hoped he might see a pair of magpies as an additional omen of good fortune but saw none. With every stride carrying him higher towards the moors and away from this eerie spot, he found himself perspiring beneath his heavy overcoat. Half-way up the climb, he paused to ease his breathing and decided to eat his snack as he surveyed the landscape and gill below. Sitting on a large boulder, he could easily follow the route of the water, its path marked with alders, oaks, silver birches and a few conifers. When it reached the floor of the dale, a short distance beyond the pool where the body had been found, the water glistened in the sunlight, its presence being highlighted like a winding silver ribbon as it meandered along the floor of the dale. At that stage it was a gentle flow, not the rushing cascade of this hillside route. Its path along the dale took it through farmland as it twisted and turned through the fields, and even from this midway vantage point Pluke could plot the route as it journeyed to the river, some five miles away.

Then his mobile phone bleeped. 'Pluke,' he answered it swiftly.

'Horsley here, Montague.' The voice was easy to recognize. 'I've got the keys to the church hall in Gunnerthwaite, it's ideal for an incident room.'

'Well done,' said Pluke.

'So shall I book it? We don't know if the death is suspicious yet, do we?'

'Yes, book it.' Pluke was not afraid to make that decision. 'We do need a base, even if it is only temporary. We've got to get her identified if nothing else.'

'Fair enough. You'll be coming soon, will you?'

'I'm examining the scene and will be a while, but you can order the necessary office equipment, telephones and so forth. Between you and me, Inspector Horsley, I do feel there is something very odd about this death and I have experienced a dreadful sensation of evil in this area. I want a very thorough investigation.'

'You're the boss, I'll get things moving.' Horsley had had previous experience of Pluke's uncanny sensitivities. 'Shall I call out more detectives?'

'No, not yet, there's enough to commence enquiries in Gunnerthwaite. We can draft in more if murder is confirmed. Detective Sergeant Wain is on his way to you, he'll begin the house-to-house enquiries. I'll be there shortly.'

Moments later and suitably refreshed, Pluke pocketed

his mobile phone, rose to his feet and continued to the top of the unsurfaced lane. Each stride took him higher and for each new elevation there were more stunning views down the dale but he did not have time to stand and stare. He plodded onwards and upwards, puffing and perspiring, stopping from time to time to regain his breath and to enjoy the incredible views below. The four farms, surrounded by their outbuildings, were clearly visible, each sitting like a broody hen among its clutch of chicks, and in the distance he could see Gunnerthwaite, a haven of peace deep within the moors. As he neared the summit, he could see members of the Task Force working around the edges of the peat ponds some way across the moor. When Inspector Theaker spotted Pluke, he hailed him.

'Montague,' he called, his voice threatening to disappear on the wind. 'Montague, the ponds are over here, old peat bogs, you might want to look at them.'

'I'll come over.'

But then, as he prepared to leave the track and tramp through the deep heather, he noticed a tractor and two-wheeled trailer parked on the edge of the moor at the other side of the lane he was using. It was about a hundred yards away and two men were near the vehicle. Pluke hailed them and they waited as he approached. The older man was carrying a shepherd's crook with an ornate curved horn handle. He was a sturdy, thick-set man in his early fifties and wore a flat cap, tweed jacket and stout brown boots. A black and white dog was at his side. His companion was much younger – around thirty – with a mop of unkempt dark brown hair and a few days' growth of beard. He wore a thick green sweater and dirty jeans.

'Now then,' the older man greeted Pluke. His companion, a powerfully built copy of the elder, said nothing but moved away to shelter behind the trailer.

'Now then,' responded Pluke in the manner of the moor folk. The Task Force officers remained at their posts some distance away, content to wait as Pluke conducted this brief on-the-spot enquiry.

'Hiking party, is it?' the man asked as Pluke came to a

halt before him, a flick of his head indicating the Task Force men. 'Rightfully roaming and got lost, have you? Disturbing wild life hereabouts? Helping to spread foot-and-mouth?'

'No, we're police officers and this area is free from the disease,' Pluke responded with as much dignity as he could muster. Plodding through thigh-high heather in his long and heavy coat was not easy.

The farmer leaned on his crook and eyed the approaching Pluke with evident curiosity. This was not his idea of how a policeman should appear. As the sheep dog lay down at its master's feet, the younger man began ostensibly to tidy some empty sacks on the trailer, keeping the unit between himself and Pluke as some kind of safety barrier while eyeing Pluke with a mixture of suspicion and curiosity.

'Police?' It was clear that the farmer wondered if this odd fellow in strange clothes was telling the truth.

'Detective Inspector Pluke of Crickledale CID.' Pluke identified himself.

'Oh, aye? Well, we get all sorts on these moors, mostly townies who drop litter, light fires and let their dogs chase my sheep. And then there's roaming ramblers who always manage to get lost and don't worry a toss about foot-and-mouth, and then there's motorists who can't cope with these hills . . . we get 'em all up here, we do. They think we're a theme park or summat. I can't say we get much call for detectives up here though. Summat going on, is there?'

'Are you local to the area?' Pluke asked.

'Aye, I am,' but the man volunteered no further information.

'Do you live nearby?'

'Aye, I do,' was the brief response.

'Both of you?'

'Aye.'

Pluke knew these men would be interviewed later but this was an opportune moment to seek useful information from a local person. That's if he would be persuaded to talk about himself.

Pluke saw that Inspector Theaker was still observing this conference from a distance so he raised his hand in a gesture which he hoped Theaker would interpret as 'Won't be long.'

'The body of a young woman has been found,' Pluke told the man. 'In that deep pool at the bottom of this gill. She's dead, we're investigating the matter.'

'Oh aye.'

'We don't know who she is, the doctor has no knowledge of any local woman who's missing. We'll be calling on everyone to ask if they can help us.'

'You're welcome to pay me a call any time, not that I can help. Can't say I know anybody who's gone missing. How did she die then? Drowning, was it? She won't be the first to die in that pool, that's summat I do know. Devil's Dump, they call it. Nasty place, I keep well clear of it, not that I can swim.'

'We don't know how she died, that's to be determined. Because she was found in the gill, she might have drowned. We have to consider every possibility. Do you know the pool near the bottom of this lane?'

'I drive past every day on my tractor but never go down there, as I said, I keep away from it. Devil's Dump, nasty spot. By my reckoning, though, yon gill's too shallow for folks to get drowned in it. Unless somebody held their heads under. All except that pool, I mean. You could drown there, they reckon, they say there's deep holes under that water.'

'You said someone had drowned there?'

'In the pool, I mean, not the gill. A young lass drowned there, summat like a hundred and thirty years back, only six year old she was. Accident, they said. Then there was a shepherd who drowned there fifty years before that. Sad spot, yon pool. Nobody knows whether that chap died through an accident or if somebody pushed him in or held his head under. Anyway, no fish has ever been caught

41

since that lass and some folks say it's haunted. I take it we're talking about the same pool?'

'It's at the bottom of the hill, just past Trough House, near a grassy area. We're parked there. It's a large round pool.'

'Aye, that'll be it. Devil's Dump's the only decent-sized pool there is in this top part of Thordale Gill. There's others, but they're smaller. All them tree roots around it are like cages – I've had ewes swept in there during floods. Like a Venus fly trap it is, catching everything that swirls near it, rabbits, sheep, tree trunks . . .'

'The post-mortem will reveal the exact cause of the woman's death,' Pluke told him. 'I understand the gill floods from time to time and that it can produce a very heavy and powerful force of water.'

'Aye, it does and it can. We get sudden storms up here, thunder, lightning, cloudbursts, gales, melting snow, the lot. When that happens, you can hear the flood coming down from those moors, roaring and crashing, it sounds worse at night. I reckon Victoria Falls must sound summat like that. In these parts, it's not a very happy sound, I can tell you. They reckon it could knock a house down if it was in the way. There's no wonder folks keep clear of Devil's Dump, especially when them storms are about.'

'Clearly, you know the district? Very well, I should imagine.'

'Born and bred here, and my father before me and his father before him. Cragside Farm, at the dale head. Pyman's the name. Reuben Pyman. Like my dad, and his dad and his dad before him. All Reubens, a family name.'

'And this young man is your son?'

'I'm not wed, never have been. This is my hand, Winston. Winston Livingstone. He can't say hello, he's deaf and dumb but he's a good hard worker.'

Pluke raised a hand as a greeting, but Winston turned his head away and moved to hide behind the tractor.

'He's a bit on the shy side,' Pyman told him.

'Does he live with you?'

'Oh, no, he's from Gunnerthwaite, lives with his mum. He bikes up here to work every day. Never misses.'

'I see. Now, you said you come up here every day, so does this moor belong to you?'

'Oh, no, it doesn't belong. My farm's my own but the moor belongs to the Estate – Gunnerthwaite Estate. I just rent it out for my sheep. I've five hundred up here, I come and see to 'em every day, like now. Bring 'em nutrients, check 'em over, that sort of thing. We'd had a worrying time this year, me and Winston, checking for foot-and-mouth but we kept clear. It takes time to see to 'em all, but it's got to be done. Then what with my pigs at Cragside, we never have a minute.'

'So, have you seen anyone behaving oddly? Looking suspicious?'

'I can't say I have. As I said, we do get all sorts on these moors, but I've seen nowt that would make me suspicious.'

'Now, those floods,' began Pluke. 'Can you remember the last one?'

'There was a real bad 'un last July, it moved rocks and tore trees down, ripped up acres of moorland and heather, a real cloudburst. And it killed a few ewes, most of 'em were never seen again. Not mine, happily, they're further up the moor and didn't get harmed. And it has flooded on and off since then. Nowt quite so bad though. We had a fair bit of rain last week, if you remember.'

'I do indeed, but that severe flood, could it kill a human being who was caught in the heavy water?'

'There's times I reckon it could, Mr Pluke. A sudden wave could knock somebody over, mebbe they could bash their heads against a rock or a tree.'

'Powerful stuff!'

'Very powerful. You make sure you keep away from the gill when it's in spate.'

'Thank you, you've been a great help. I won't keep you any longer, but either I or my officers may want another chat with you.'

'You're welcome to call at Cragside any time. I'm never

far away. If I'm out, I'll be up here seeing to my sheep and won't be too long. You can see my farm from here, that 'un with the red roof, top end of the dale, on your right from here.'

Pluke followed the direction of his pointing finger and identified the sturdy complex of buildings with the winding road leading from the route down the dale. Then Pluke spotted a movement in the foldyard.

'There's somebody in your yard.' He pointed too. 'Walking about.'

'By gum, you've sharp eyes, but then you are a detective. Aye, that's Sylvia, she sees to things for me, cleans, cooks a bit, washes my clothes. Winston's mum, she is, she comes from Gunnerthwaite three times a week, this is one of her days. She'll have our dinners ready when we get back. It's about time we finished.'

'So long as it's not an intruder. Well, thank you, Mr Pyman. Now, if you do hear anything about a missing woman, or if you recall any unlikely happenings hereabouts in recent weeks, perhaps you'd let us know?'

'Allus glad to help you chaps,' he said in a note of finality.

'We are establishing an incident room in Gunnerthwaite church hall. You can always contact us there.'

'You don't think she was swept right down from them ponds, do you?' the farmer asked. 'If she'd died up further up the moor, she'd never get swept down to Devil's Dump, the channels are too shallow and too narrow. Like gutters. You're wasting your time looking any higher up than those old peat bogs. They can overflow into Thordale Gill – and oft times do in a sudden storm.'

'We want to examine the gill every inch along its course to Devil's Dump,' Pluke told him. 'We have no idea how or where she got into the water, she might have died elsewhere and been placed in that pool . . . We've got to consider every possibility, however unlikely.'

'Aye, well, you know your job. Mustn't keep you. I'll be off then,' and he turned to his tractor, clambered into the driving seat and started the engine. Winston clambered aboard the trailer and the dog followed as they departed. Pluke saw they were heading for home as he made his way to Inspector Theaker.

'Useful witness, was he?' enquired Theaker as Pluke approached.

'He's a local farmer,' and Pluke explained about Pyman's knowledge of the moors, peat bogs and gill, stressing that he might be a useful source of expert advice about the vagaries of the water in flood conditions. 'He knows of no missing women and reckons it's highly unlikely anyone could accidentally drown in the gill – except for the pool at the bottom where our victim was found. He calls it Devil's Dump, it's where a young girl and a shepherd died many years ago, in separate incidents, and he says no fish has been caught there since. He also claims it is haunted. I thought this place had a strange atmosphere. He did confirm that a flash flood coming off those moors could be severe enough to kill anyone caught in it, however.'

'It's happened on the Swale, people caught in flash floods. But here, well, you can't beat local folklore for making places sound eerie,' smiled Theaker. 'Now, Montague, this is the situation from my point of view.'

Theaker explained how centuries of peat digging on the moors had created a number of deep excavations which covered several acres each; over the years, these had become exhausted or disused due to the increasing use of modern fuels. The old workings had filled with water to form large ponds. Most of the time, the water was static, perhaps seeping into the spongy moorland to eventually find its way into Thordale Gill, but periods of heavy rain or melting snow could cause the ponds to overflow. When that happened, the water raced through natural gullies or across the surface of the moor between the heather and rocks as it made its way to Thordale Gill, helping to swell the flow which came from dozens of other sources.

Pluke examined the nearest peat bog, its steep sides sheer where the peat had been sliced away to form a pit some ten feet deep by fifty yards wide and over a hundred yards long. Here, there were a dozen such pits, all full of calm water.

'It wouldn't be difficult to cut a grave in this peat, would it?' Pluke asked.

'Not at all, you could do it easily with an ordinary garden spade although they use special cutters to shape the peat into blocks for burning on fires. We'll look out for a grave, Montague, although I doubt it won't look much like a grave now.'

'And don't forget a possible murder weapon!'

'We won't!'

Some two hundred yards to the north, Theaker showed Pluke a parking area, just off the road, where tourists could leave their vehicles for a walk across the moors, a stroll around the old peat workings or merely to sit and enjoy a picnic. At this elevated point it was possible to see most of the network of gullies and natural drains which carried surplus water into Thordale Gill.

'In spite of its remoteness, visitors do come here,' Theaker said. 'The victim could have been brought by car but I'm not sure she could have been washed down from these peat ponds and moors. We need to follow the course of the main part of the gill, where it widens sufficiently to carry something as large and heavy as a human body.'

'But if cars park here and people trek across the moors, then we do need to search the whole area, Mr Theaker. We need to know who has parked here and when. The fact that there is no abandoned car could suggest she did not come alone.'

'We'll check the area for tourist litter, Montague. Who knows what we might find!'

'We must establish whether she was brought to this place dead or alive. Was she buried up here? If so, where? Or did she die from exposure or natural causes and lie on the moor until she was swept into the gill by the flood? And don't forget those missing shoes. And now I shall leave you to your work as I descend via the gill itself.'

'Don't fall in,' smiled Theaker.

Pluke found an elevated mound from which he could

survey the area surrounding the peat bogs, noting that farmer Pyman and Winston had disappeared. The whole area had been subjected to widespread earthworkings – the digging of the peat, ancient burial grounds, primitive paths and roads, attempts at removing heather – and even now some areas comprised bare earth, apparently scoured by waves of floodwater or some other powerful force, natural or man-made. The patches of bare moorland formed small islands among the thick, expansive carpet of heather; some were water-filled while others were rocky and infertile, but all were part of this rough and inhospitable moorland terrain. He knew that, in times past, men had fallen here in blizzard conditions and their bodies had not been found for months or even years . . . the dense layer of heather concealed a great deal. Smooth and beautiful along its surface, especially when viewed from a distance, it obliterated a great deal below that handsome surface.

Pluke now walked towards the dip in the landscape which marked the downward flow of countless small watercourses, all merging into Thordale Gill. Most were only inches wide and inches deep, tiny but effective drains, and, realizing none was wide enough or deep enough to have borne the corpse, he concentrated on the main stream. Quickly, he reached a lofty pool, one which appeared to gather most of the moorland water before spilling it over the edge and into the gully below. This pool, much smaller than Devil's Dump and not as deep, appeared to be a sort of concourse – several drains trickled their waters into it, some peat-coloured and others clear, and the surplus water poured over a natural dam of rocks and boulders to mark the effective beginning of Thordale Gill.

Down the ages, the water had scoured out a deep crevice between rocks and earth and now it cascaded down in a series of small rapids and waterfalls. Pluke found he could negotiate the route along the bank nearest the road. In some places, the gill dropped a long way, in others it meandered for a hundred yards or so before rippling down a series of small natural steps, and as it tumbled down the hillside, so it broadened as it accepted yet more water from rivulets and drains. Half-way down, the gill's watercourse was about six feet wide, running through a miniature canyon about ten feet deep; there were small rocks on its edges with boulders midstream and plants like ferns, valerian and infant rowans clinging to the rock faces above water level.

Pluke could imagine this with the gill in spate. The downpouring water would gush through this limited space with all the force and weight of a burst dam, carrying all before it. And so it continued down to Devil's Dump, a series of narrow stonewalled channels opening into broader runs, and all bearing marks of regular flooding. There were bare rocks, debris lodged behind bushes growing from those rocks, occasional pools, small and shallow with stone bottoms, and a watercourse otherwise clear of rubbish and plants.

Then he was back at Devil's Dump, having not found the grave or anything that could be construed as evidence material to the girl's death but having gained a valuable impression of Thordale Gill in its quieter mood. He could now visualize it when it roared into action to cope with those fearsome floodwaters from the moorland. Standing in silence as he gazed across Devil's Dump towards the cavern which had held the unfortunate young woman, he did consider venturing across to search the debris which would have been washed inside. But, on reflection, he decided to leave that to Inspector Theaker and his Task Force – after all, that was their job and whatever they found might have some relevance to other things found elsewhere. So he left it alone.

From the grassy area where Millicent had earlier parked, he felt another shiver ripple down his spine and, although he would have loved to spend more time at Trough House, he realized that could not be. He was a policeman on duty, he was not trough hunting, and so he turned to leave. Then he remembered he did not have any form of transport. Millicent had gone home, Wayne Wain had gone to

Gunnerthwaite while Theaker and his teams were busy on the moor. As he needed to reach the incident room, he decided to ring Wayne Wain on his mobile telephone. Happily, he responded.

'All right, sir,' he agreed. 'I'll come and collect you. Quarter of an hour or so.'

That gave Pluke a few minutes to snatch another fleeting visit to Trough House.

Chapter Four

With only some fifteen minutes before the arrival of his transport, Pluke's second examination of Trough House had to be brief. He hurried up the lower section of the hill, pushed through the decaying wooden gate and strode towards the tumble of neglected stonework. As he'd already viewed the remains of the house, he now sought signs of troughs within its curtilage. He reasoned that if cattle or horses had been housed here, then the area must have supported at least one trough or even more. There must have been a supply of water too, a natural source from the moors. Thordale Gill was too far away, unless some kind of diversionary aqueduct or mini-canal had been constructed, but of that there was no sign. More than likely, water would have flowed from the moors directly behind the house and been channelled into a pipe which in turn would have supplied the trough or troughs. He peered at the heathery, rock-laden slope, trying to identify an existing or former gully, and then, without too much surprise, he located one.

It was dry now and clearly unaffected by the recent floods but he could identify the remains of a narrow, rock- and pebble-based channel, a thin heather-free line weaving its way down the slope, bypassing boulders and chunks of rising ground until it snaked its way towards the farm-yard. And there it stopped. Sensing triumph, Pluke hurried towards its terminus and found that the channel vanished into a lead pipe which in turn disappeared into a small hillock. Excited, he hurried to the other side of the hillock and found the emergence of that same pipe.

There was a dense patch of nettles, briars and weeds but when he parted a section and looked beneath, he found a large stone base which had undoubtedly supported a substantial trough, perhaps a double-header which had been fed with water from the moors. He next sought an overflow and, with his expertise, quickly traced it to the western end of the trough's base. It was a simple hole in the ground. It would have been kept clear, he knew, and linked to the farm's drainage system.

But of the trough itself there was no sign. In his role as Custodian of Horse Troughs, he'd have to make every attempt to locate it – but not now for he had other duties to concern him. Even so, he had a quick look to make sure the trough hadn't been smashed into small pieces, nor was there any sign of it lying neglected and unwanted in some hidden corner. He wondered, for a fleeting moment, whether the woman had been buried somewhere within these grounds, but he encountered no sign of a deserted grave. Besides, the floodwaters hadn't reached this point; they'd been diverted somewhere on the heights above.

Then he heard a car horn. Wayne Wain was reversing his unmarked police car on to the patch of ground near Devil's Dump, and as Pluke emerged through the gate he waved to attract Wayne's attention.

'Found anything interesting?' Wain asked as Pluke settled in the front passenger seat with a huge smile of achievement on his face.

'Indeed I have, Wayne,' beamed Pluke, clearly delighted with his excursion. 'I have found the site of the Trough House trough, and its water source. It just remains for me to trace and even recover the actual –'

'I was referring to our enquiry, sir, the dead woman,' Wayne interrupted. 'I thought you had been to the source of Thordale Gill? Where the Task Force is working?'

'Ah, yes, yes indeed,' and as Wayne drove away towards Gunnerthwaite, Pluke outlined his experiences, adding that he had not found any sign of a deserted grave although expressing a view that the action of the floodwaters could have obliterated any shallow depression in the earth.

Wayne listened as he drove confidently down the dale. 'So what now, sir? Where do you want to go?'

'I was intending to visit the incident room,' Pluke said.

'It's not fully operational yet,' Wayne told him, ' but I've teams out on house-to-house, trying to get the woman named. There's lots of bed-and-breakfast places and holiday cottages in and around Gunnerthwaite. Tracing short-term visitors won't be easy and we have to remember our victim might be such a person. Maybe no one knew she was in the area?'

'That's why it's important to get her identified as soon as we can. Let's make a bold start, Wayne, by calling at some farms during our trip down Thordale.'

As they had already talked to Reuben Pyman of Cragside, Pluke decided to call at the next farm they passed – it was Dale Head which occupied a spectacular south-facing site on the northern slopes. Leaving the dale road, they drove along the well-kept tarmac drive towards the solid stone dwelling house and its nest of satellite buildings. It was already mid-afternoon, and as Wayne eased the little car to a halt outside the back door, a large and very thick-set woman emerged.

She was almost six feet tall and in her early fifties with a red face, grey hair and horn-rimmed spectacles. She wore a flowered apron over a thick skirt and a short-sleeved blouse. With black wellington boots on her feet, she carried a teapot which she emptied into a drain, then awaited them with a facial expression which shouted 'You go no further!'

'We only see reps by appointment.' She looked as immovable as a bull elephant. 'And whatever you're selling, we don't want any. We've got enough.'

'We're not selling anything, we're police officers,' and Wayne produced his warrant card. She inspected it closely, then nodded.

'Aye, well, you'd better come in then. Frank'll be here in

a minute, he allus comes in for his 'lowance break at half-past. Sit yourselves down,' and she indicated a huge pine kitchen table surrounded by eight Windsor chairs, worth a fortune in any antique shop. As she busied herself at the Aga, she almost commanded, 'You'll have a cup of tea and a scone?'

Wayne looked at Pluke for guidance, Pluke being very cautious about accepting unsolicited gifts from strangers, but in these moors such hospitality was traditional. Anyone visiting a farm at mealtime was expected to join the meal – it was ill-mannered not to – so, somewhat to Wayne's surprise, Pluke agreed, knowing this was no attempted bribery of a police officer. 'We would be delighted to join you. I am Detective Inspector Pluke and this is Detective Sergeant Wain.'

'How do you do. I'm Mrs Hepworth. Sugar, is it?'

'No thanks,' they chorused. 'Milk, but no sugar.'

'Well,' Pluke began, 'we are here because –'

'If you wait until my Frank gets here, you can tell us both at once, that'll save telling the tale all over again, won't it? Time's precious for farmers, we've no time to stand around all day talking. He'll be wanting to get on with his milking after he's had his 'lowance. Butter?'

'Thank you,' She worked on their snack, buttering about a dozen scrumptious scones, smothering them in strawberry jam before placing them on a large plate. Then she organized some huge mugs, a massive brown teapot, a can of fresh and creamy milk from the pantry and some slices of fruit cake. She placed all these on the table and said, 'Frank's here now.' In walked a diminutive man in brown overalls and flat cap, followed by a black and white mongrel and a Jack Russell terrier; both animals sniffed at the visitors, then trotted over and flopped in front of the Aga. Without a word, the newcomer placed his cap on a hook at the end of a kitchen cabinet and washed his hands in the sink. He then sat at the end of the table near Pluke. He had a thick head of iron grey hair, roughly cut, a weathered, pinched and sharp face with a long pointed nose and sharp, penetrating blue eyes, without spectacles. He had a

53

growth of whiskers on his face which smothered most of his hardened complexion.

'Now then,' he nodded, reaching for the teapot and a mug. Because strangers at one's table were a feature of life on these moors – his wife's department in fact – Frank ignored the visitors and got on with his meal.

'Good afternoon.' Pluke took the initiative. 'Mr Hepworth, is it?'

'Aye, who else would it be?' He poured his tea, slopped in a generous helping of milk, and then hauled the plate of scones closer to him without offering them around.

'I am Detective Inspector Pluke and this is Detective Sergeant Wain. We're from Crickledale CID.'

'A bit out of your way, aren't you? Looking for a cottage mebbe? 'Cos if you are, we don't have any. Ask at the post office in Gunnerthwaite.'

Mrs Hepworth now settled at the other end of the table and, after making sure Pluke and Wayne had a plateful of scones and cake, and full mugs of hot tea, she said, 'I said to wait till you got here, Frank, to tell us what they want.'

'Right.' He munched a scone and wiped his lips with the back of his hand.

'We are here on enquiries about the death of a young woman,' Pluke tried again. 'She has been found dead in the stream at the dale head, in what's locally known as Devil's Dump.'

'Oh my goodness!' cried Mrs Hepworth.

'Suicide, is it?' asked Hepworth without emotion. 'We get some funny folks staying in this dale, in holiday cottages. Them with stress and daft tourists. Wouldn't surprise me if one of 'em had tumbled in – or mebbe chucked herself in.'

'This is dreadful, Mr Pluke, awful, so what happened to her?' asked Mrs Hepworth, clearly shocked by the news.

'We don't know what happened nor do we know the cause of death,' Pluke continued. 'Our immediate task is to find out who she is and where she is from.'

He followed with a brief description of the casualty.

54

'Could be anybody,' admitted Hepworth, 'from any-where. She's not a local lass, I can tell you that. We've nobody like that living round here.'

Mrs Hepworth chipped in. 'Have you asked at the cot-tages in the village? Young people rent them and get up to all sorts, not that it's anything to do with me how they entertain themselves but when young lads and lasses have parties with drinks and drugs, well, you never know what they get up to. Young locals can't afford to buy these cottages, so we get townies snapping 'em up then only living here two or three weeks a year. And they fetch all their own food. No good for us, that sort of going on. They should be bringing money into the countryside not taking the countryside away from us, stone by stone, house by house –'

'We are conducting enquiries in and around Gunner-thwaite,' Pluke cut short her outburst. 'We shall be visiting every house and and cottage.'

'The post office has a list, she acts as a sort of booking agent, she's as helpful as anybody, there's not a lot she doesn't know about this area.' Mrs Hepworth actually smiled. 'She might recognize that young woman, she might have called in.'

'We'll speak to her,' Pluke assured her, then addressed Mr Hepworth. 'Mr Hepworth, do you have sheep on the moor?'

'Aye, I do, but I missed a few weeks – foot-and-mouth, you know. I kept my sheep down here while it was rife, just in case. We were never infected though.'

'And usually you drive up there from time to time? To attend them?'

'Aye, once a day at least when things are normal, more in winter.'

'I just wondered if you'd come across anyone hanging about on that lane near Trough House or around Devil's Dump, somebody behaving suspiciously, cars parked in odd places, the sort of thing you'd think was unusual?'

'Nay, Mr Pluke, I can't say I have seen owt out of the ordinary. I mean, ramblers use that lane a lot and cars park

on Rockdale Moor top beyond the peat bogs and sometimes you get tourists finding their way down the dale but
that's about all. But I do tend go up there early on, seven
o'clock on a morning, and I've not seen anything funny
then. I can't speak for what's happened later in the day.'

'How do you travel? I am wondering if you'd walked
past Devil's Dump recently?'

'Nay, not me, Mr Pluke, I've no time for walking beside
pretty pools. I take my tractor up, straight there and back
again, time's precious.'

'Thanks, but if you do recall anything, you'll get in touch
with our incident room in Gunnerthwaite?'

'Aye, I will and now it's time I was off, milking won't
wait,' and suddenly Hepworth downed the last of his tea,
stuffed the last piece of cake into his mouth and got to his
feet. 'But I know nowt, Mr Pluke. I seldom get off these
premises except to see to my ewes, Mrs Hepworth does all
the running about and gossiping, so if she knows nowt,
then we both know nowt.'

Pluke was about to ask Hepworth if he knew anything
of the whereabouts of the Trough House trough when the
little farmer snatched his cap from its hook, plonked it on
his head and departed with the two dogs at his heels.

'You'll have a top up, Mr Pluke?' Mrs Hepworth waved
the teapot at him. 'And Sergeant?'

'No thanks.' Pluke rose to his feet and prepared to leave,
with Wayne Wain doing likewise. Any questions he might
have asked about Trough House would have to wait. 'We
must be getting along, we mustn't hold up the work of the
farming community. Thanks for your co-operation and
refreshments.'

Wayne set off towards Gunnerthwaite but Pluke asked
him to pull on to the verge while he consulted his map.
After perusing it for a moment or two, he said, 'There
are only four farms in this dale, Wayne. I've had brief
words with Pyman of Cragside and we've just seen the
Hepworths of Dale Head, but there are another two along
our route to Gunnerthwaite. I suggest we call now.'

'Seems a good idea to me,' agreed Wayne and so, within

six or seven minutes, they were drawing into the yard of Ling Garth.

This was a very well maintained and tidy complex of farm buildings remarkably similar to Hepworth's spread, but built on to the southern slopes of the dale. The owners were Stephen and Marjorie Booth, a modern couple in their mid-forties with a son called Mike who was twenty-two. Mike was away, helping a friend to move house in Malton, but the couple welcomed Pluke and Wayne. They said they had no idea who the victim might be but would pass on any information they received. They did confirm, however, that they had two cottages on the premises, both converted from one former barn. They were called Number 1, Ling Garth Barn and Number 2, Ling Garth Barn. Both had been let throughout the summer but currently there were no tenants. The Booths did not run sheep on the moor, preferring to maintain a dairy herd – which had avoided the foot-and-mouth outbreak – and to breed horses; for that reason, they seldom if ever used the lane which led up to the moor past Trough House. The description of the dead woman meant nothing to them, although they promised to ask Mike when he returned. He was spending tonight – Saturday – with a friend but would be home tomorrow. Like any young man, he was out and about a good deal in his leisure time, attending pubs and clubs in the area, going to agricultural shows and such, so he might have come across the victim or heard some reference to her. His daily work was on the farm however, where he was in partnership with his parents with a view to eventually taking over the entire business – with a wife or partner if and when that happened!

The fourth farm, Throstle Nest, was on the northern slopes with fields adjoining those of Dale Head. This was a rough, untidy place in need of care, maintenance and lots of paint. Eric Hall, the owner, was a scruffy, long-haired individual in his late sixties who was trying vainly to start an ancient Ford Escort when Wayne's car eased to a halt in his yard. He wiped his hands on a filthy rag and went across to the detectives.

'Eric Hall,' he said in a surprisingly cultured accent. 'What can I do for you gentlemen?'

When Pluke explained, Hall looked shocked at the news but shook his head.

'Sorry, Mr Pluke, she means nothing to me but come inside and meet the wife, she might be able to help.'

Sally Hall, a neat and tidy blonde who looked ten years younger than her husband, was baking apple pies and the kitchen seemed full of pastry, apple peel and baking tins. Up to the elbows in flour, she listened to Pluke then shook her head. 'Oh, that's dreadful, really dreadful. The poor woman. I'm sorry, though, I can't say I've seen her and I'm sure she's not local. You could ask the boys, but they're both at work.'

'Boys?'

'My sons, Alec and Patrick. They're twins. There's not enough work for them on the farm so they've day jobs, Alec works for an estate agent and Patrick runs an off-licence in Malton. They live at home, though. They'll be back just after six, Mr Pluke.'

'Some of my officers will call on them, Mrs Hall, thanks. Tomorrow perhaps?'

'Yes, fine, they'll be out tonight, being a Saturday,' Eric Hall told them. 'They're musicians in their spare time. Country music, they sing and play guitars in the pubs and clubs. Busy lads. I never know where they are from one minute to the next. Saturday usually means a gig some-where.'

'They might have seen the girl, then, if she's spent time in the area,' Wayne Wain realized. 'How old are they?'

'Twenty-seven,' said Mrs Hall. 'It makes me feel old! I'll tell them to expect your officers tomorrow.'

'Or they could pop into the incident room in Gunner-thwaite church hall,' Pluke said, 'if they've other com-mitments.'

'I'll tell them,' said Sally Hall.

'Now, sheep and holiday cottages,' Pluke continued. 'Do you own any?'

'Me own a cottage?' laughed Eric Hall. 'I can hardly

58

afford to run this place let alone buy cottages. No, sorry, Mr Pluke. Not us, that's not our line of country. I'm all for diversifying but I've enough on my plate with my pigs. And I do have a few sheep on the moor, we didn't get foot-and-mouth, a big relief I can tell you. Why do you want to know about holiday cottages? Are you wanting to rent one?'

'No, but I understand there are lots in this area. Our victim might have rented one, which could explain why she is not known locally.'

'Good point. If I were you, I'd try the post office,' smiled Hall. 'That's the fount of all knowledge in this part of the world.'

'Thank you, now your sheep. Do you run them on the moor?'

'We do, we've four hundred or so, not much money in 'em nowadays, but we keep going.'

'And do you use the lane past Trough House?'

'We do, but if you're asking whether I've seen anything untoward up there, the answer's no. Certainly not that lass, and nobody hanging about, no campers in tents, no cars parked at all hours, no odd-looking folks mooching about the place, nothing like that. Mind you, Rockdale Moor top can be very busy with tourists in the summer, weekends especially. You never know who's up there.'

'We hope we might trace some visitors,' Pluke said, 'but in the meantime, if anything does come to mind . . .?'

'I'll get in touch, I promise.'

'Thank you,' and so another interview concluded with little or no useful information stemming from it.

Back in the car, Wayne Wain asked, 'Well, sir, what now? We've done the farms and farmers – without visiting Crag-side, that is – so what about some of the cottages in Gunnerthwaite? They're not all holiday accommodation.'

'I'll leave those to your teams,' Pluke told him. 'I don't want to interfere with your routine, besides this is not yet a murder investigation. To the incident room if you please.'

'As you wish,' smiled Wayne Wain as he started the engine and drove away.

The church hall was a splendid and surprisingly spacious stone built, red-roofed building just beyond the parish church as Pluke and Wain entered from Thordale. With fresh green woodwork and a smart appearance, it had ample car parking before it and the lights were burning with signs of activity inside. Wayne eased to a halt close to the double main door. Inside was an entrance foyer with ladies' and gents' cloakrooms at either side, and beyond that the body of the hall. At the far end was a stage complete with curtains, and to the right of the stage was a short flight of steps which gave access to further rooms behind the stage such as an ante-room, kitchen and changing rooms.

The place was ideal for accommodation of an incident room. Already, desks were in place, telephones had been connected, word processors, a photocopier and a scanner had been installed, while a blackboard stood on the stage bearing a heading with today's date, a note of the prevailing weather and details of the discovery in Devil's Dump. There was a description of the dead woman along with some early photographs and details of the Devil's Dump location with its map reference. Half a dozen detectives, men and women, were working in the room. Pluke spotted Inspector Horsley, the man in charge of this part of the enquiry.

'Ah, Inspector Horsley.' Pluke greeted him in his formal manner. 'Things look businesslike, you've done well.'

'The telephone lines have just been made operational,' he said. 'So, yes, we're now up and running. All ready to tackle this investigation.'

'So what's the position so far?'

'Not a lot to report, Montague. We've detectives in the village trying to get a name for our victim and I've circulated all police forces, nationwide, for details of any women in the twenty to forty age bracket who are missing. That's about all.'

Pluke updated Horsley on his progress, all of which

would be entered into the computerized filing system known as HOLMES, should this develop into a murder investigation. The phone rang. A woman detective answered it then said, 'It's for you, Mr Pluke. Dr Meredith from the Path. Lab.'

'Ah!' Pluke stepped forward to take the phone. 'Good afternoon, Dr Meredith. Good of you to call so soon.'

'I got busy immediately,' said Meredith. 'Luckily, I was not overburdened with bodies. However, several interesting things have emerged. First, I believe our victim has been dead for a month or six weeks, something in that region. This recent summer is a likely time of death. I can't be more precise. Next, my examination of her outer clothes, hair and nails shows they are full of very peaty soil. It's rather more than I would expect from immersion in dirty water. As you thought, it suggests she has been buried, Mr Pluke. Only for a short time, I think, but buried nonetheless. In peat. Partial preservation of the flesh and light staining of her skin supports that theory. Now, the body did have injuries, Mr Pluke, which were consistent with a battering against rocks, and that supports our theory that she was swept down the gill in a heavy flow, flood conditions more than likely. But there are head injuries too – a good defence barrister might claim they were the result of that same battering but there is a possibility they were done with a blunt instrument of some sort. A blow on the head, Mr Pluke, with something very heavy and solid. I did wonder if she'd hit her head on the corner of a step or table, a table leg even, or perhaps been attacked by a madman wielding a chair leg or something similar. Something with corners on it, Mr Pluke. I'll make sure you get photographs of the injury. Other than those ideas, I can't suggest a weapon although I can rule out something with a small base like a hammer, iron poker or even a heavy candlestick. The injury's bigger than that. If you find a likely weapon, I'll try to match it with the injury. So there you are, Mr Pluke, I'll state her death was due to a blow on the head, a depressed fracture of the skull resulting in brain damage and death.'

'Not an injury resulting from being battered against rocks by the floods?'

'I doubt it. It is somewhat similar to being struck against a sharp edge of rock but I'm confident that blow was inflicted *before* death and that her other injuries occurred after death. She did not drown, Mr Pluke, she did not die of a heart attack and there are no other indictions of injuries. That head injury did it, Mr Pluke.'

'So I have a murder to deal with?'

'You have. That is my opinion. I'll go further and say it's a very cunning murderer, bearing in mind that dress. It is very old, Mr Pluke, probably from the early years of the twentieth century – pre-First World War, we think – but the body has not been buried all that time. I think the killer wanted people to think the body was of that era, should it ever be found. There are no modern articles upon the body but the give-away is that the remnants of nail varnish are modern. I am having the varnish analysed but that will take time. We might determine the manufacturer and date it was sold. So there you are, a modern young woman with a very suspicious head injury.'

'Thank you, Dr Meredith, I'll inform my officers immediately.'

'And one other thing, Mr Pluke. She was a virgin – rather odd for a modern young woman, don't you think?'

Chapter Five

'Murder, eh? A woman who has not been raped. Killed by a blow to the head. Robbery, you think?' Horsley put to Pluke when he told him. 'There's no sign of a handbag, no watch or jewellery on the body.'

'That could be a motive, but would a robber spend time burying his victim? I think he'd get away as fast as he could,' Pluke suggested. 'It means we need to consider all aspects with great care as we examine other possibilities.'

'Well, while you're thinking about it, shall I arrange a full call-out?'

'We've all the support services we need,' Pluke conceded, 'and I'm not sure we need a full complement of detectives. If we bring too many, they'll swamp the village and there'll be nothing for them to do, there's not many people living here so they'll be chasing each other around in circles. And the killer might be local.'

'We can't be too sure about that,' Horsley countered. 'The place does attract visitors.'

'Nonetheless, this has the hallmarks of a crime committed by a local person. I feel we should concentrate on the immediate locality.' Pluke sounded determined. 'I have what is called a gut feeling, Mr Horsley, not a phrase of which I am particularly fond, but one which gets over the message quite succinctly. My feelings are perhaps mere instinct but I did experience an odd sensation of evil near Devil's Dump. Others have died there, there is the question of that dress, the likely mode of burial, the fact that she has no shoes or belongings, that she is a virgin . . . all very relevant, Mr Horsley.'

'Even if she may not be a local woman?'

'That has yet to be determined, Mr Horsley. We do not know who she is.'

'But no local woman is missing, Montague.'

'None of whom we are aware, Mr Horsley,' stressed Pluke, studying his watch. It was quarter past five. 'Now, we need to check whether anyone living locally has a criminal record or unsavoury reputation which might be linked with a crime of this type. Then we shall need a news conference, but we're too late for the regional television bulletins or the local evening newspapers. It will be a waste of time asking the press to attend this evening so we should fix one for ten thirty tomorrow morning.'

'Right, I'll check with the local police, but our teams need to be told murder has been confirmed,' Horsley reminded Pluke. 'In anticipation of such a development, I've already instructed them to return here at six, for an update. And I radioed Inspector Theaker on the moor top, one of his men will attend.'

'Well done. I shall wait until six and address them,' Pluke said. 'Have we anything from other forces about missing women?'

'Quite a few possibles, but no matches yet. Most are shorter than her and not all have pierced ears. We're getting some useful feedback anyway.'

'Then there's not a lot I can do at the moment but I do wish to visit the post office. I shall go now, and will return at six. Wayne, I think you should accompany me.'

Gunnerthwaite post office, which also served as the local shop and newsagent, occupied a former stone cottage in the centre of the village and boasted a huge plate glass window which displayed items of interest to tourists. There were guidebooks, picture postcards, souvenirs of all kinds, watercolours of the surrounding moors by a local artist and mugs bearing the logo of Gunnerthwaite. There were even a couple of dark green T-shirts with 'Gunner-thwaite' printed across the back. Outside, the pillar box was built into the thick wall and almost smothered in bright red paint; it still bore Queen Victoria's initials and crown. Pluke and Wayne pushed open the equally bright red door at which a bell sounded in the private section. They waited at the dark wooden counter as a woman materialized from behind a curtain and moved into position. The post office section was closed but the shop was open. The lady was about seventy, stout and grey-haired with a round, cheerful face, ruddy cheeks and warm brown eyes; she wore a red apron over her brown dress.

'Yes?' She peered at them short-sightedly.

'We're police officers –' began Pluke, waving his warrant card at her.

'I've had your chaps in already,' she said, even before he could announce their identities. 'Asking about that lass in the gill up Thordale. Nasty business, a sorry state of affairs. But, as I said, I can't say I know who she is, she's not a local, I do know that. We do get visitors in Gunnerthwaite, folks I never set eyes on, youngsters coming for parties and things. They never come in here, too busy with their booze and loud music and sleeping in till all hours of the day. Most of them fetch their own food and drink, so it's the older folks who generally pop in here for things.'

'It is now a murder investigation, not merely a missing person enquiry.' Pluke realized that if he told the lady in the post office – who, it seemed, was the village communications system, a highly efficient form of bush telegraph – then the population of the entire district would quickly become aware of it.

'Murder? But your men said she might have drowned, an accident mebbe.'

'We felt that was a possibility during the very early stages of our enquiries but the post-mortem examination suggests she was murdered.' Pluke had decided not to reveal the precise cause of death. His news would prompt a surge of speculation and gossip within the community. Just what he needed!

'That is terrible, just terrible . . . you don't expect that sort of thing in Gunnerthwaite or even in Thordale . . .'

'We must talk to everyone living here, and we have to trace occupants of holiday cottages, as well as any other visitors or incomers.'

'You've shocked me, you have, this is dreadful . . .'

'So, er, for our records, might I have your name?' asked Pluke.

'Miss Pyke.'

'And your first name?' Pluke had now produced his trough notebook which, in the mind of Miss Pyke, looked like a police notebook. This move transformed their chat into something much more formal and a look of horror flashed across her face.

'Well, I'm not sure I want my details in police records.' She backed away from her counter. 'I mean, I'm not one for making a fuss about things and besides, everybody calls me Miss Pyke. I can't see why you need my Christian name, that's something very personal to me. I've been Miss Pyke ever since I was fifteen.'

'We must differentiate between you and any other Miss Pykes,' tried Wayne.

'Then you can write Miss Pyke of Gunnerthwaite post office,' she retorted. 'So long as you don't get it mixed up with Gunnerside or Gunnerton. Some do, you know, get these places confused. I've had tourists here looking for Gunnerside and that's up in the Yorkshire Dales, half a day's drive away from here.'

'I have no wish to upset a lady, so Miss Pyke it is,' agreed Pluke. 'So, what I need, Miss Pyke, is a list of holiday cottages, by that I mean the names of their owners or those responsible for letting them. I am told you act as a kind of agent.'

'Keyholder more like,' she said. 'I keep some of the keys here and I do have lists of when the cottages are available, I keep in touch with the owners. I sign the keys in and out, but if it's just a list of every house you want, there's the electoral register. You can look at that.'

'We can get copies of the electoral register, it's contacts for the letting of the cottages I need,' Pluke explained. 'I must get as many names and addresses of tenants as

I can, so we can check every one of them before eliminating them from our enquiries.'

'I do keep a book,' she said. 'It has lists of those I see to.'

'Can I borrow it?' Pluke asked. 'Just long enough for us to photocopy it, then you can have it back. We'll go through all the names, we want to make sure no one is missing from their usual haunts.'

'Well, if it'll help find out who she is and who did this, you can have it – but I do need it back as soon as I can. Folks never stop ringing up for vacancies and prices and so on.'

Pluke and Wayne remained a while to explore her knowledge of local domestic strife, neighbourly battles about hedges, fences and access roads, disputes over cats digging up gardens and dogs messing on lawns, or any of that host of trivial things which cause neighbours to fight, friends to fall out, families to grow apart, solicitors to be contacted or the police to be called. However, if Miss Pyke was to be believed, then Gunnerthwaite seemed a blissful place in which to live and work with few problems other than seasonal ones involving tourists, caravanners and litter-droppers. Pluke and Wayne left with her precious book of holiday cottage addresses, but with no useful information about conflicts in the undercurrent of life in Gunnerthwaite.

'I respect what Miss Pyke has told us, but I can't believe it's all sweetness and light, even in this small place,' observed Wayne Wain as they made their way back to the church hall.

'There's bound to be friction between members of any community,' was Pluke's philosophy. 'Some people manage to keep problems private and concealed from the ears and eyes of everyone, even from their immediate families. Yorkshire village folk are particularly good at that, they keep things very quiet and personal, they don't shout about their disputes or have fights in the street, Wayne, they don't bother with courts and legal solutions. Well, not many of them. So even if Miss Pyke does not know of any local strife, there may be some. Even in a peaceful place like this, there might be a drama of sufficient intensity to generate a murder. Something has prompted this death, and it is our duty to identify that cause.'

'She could have been killed elsewhere and dumped here,' Wayne reminded Pluke. 'That seems very likely. Some prostitute upsetting a client, some poor girl working as a prostitute on the docks or in an inner city, trying to earn a crust, and this is her reward, some villain's mistress who's passed her use-by date . . .'

'The pathologist did not suggest she led the life of a prostitute,' Pluke told him. 'He suggests just the opposite – she was a virgin. I know a woman can be a prostitute and remain *virgo intacta*. When I was on my detective training course, we were told –'

'I do know what you mean,' smiled Wayne Wain. 'This woman could have been a prostitute, or involved in some business of a sexual nature, while remaining a virgin, or she might be as pure as driven snow and been killed for some other reason.'

'I favour the latter prognosis,' was all Pluke could offer as they arrived at the church hall. 'But whatever her personal background and morals, we shall investigate every possibility with the utmost vigour. Now it's six o'clock and time for our first conference of detectives.'

Inside and before speaking to his teams, Pluke swiftly examined Miss Pyke's 'Record of Lettings'. Although it did contain details of the cottage owners, dates of occupancy and a record of the issue of keys by Miss Pyke, it did not provide the addresses of those temporary occupants. It simply gave a surname because the lettings were arranged by the owners or their agents, and it was the issue of the keys that was delegated to Miss Pyke, after the appropriate liaison between the relevant parties.

Pluke handed the book over to Horsley. 'We need to interview all those house agents and owners,' he said. 'There must be some record of the tenants' addresses.'

'I'll put a team on to it,' Horsley promised. 'All we have

to do is find some unfortunate woman among this lot who hasn't returned home.'

'If that had been the case, surely her relatives would have been making a fuss?' suggested Pluke.

'Not if she lived alone and not if her friends, family or workmates had no idea where she'd gone for her holiday or how long she was likely to be away,' countered Horsley. 'And how far back do we go? A year? Two? Just a few months? This is not a comprehensive list of holiday cottages hereabouts, Montague – there are others not on this list, remember. But leave it with me, it'll be a good exercise for our newest detectives. I'll start at the beginning of this summer season.'

'Excellent. So, is everyone here?' Pluke asked.

'We are,' confirmed Horsley.

'Then I shall address them.'

A group of only two dozen detectives had assembled instead of the usual forty or so, although their number was increased by the specialists – Task Force, Scenes of Crime, incident room staff and so forth. Pluke's immediate task was to confirm the murder, saying that the woman appeared to have been struck on the head with a blunt instrument or object of some kind, the nature of which had not yet been ascertained. Photographs of the injury were available as was a video of the body and its post-mortem examination – he asked his officers to consider any object which might have inflicted the fatal injury. He then ordered them not to reveal to the public at this stage the precise means by which death had been caused.

As her identification was of paramount importance, along with a need to trace her last movements and contacts, her physical description was repeated and now appeared on the blackboard. A video of her final resting place had been made in addition to still photographs and digital pictures for transmission via email and on the Internet – these would assist other forces in the searches of their own records. Her apparent lack of any sexual life was considered important as was her unusual dress and the fact she might have been buried for only a short period.

How and from where her body had arrived at Devil's Dump had yet to be determined as was the precise date of the flash floods. Pluke stressed the need to make intense efforts to trace anyone who might have been in and around the vicinity of Devil's Dump or near the peat ponds over the past few months – people behaving in an odd or suspicious way, digging on the moor, carrying a heavy object, acting oddly, parking for long periods at strange times or being furtive in their behaviour.

Her grave must be traced as well as any jewellery, handbag or clothes she may have worn prior to death or burial, especially her shoes. They could have been thrown across the moor, well away from the path of the flood-water, or they might have been disposed of elsewhere. And what was the murder weapon? Had it been buried with her? Disposal of her body might have also provided a means of concealing the murder weapon. Or had the floods disturbed it too? If so, where was it? Washed into a crevice somewhere? He also reminded them that the woman's death may have coincided with the peak period of the outbreak of foot-and-mouth disease, a time when tourism was restricted on the moors and when few people would be around. Her asked them to bear in mind its impact on this rural community. Having completed his presentation, Pluke asked for questions or comments.

Sergeant Browning of the Task Force raised his hand.

'Inspector Theaker asked me to say that we have searched the entire area around the peat bogs, sir, and down the watercourses towards Thordale Gill for about two hundred yards. We have lots of items of tourist rubbish – plastic sandwich wrappers, drinks cans, sweet papers, that sort of thing – and he has retained it all for examination. But that's all so far. No sign of a grave or murder weapon. We've still got to search the gill itself.'

'Thank you, Sergeant. You may convey to him that this is now a murder enquiry.'

'Yes, sir, I will. He said we will continue until eight o'clock, unless it gets dark too early.'

'The incident room will remain open until nine,' Pluke reminded them. 'Now, anyone else?'

A woman detective raised her hand.

'Sir,' she smiled. 'There is a weather forecaster in the village, he writes notes for the local paper. I heard about him during house-to-house enquiries, a woman told me, she's his neighbour, but he's out just now and usually gets home about half-past six. I thought he might know the date of the flood.'

'Wonderful! Talk to him as soon as you can.'

'Yes, sir.'

Pluke's mini-conference occupied about forty-five minutes, and after his teams had refreshed themselves with tea and biscuits, they returned to their enquiries for the final hour or so, stimulated by the fact that this was now a murder enquiry. Pluke spent some time reading the statements already filed and then checked the early returns of women missing in other parts of the country. Some twenty files had been received by this time, along with fairly detailed descriptions, and Pluke saw that nine of them were roughly similar to the woman from Devil's Dump. Positive identification might require careful comparison of fingerprints, DNA profiles or dental records before any relatives would be invited to inspect the remains – but at least his enquiry was receiving positive and useful feedback. Tomorrow's news conference would be a great asset too – inevitably, that would produce a description of the woman which would also generate suggestions from the public as to possible identities.

'There's no need for you to hang about here, Montague,' Horsley said to Pluke. 'Things are moving along nicely and I can see to the booking-off routine and recording of final statements. If something dramatic does occur, I can get you on the mobile.'

'I have no transport,' said Pluke. 'It would mean Detective Sergeant Wain leaving too, and he's out with his teams just now.'

'Fair enough. But don't feel obliged to hang around if there's nothing to do.'

71

'That young detective, the one who mentioned the weatherman. Can you raise her on the radio? If she's going to revisit his house shortly, I'd like to accompany her.'

'I'll try,' promised Horsley.

Twenty minutes later, Pluke was walking beside Detective Constable Laura Brackley as she led him to the home of Gunnerthwaite's weather expert. He was the appropriately named Clarence Fairweather. On the way, Laura explained that Clarence worked as a shop assistant at a gents ' outfitters in Pickering, commuting daily by car, but in his spare time he maintained records of the weather and submitted articles to local papers and magazines. Locally, he was quite famous – at least, that's what his neighbour had said – and was frequently called upon to make forecasts by studying nature and saints' days. His Fairweather Forecasts were often printed in the national daily papers, the neighbour had said in considerable awe.

Clarence Fairweather lived in Spring Cottage, a detached handsome stone structure at the eastern end of the main street. Its name was on the neat white front gate and Pluke wondered whether it referred to the weather, or to the fact that it lay at the edge of the moors, near the foot of a slope where springs must surely emerge. This was good horse trough country – for them, a reliable supply of high quality spring water was essential. The cottage had a neat privet hedge and a smart front door with a brass knocker, brightly polished. The detectives strode up the sandstone garden path, Pluke activated the knocker with some vigour and Fairweather responded by opening the door almost immediately. In his early sixties, he was a small man with a bald head adorned with wisps of fair hair around the neck and ears. He had bright blue eyes behind horn-rimmed spectacles and wore a blue apron over his clothes. In his right hand there was a large wooden spoon with something clinging to it and in his left, an oven cloth.

'Yes?' There was almost an aggressive tone in his voice, no doubt because he'd been interrupted in the middle of making his evening meal.

'I am sorry to interrupt,' Pluke apologized. 'I can see you are busy.'

'I'm preparing my supper.' Those bright blue eyes peered at Pluke. 'If you're Jehovah's Witnesses or selling something, I'm not interested.'

'I am Detective Inspector Pluke and this is Detective Constable Brackley, we are investigating a murder in the dale.'

'A murder? My God . . .' and Fairweather's aggression evaporated in an instant, his hands falling to his sides and his mouth opening in shock.

Pluke saw that his opening gambit had shaken the fellow; clearly, the news had not yet reached him but at least Pluke had gained his undivided attention.

'A young woman has been found dead at the head of Thordale,' Pluke began to explain. 'In the pool known as Devil's Dump.'

'But . . . but . . . but . . . you don't think I had anything to do with it, do you?' spluttered Mr Fairweather.

'That never entered my head.' Pluke was honest in his remark. 'We are here to seek your help in establishing some material facts about the weather.'

'Oh, oh,' and a huge sigh emerged from the little man. 'Oh, I see . . . the weather, well, you'd better come in. Do forgive me, I'm making my supper, I live alone . . .'

'We can call back,' Pluke offered.

'No, there's no need. I'll just put it in the oven, it only needs a final stir. Sit in the lounge and I'll join you in a second or two.'

Fairweather admitted them to his small but neat lounge, settled them in the armchairs and asked if they'd like a cup of tea as the kettle had just boiled. Pluke declined, saying they'd just enjoyed a teabreak, so after disposing of his meal, spoon and oven cloth, Fairweather joined them. He sat on the edge of the settee, his hands revealing his nervousness.

'You gave me quite a shock, Inspector . . . did you say Pluke? You're not the horse trough Pluke, are you?'

'Well, as a matter of fact I am,' and Pluke did expand

his chest just a little, such was the pleasure at being recognized.

'I have all your books, Mr Pluke, so well researched, such a valuable contribution to local history . . . but I mustn't side-track you. A murder, you said? In Thordale? I find that quite staggering, quite upsetting, so close to home . . .'

Pluke outlined the facts and Fairweather listened intently, first saying he had no idea who the dead woman might be, and secondly saying he'd not walked that area for some months, adding that he would help as much as he possibly could. Pluke then turned to the weather.

'I am told there was a flash flood during the summer. We have reason to believe the deceased was washed into a small cavern beneath some tree roots at the side of Devil's Dump, Mr Fairweather. It would require a tremendous force of water to achieve that. Our enquiries suggest a severe flash flood may have occurred on Rockdale Moor but none of our enquiries has established the precise date, although we understand it was during the recent summer – July, I believe.'

'Ah, yes, well, you are right, of course. It was one of the Margaret Floods, not generating quite as much ferocity as Langtoft in 1892, but remarkable nonetheless.'

'St Margaret's Day, you mean?' Pluke did have a knowledge of saints' days and St Margaret's Day, 20th July, was noted for the floods which frequently occurred around that time. They were often associated with short but extremely violent thunderstorms and major cloudbursts.

'You know the old lore, Mr Pluke? Yes, well, the Thordale flood did occur actually on St Margaret's Day this year, 20th July. Right on time.'

'And what happened?'

'It was rather like the Langtoft flood, but less severe, Mr Pluke. Let me remind you about Langtoft in the East Riding, a village in the Yorkshire Wolds. In the evening of 3rd July, 1892, there was a violent thunderstorm on the hill behind the village, a most dramatic storm, a cloudburst of biblical proportions. More like an earthquake, they said. A huge torrent, like a tidal wave, washed down the hill and raged through the village – it was seven feet deep, Mr Pluke. Imagine that. A wall of water powerful enough to sweep away haystacks, farm buildings, cattle, horses, hedges and even houses. No human lives were lost – that was remarkable in itself – but even today, the scars of those floods remain on the hills behind Langtoft.'

'I know about it,' nodded Pluke. 'A storm of the most unbelievable ferocity.'

'Our Thordale flood was not quite so severe, Mr Pluke. For one thing, there are no houses at the head of Thordale other than the ruin of Trough House and it bypassed that. It was an epic cloudburst, though, right above the peat ponds. The ponds and nearby moorland overflowed, they just could not cope, and a surge of water gathered on those heights. It flooded the peat ponds and found its only means of exit – down the gill at Thordale Head. Quite literally, it gouged its way down the gill, Mr Pluke, ripping up trees, dislodging boulders, tearing away the earth down the sides of the gill and killing several sheep. Their bodies were never found, they'd been swept a long way downstream – but because the bed of Thordale Gill is deep and wide at the top, it coped. The water was channelled into it like a giant funnel and it coped. By the time it had reached the lower dale, the force had dissipated. There was some slight overflow downstream but it was not serious.'

'So the cloudburst caused little damage?'

'It scoured several routes through the peat, Mr Pluke, and demolished some trees – there used to be a clump of lovely rowans just below the summit of the gill, the Rockdale Rowans, but they've all disappeared, smashed to matchwood by the flood. Happily, because the storm occurred in such a remote area, other damage was minimal. Had it occurred on the moor immediately behind this village, I cannot bear to think of the consequences.'

'There was a similar flood at Holmfirth in West Yorkshire, I believe,' said DC Brackley.

'Yes, in 1852, but that was due to a burst dam,' Fairweather told her. 'Ninety million gallons swept through the town, destroying houses, mills, bridges and trees, and it killed almost a hundred people. But ours and the one at Langtoft were due to cloudbursts, not faulty dams.'

'Did you visit the area of the flood?' asked Pluke.

'Not at the time. I was at work when it happened – it was a Friday – but I did go up there the following Sunday, the foot-and-mouth restrictions had been lifted by then. The moor was devastated, Mr Pluke, huge areas of heather and peat swept away, devastation of trees and shrubs in the gill, rocks and and boulders shifted . . . it really did transform the landscape. It bears no comparison to what it was like prior to the flood – although the ponds remain and the gill has reverted to its normal level and path. Much of the floodwater came down the lane nearby.'

'I could see the marks it left. Now, would the flood be powerful enough to dislodge a body from a grave?' Pluke put to him.

'Oh, yes, I'm sure it was capable of that, certainly if the grave was a shallow one in the direct line of the flow, or among the peat up there . . . oh dear, is that where your victim came from?'

'I do believe so,' Pluke said. 'I believe her body was transported to the moors by a vehicle of some kind – you'd need a vehicle to carry a body – and buried near those peat ponds, then swept by the flood to its resting place in Devil's Dump. If the flood occurred on 20th July, she must have been murdered before that date. My problem is knowing precisely how long before.'

'Sadly, Mr Pluke, I cannot help with that. All I can say is that the flood occurred on that date, and there has been nothing comparable since although we did have some heavy rain last week, enough to cause the gill to rise higher than normal. Quite often, it's such a secondary or sub-sequent rise in the water level which dislodges debris produced by the first wave of floodwater. Over time, things can be swept a long way, Mr Pluke, even heavy things like animals' carcasses and tree trunks. They can end up in some very odd and otherwise inaccessible places.'

'So this body could have been dislodged a second time from an earlier resting place? By the second, lesser flood? Or lodged or moved deeper into its original site?'

'Very possible in either case, Mr Pluke. Now, you do realize that peat preserves bodies, don't you?'

'I do indeed, Mr Fairweather, I recall the famous 1984 case of the corpse known as Pete Marsh, preserved for centuries.'

'Yes, but the point I am making, Mr Pluke, is that if that woman had been buried in peat, she might have been there for a very, very long time.'

'That was our first thought, Mr Fairweather, but ours is a modern lady, of that we are certain.'

'Oh, dear. Well, I don't know of any ladies missing hereabouts.'

They remained a few moments longer, chatting about the weather, and then Pluke returned to the incident room to programme 20th July into the system, and to make all the detectives aware of its significance.

'But there is another problem,' Pluke told Horsley.

'Which is?'

'If she died or was buried on those moors near the peat bogs, or even along the route of the gill, it means that the scene of our crime may have been totally obliterated. Whatever forensic evidence there might have been will surely have been washed away – and perhaps the murder weapon with it,' Pluke reminded them. 'She might have lain there for centuries had it not been for St Margaret's Flood.'

'So you've not got a lot to go on, have you? No identity, no scene of crime, no grave, no forensic evidence, no weapon, no suspect!'

'There is always a clue somewhere.' Pluke tried to sound confident, adding, 'And I must find it. Now, it is time to conclude my day's duty. I need time to think about this crime so if I can find Detective Sergeant Wain, he can take me home.'

*   *   *

77

Because it was Saturday night, Millicent grilled a succulent juicy steak and as Montague should have been enjoying an off-duty evening, she agreed they might both enjoy an aperitif, a nice sherry. It was while savouring those quiet domestic moments that Millicent presented his gift, neatly wrapped.

'But Millicent, it's not my birthday!'

'No, my dear, but when I saw this I couldn't resist it,' she told him as he began to unwrap it. 'I thought you would like it, especially as your visit to Trough House was interrupted.'

Like a child opening a Christmas present, Montague tugged feverishly at the wrapping until the contents were revealed. It was a print of a watercolour signed by the artist. It was in a wooden frame with a glass front and on the rear was a sticker bearing the name of the firm who had framed it – Crickledale Framers.

'But it's Trough House!' he exclaimed with evident excitement after a few moments. 'In its original state, not the ruin I saw . . . Oh, Millicent, this is wonderful and look – the trough is there, just where I thought it would be! See, the trough's even got the name Trough House carved along the front! I wonder if that is an accurate portrayal? If so, the trough might still exist somewhere . . . but the painting looks modern, that frame is new, I know Crickle-dale Framers, they're just off the market place. Where did you get this?'

'At the post office in Gunnerthwaite after I left you this morning. And look, it shows a shepherd on the moors behind the house. The artist always puts a shepherd in all her paintings of the moor.'

'This is remarkable, Millicent, truly remarkable. I must speak to the artist,' he said. 'In my own time, of course, when this enquiry is over. The artist must know what the house looked like and where the trough was located, how could she know that? She's even included the name on the trough –'

Millicent interrupted him with a smile. 'Her name is Susan Miller, she's signed it at the bottom right-hand corner. If you are busy solving a murder, I could try and find her, couldn't I? It won't take long, I can start with the firm who framed it, they're in Crickledale, you know. Or I could ask the woman in the post office where I bought it. But tomorrow is Sunday and they will be closed.'

'I can wait – and I think we should celebrate, Millicent. Without doubt, this justifies another sherry,' beamed Pluke.

Chapter Six

Montague Pluke had performed all his luck-enhancing morning rituals, such as getting out of bed on the right side, stepping from the bedroom with his right foot first and making sure his rabbit's foot was in his trouser pocket. Sensing that good fortune would accompany him throughout today, he was further enlivened at the sight of a pair of magpies at the far side of his garden. Two for joy, he thought, another omen of good fortune. Verily, he realized, today will be a lucky one, and such was his happiness and confidence that he was humming tunelessly as he entered the kitchen for breakfast. He made sure he entered with his right foot first.

'You appear to be extremely happy, Montague,' smiled Millicent at the stove. 'It is such a shame you have to work today, I was really looking forward to an outing into the countryside.'

'The reason I appear to be happy is that I *am* happy, my dear, and I am happy thanks to you. Furthermore, I feel lucky and am sure I shall be successful in this investigation. Then we can explore the countryside at leisure, without the burden of an unsolved murder. I am sure that you, on your own, can pursue the puzzle of the trough in that painting. If the Crickledale picture framers are closed today, you could visit a tourist area, a place where similar paintings are sold. I am sure such places will be open on Sundays, even at this time of year. I must find that artist, Millicent, I must investigate the whereabouts of that trough. It is my first real challenge as North Yorkshire's Custodian of Horse Troughs.'

'I will see what I can do,' she assured him. 'Now, get a good breakfast, you never know whether or not you will have time for lunch, and tonight I shall have a nice meal ready for you.'

'On Sundays we tend to close the incident rooms earlier, at seven,' he said. 'So, unless there is some untoward development, it will be a reasonably early finish today.'

'I look forward to it. Now, I have your two fried eggs, bacon, black pudding, sausage, mushrooms, tomato, baked beans and fried bread in the oven, all nice and warm. Do you want your porridge first?'

'Porridge is so good for the system,' he said. 'A man must have his oats very regularly, so yes, I'll have it first.'

Pluke was collected by Wayne Wain and they drove the route taken yesterday by Pluke and Millicent. When they reached the top of the moorland road which led down to Devil's Dump, Pluke asked Wayne to pause because he wanted another look at the locality. Wayne drew to a halt in the day trippers' car park, a flat and spacious area within sight of the peat ponds. It provided stunning long-distance views down Thordale and beyond.

'What are you looking for?' Wayne Wain asked. 'The Task Force won't be here yet.'

'I am trying to visualize how this area must have looked before the Margaret Floods,' said Pluke.

'Much the same as now with the ground not so disturbed, I expect,' contributed his sergeant.

'Not entirely, Wayne. Yesterday, Mr Fairweather referred to the Rockdale Rowans, a clump of them near the summit of that lane. They were destroyed by the flood, he told me, so I need to see what is left.'

'I can't see what they've got to do with a murder!'

'We've considered this moor to be open, Wayne, with no concealment for anyone performing an illicit act – but if those rowans were growing in a clump, then they would offer some shelter, a shield perhaps? And they were close to the summit of the lane, which in turn means they were near the gill. So I am going for a quick examination of the likely spot. And in the past, the presence of rowans often indicated a burial ground. Come along, the fresh air and walk will do you good.'

As they walked towards the lane which led up the hill from Trough House, they could see the result of the mighty natural forces.

'It's like the effect of a huge glacier on the move,' commented Wayne. 'As the rocks and boulders were moved by the water, it would produce a giant sandpaper effect, scrubbing the surface from the ground and carrying with it plants and movable objects. I can see now how it must have transformed this landscape, certainly enough to dislodge a body in a grave.'

'A shallow grave, yes, Wayne. A hurriedly created grave. And enough to shatter a copse of rowan trees which stood in its way. See, over there, the smashed remains on the crest of that hillock?'

Slightly below their elevation, Pluke had noticed the remains of a small copse, broken trunks among a pile of rocks; some damaged trees lay smashed on the ground and tangled with the short relics of the trunks of others. It was as if the entire copse had been crushed to matchwood by an enormous weight, and it was evident that most of the ruined trees had been washed into the gill by the flood-water. A few sad remains were all that was left; not one complete tree had survived. Pluke walked towards the devastation, taking a wide-angled approach. Wayne followed, not really understanding Pluke's intense interest in this copse.

Then, facing east along the escarpment below the copse, Pluke said, 'See, Wayne, see this.'

Wayne followed the line of his gaze, squinting into the bright sunshine. 'What, sir? What are you looking at?'

'Shadows, Wayne. See, below the copse, that level part of ground, like a step almost . . . the sun is beaming across it and you can see the sharp outline in the ground . . . a shallow hollow, Wayne, orientated east-to-west . . . Come, let's take a closer look.'

'The grave, you mean? Is it the grave?'

'What else would it be, Wayne?' and Pluke was striding purposefully down the heather-covered slope until he was below the trees and standing on the small flat plateau. Then he stood at the western end of the hollow; Wayne joined him and together they stood and peered at the shallow depression.

'From here, it could be anything,' admitted Wayne.

'An oblong hollow in the ground, Wayne, approximately two feet wide by six feet long and eighteen inches deep. I can see it's been battered by the flood which first hit those rowans and then swept down here before rushing into the gill, but how symmetrical, Wayne. Man-made, I would suggest, it's too precise to be the work of nature. And I think it's now got some silt in the bottom, it doesn't match the surrounding moorland.'

He went forward, stooping to peer at the ground as if hoping to discover some evidence of his theory, but there was nothing. Then he dug his heel into the earth, finding it was soft and sandy, unlike the peat covering of the surrounding moorland. And the approach was fairly level, certainly good enough to permit access by a vehicle.

'We'll never prove that was a grave, sir, or that she was buried up here. The whole place has been washed clean by the flood.'

'If she was buried on these moors, Wayne, this is one likely place – there's shelter for the grave digger, it's out of sight behind those trees, it's a soft piece of ground and you can see how the flow of the flood from here would wash her into the gill, and then to Devil's Dump. Even if I can never prove this was her grave, I'd stake my reputation that this is the place.'

'Fair enough, you know what to look for, but why is it so important to determine her place of burial if all the likely evidence has been washed away?'

'Because we must find the sort of person who would

bury her here, Wayne. Not everyone would do that or even think of doing that.'

'That's true, sir. I'd pick somewhere secluded, hidden away, with soft earth, somewhere I could dig out of the sight of men walking dogs or tending sheep, or tourists and ramblers.'

'Precisely, Wayne. Now, take me slowly down the hill, I want another look at Devil's Dump, its relationship to the location of the farms en route and even a quick glance at Trough House . . .'

'And all before our day's work begins!' smiled Wayne Wain. 'All right, sir, you know what you're doing.' And they returned to their car.

On the grounds that he had not yet started his police duty for the day, Pluke entered the site of Trough House, albeit very briefly, just to see if the artist had portrayed it correctly. Although he did not have the painting with him, he felt sure her portrayal was accurate. He could visualize those fallen walls at the peak of condition, forming a handsome and sturdy house in the remotest of places. He peered into Devil's Dump once again, looking across at the cavity in the shadows beneath the tree roots and appreciating how difficult it was to see anything concealed inside. Then they cruised down the dale noting the distances between the farms and the peat ponds. By the time Pluke arrived at Gunnerthwaite, he had reappraised the entire scene.

Wayne pulled up in the car park of the church hall and Pluke said, 'Wayne, it is vital that we concentrate on finding out who, among the local people, has been up to the moor near those peat ponds in recent months, and when, and why. And who they saw when they got there. We need a list of those making regular visits.'

'Right, sir, will do. I'll get my house-to-house teams to concentrate on that, revisiting earlier houses if necessary. The trouble is we have no time-scale as a basis for enquiries, have we? Except an unknown period prior to 20th July. And around that time, the foot-and-mouth outbreak would have deterred a lot of visitors who might have been protential witnesses.'

'True, but it is said that a murderer always returns to the scene of the crime, Wayne, so we can't ignore anyone who has been on the moors recently.'

'Checking that the body was still buried, you mean?'

'Or wondering if it might have been dislodged by the flood,' smiled Pluke.

'But if he went to look for it after the flood, he'd have found it, surely, like Mrs Pluke did? A local killer would realize it must have been washed down the gill, wouldn't he? If he found the grave empty, there's nowhere else it could have gone.'

'If it got swept into the rear of that cavern, it might have been out of sight for some time, even hidden behind debris. Maybe the second, minor flood dislodged it and floated it to the front, to the place where Mrs Pluke found it. But suppose the killer had found it, what could he do?' Pluke asked. 'You and I know how difficult it is to carry a dead body, even with assistance, let alone extract one from that position without help of any kind, and then carry it away for reburial or disposal. I would suggest the killer, if he had found her, would leave the body exactly where it was. He'd hope that nature would dispose of it before anyone else discovered it – but thanks to Mrs Pluke, that did not happen.'

'Or he could report finding it, as some murderers do?'

'He could, but he didn't, Wayne. That is another reason I think the killer is local – it's someone letting nature take its course, as it does with dead sheep or cattle if they are not recovered. He'd know how it works, it's nature in the raw, Wayne; she'd suffer the attention of animals, birds and insects, the effects of a lesser flood or two, or even heavy rains refilling the gill from time to time – all would help to dispose of those remains, quite speedily too.'

'Even so, it would still take some time . . .'

'Yes, but time was against the killer, Wayne, even though the body was in a very fragile state. It wouldn't have taken much more treatment by nature to disintegrate it – I've known the carcasses of sheep disappear in a matter of days due to nothing more than the effect of the weather. It's a good job we found her when we did.'

'So we're looking for someone who knows the moors well enough to bury her up there, and someone who is content to leave her to nature now? A cool customer, I'd say, sir.'

'That is my feeling too, Wayne. But come along, our teams will be waiting.'

The well-established routine of any incident room meant the detectives and civilian support staff assembled before nine each morning. Coffee and biscuits were enjoyed after the drive to work and in preparation for the long day ahead. At nine thirty, the officer in charge chaired a conference of detectives and civilians, the purpose of which was to pool all the information gathered to date, to highlight any particular lines of enquiry, to discuss problems and to plan the coming day.

Pluke's incident room followed this pattern. After a private discussion with Inspector Dick Horsley to assess the information which had arrived overnight, and a further chat with the press officer, Inspector Paul Russell, Pluke stood on the stage to address the troops. As this was the first formal conference, he reiterated the facts of the case, stressing the immediate need for positive identification of the victim and her last known movements or contacts. He followed by highlighting the need to determine the movements of anyone who might have visited the peat ponds area and added that a trawl of local criminal records had not revealed any likely suspects.

'I may have located the grave,' he added, following with a description of the site while pinpointing it on the map. 'Inspector Theaker – that's a job for you. Examine it, take photographs. You'll see the indentation in the ground below the broken rowans.'

Continuing his address, he asked the teams to trace people walking dogs or sightseeing. Sheep farmers running sheep and parties of grouse shooters should be traced and interviewed even though the flood had occurred prior to the start of the grouse season. He asked in particular that detectives interview Mike Booth of Ling Garth Farm, Alec and Patrick Hall, the musicians of Throstle Nest, and Winston Livingstone of Cragside in the hope they might be able to convey some information. Further efforts must be made to uncover the undercurrents of life in Thordale and Gunnerthwaite, a motive must be found for the murder and suspects identified. Following his chat with Horsley, he was able to confirm that several possible names for the victim had been put forward by other police forces. Actions would be allocated in an attempt to determine whether or not one of them was the woman found in Devil's Dump. After his delivery, Pluke asked for questions or comments, adding that a news conference had been arranged for ten thirty so that, by tomorrow, the murder would be widely known – but, as it was Sunday, there was no regional news on television tonight and no evening newspapers. He fielded one or two questions and then dismissed his teams to their duties while he adjourned, with Inspector Russell, to the ante-room to prepare for the news conference. During their discussions, he advised Russell to stress the two main thrusts of the enquiry – identification of the victim and the movements of people near the peat ponds – both of which would benefit from press publicity.

The chief events of the morning having been determined, Pluke decided he should get outside and spend time in the village, soaking up the atmosphere, talking to residents, trying to relate this small community with the more remote Thordale and chatting to anyone he might encounter. He told Inspector Horsley of his intentions. It was quarter past eleven when he left the bustle of the incident room and he was just in time to see the congregation leaving the parish church. It was Church of England, he noted, not Catholic or Methodist. Not wishing to jeopardize the house-to-house enquiries already planned for the village, he walked briskly ahead of the emerging faithful – all six of them – and soon found himself passing the post office. There he halted to look into the window – it was an old police trick to gaze into a shop window so that one could observe the passing scene in the reflection from the glass. Instead he found himself attracted to the paintings on display.

Millicent had purchased his print here and, judging by the appearance of others on sale, they were the work of the same artist. As he studied them, he saw that each was of a different scene within the moors – a grouse butt, a grouse perched on a dry-stone wall, a stretch of purple heather, a farmhouse, a pack horse bridge, a moorland cross, sheep sheltering in a blizzard, a kestrel hovering near a patch of water and a stone footway vanishing over the heathery horizon. All were based on original watercolours, all framed and all the work of Susan Miller. And, he noted, every one of them had the small figure of a shepherd somewhere in the background, complete with crook and a black and white dog.

'Hello,' said a woman's voice. She had approached without him realizing – she'd not yet walked into the range of his reflected vantage point – and when he turned, he saw it was Miss Pyke, the postmistress.

'Ah, Miss Pyke, good morning to you,' and he raised his panama as befitting a gentleman of his stature.

'I saw you earlier, when I left church, I followed you here. We said prayers for you and your officers and, of course, we prayed for the unfortunate young woman.'

'That is most considerate of you.' He replaced his hat. 'I am sure we shall all benefit from those kind thoughts. And that reminds me, I have not yet contacted the vicar, I must speak to him before the day is out.'

'He's a visiting vicar, one of our flying clergymen. We have services once a fortnight. He is from Thorncroft, that's the next village, but he will be here until twelve – he stays behind so that people can discuss their problems with him.'

'Then I shall go immediately.'

'While you are there, you must look at our collection of maidens' garlands.'

'I have heard of them,' Pluke acknowledged. 'But I must

admit I have never seen them. I shall make a point of doing so.'

'I know you will appreciate them. Now, you like those paintings?' She had noticed his admiration of them.

'Indeed I do. In fact, my wife bought one yesterday, a present for me. Trough House.'

'Ah, yes, I remember that lady. All those prints sell very well, the price is reasonable and the pictures are full of moorland atmosphere.'

'I am intrigued by the Trough House print, it shows the house in its complete state, including the trough. I am interested in troughs, you see . . .'

'I did hear that your name is Pluke, Detective Inspector Pluke. You're not the Montague Pluke who writes those wonderful books about horse troughs, are you? I thought I recognized you yesterday although I'm pretty hopeless with faces. I really must get some new glasses. I went to a WI group meeting some time ago when you were the guest speaker . . . a wonderful talk, Mr Pluke. I had no idea horse troughs could be so interesting. Fancy you being a detective as well! I had no idea you were famous.'

'Well, I'm not really famous.' He blushed modestly. 'I just wish to record troughs for posterity, before they all get lost or forgotten.'

'What a wonderful commitment, Mr Pluke. I do admire you.'

'I would like to talk to the artist sometime – in my leisure time, I must stress, not during this enquiry – as I would dearly love to know how she knew about the trough, its position in relation to the house. In her painting it bears the name of the house – Trough House in letters carved in stone along the front.'

'Oh, I know where that is, Mr Pluke. It's in the garden of Rowan Cottage, down by the bridge.'

'The Trough House trough you mean?' He could hardly believe what he was hearing.

'Yes, you can see it as you walk past, it's a beautiful piece of carved stone.'

With his heart beating, he wanted to rush down to

Rowan Cottage, but then remembered this was not part of the murder investigation. And besides, he wanted to interview the vicar. He'd catch him now, he might leave before the house-to-house teams arrived.

'I will try to pay a visit to Rowan Cottage,' he assured her. 'But first I must catch the vicar. But tell me, why is that trough in the garden of Rowan Cottage?'

'It was moved by the people who own Trough House,' she said. 'Trough House lay derelict for years but eventually the owners of the land – descendants of the original owner – built themselves a smaller place, that's Rowan Cottage. They used stone from Trough House to build Rowan Cottage, then transferred the trough to the new site.'

'They didn't attempt to reconstruct Trough House on its own site then?'

'No, it was far too remote. No drainage, no sewage, no mains water, no electricity . . . it had been derelict for years but they already owned the land which is now the site of Rowan Cottage. It's used for holidays, Mr Pluke, but it's not on my books. I don't look after the key, I've nothing to do with it. It's only used by the family and their friends, and then only occasionally. I don't think anyone's there now but you could check. They're called Featherstone, they live somewhere near Wakefield. Wool people, I think, former mill owners. Plenty of money. We don't see much of them when they come. Well, I say they, but I mean her, the daughter. Her parents died a while ago so she comes alone now.'

'And does the Trough House site still belong to that family?'

'Yes, so far as I know, Mr Pluke. From time to time folks, visitors mainly, get their eyes on it and think it might make a site for a house or a caravan site, perish the thought! They try to buy it but we don't want our dale made unsightly by parked caravans, or our roads blocked with them coming and going. So yes, I think the Featherstones still own Trough House – or what's left of it.'

'Well, it seems the artist also knows something of its

history, I must track her down when I have a moment. Do you know where I can find her?'

'Sorry, no. I get my prints ready framed, from Crickledale Framers. I buy them through an agent – it's Miss Featherstone who owns Rowan Cottage as a matter of fact. But those pictures are very popular, Mr Pluke, tourists love them and some people try to collect every picture the artist produces. They've all got a shepherd in the background, as you can see.'

'Yes, I had noticed that,' Pluke smiled. 'What a wealth of information you have provided – and all through my wife buying that print. Well, I must be getting along, I mustn't miss the vicar.'

'Do call again, Mr Pluke, if you need help, even when the post office is closed. Just ring the bell.'

'Thank you, Miss Pyke.'

And so they parted, with Pluke now heading for the church to join the queue of those who might have spiritual requirements to discuss. When he arrived, he walked into the empty medieval building which smelled of dampness and candle wax, and his echoing footsteps caused the vicar to appear from the vestry. He was a youthful vicar, bearded and slender, with dark wavy hair and a ready smile. With a dog collar showing above a navy blue sweater, he wore jeans and trainers and smiled a welcome to his caller.

'I've no office here.' He threw his hands wide in a gesture of apology. 'So if it's private, we can go into the vestry and close the door, or if you're thinking of arranging something like a bring-and-buy sale and want my input, we can discuss it in the pews. I didn't see you at church, but my name is Cooper. Michael Cooper, call me Michael,' and he extended a hand for Pluke to shake.

Pluke shook it and said, 'I am Detective Inspector Pluke, I am here to investigate a murder, Mr Cooper, not to seek spiritual guidance. We can talk here, it will only take a moment.'

'Oh, right, sorry, I was ahead of myself, forgive me. We

did pray for the poor woman . . . So how can I help, Mr Pluke?'

'This is more of a courtesy call than an enquiry,' Pluke continued. 'But I do feel that, in these kind of circumstances, I should make myself known to the key inhabitants of a small community.'

'Ah, yes, I understand. The doctor, the vicar, the squire, the chairman of the parish council, landlord of the local pub.'

'Exactly, although there is no pub here. A dry village, not very common hereabouts. But such eminent people often have a finger on the pulse, in a manner of speaking – they know the undercurrents, the petty squabbles and the domestic dramas that often bedevil a small village.'

'Well, I'm an outsider, Mr Pluke. I come here once a fortnight and hold these surgeries, that's about all. It's sad that itinerant modern vicars don't get involved with the day-to-day life of parishioners. I've a very small congregation, sometimes I think these locals are a bunch of pagans! Apart from those regulars, I don't see many Gunnerthwaite people. But if I can help in any way, then of course I will.'

Pluke then detailed the circumstances of the woman's death, stressing the main thrust of his enquiries and asking that the Reverend Cooper keep his ears and eyes open in the hope he might come across information useful to the police. Cooper said he had no idea who the dead woman might be but promised his co-operation. Before leaving, Pluke asked, 'Like you, Mr Cooper, I am not from this locality so I am not au fait with local problems. For example, does the church suffer from crime? Vandals wrecking the churchyard, travelling thieves raiding offertory boxes or stealing furnishings?'

'I've only been coming for the past two years, and since that time we've kept the church locked,' he said. 'Thieves did take two antiques, valuable Jacobean chairs, some three or four years ago. Since we've been locking the doors that kind of trouble has ended and I've no reports of vandals in the churchyard.'

'So if a genuine visitor wants access while you are not around, is that possible? You do host a noted collection of maidens' garlands.'

'Oh yes, I'll show them to you, but when the church is closed, visitors can obtain the key from the clerk of the parish council, Hilda Weston at Greenside Cottage. We put a notice on the door to that effect. We do get them wanting to see the interior. In addition to the garlands, we have parts dating to Norman times and some very interesting tombs.'

Cooper took Pluke on a tour of the church, eventually pointing to six dusty garlands hanging from the ceiling of a chapel in a side aisle.

'I do have a little knowledge of those garlands,' Pluke explained. 'They were used at the funerals of young unmarried girls. It was a way of proclaiming their virginity. Some garlands were made with white paper and others from white linen, then decorated with streamers or coloured paper flowers. They were carried by youngsters dressed in white who walked ahead of the coffin, then after the burial, each garland was either hung in the church and left until it rotted or fell to pieces, or it was placed on the coffin. It is unlucky to remove them from the church, Mr Cooper, but in those areas where examples have survived, like here, many have been removed by over-zealous church cleaners, and lost for ever. And I am sure lots have just fallen to pieces.'

'We've lost only one since I came,' said Cooper. 'I've no idea where it went, there were seven hanging there when I arrived, and then one day, when a travel writer came to look around – a Sunday, as it happened – I realized we'd lost one. They are most fragile, though, a knock with a feather duster or even a passing bird panicking in the rafters would probably cause one to fall down in pieces. Birds do get trapped in the church from time to time and can cause havoc, starlings especially. So far as I know, the last time a garland accompanied a girl's coffin was in 1872 – that girl who was drowned in Devil's Dump – so those have been there since before that time. I think the missing one was made of tissue paper, it probably distintegrated and got swept up with dust and flower petals. We get petals and even leaves falling from floral decorations. A church can generate an amazing amount of litter, Mr Pluke!'

The vicar continued his guided tour, naming the inhabitants of the stone-lidded coffins, explaining some of the inscriptions and memorials on the walls, and providing a history of the stone font. He also escorted Pluke around the churchyard where Pluke noted some of the names on the tombstones – he saw Pyman, Featherstone, Livingstone, Hall, Booth and others he'd already encountered on this enquiry. There did not seem to be any new graves, however, although the Reverend Cooper said he would consider burying the victim if there was no alternative.

Interesting though the visit was, especially from the folklore aspect of the maidens' garlands, Pluke found little of value to his investigation and, after bidding farewell, he set off back to the village. But he could only think of the trough at Rowan Cottage – it was so near and yet so far . . . He decided he could justify a visit by undertaking legitimate house-to-house enquiries. He didn't think such a visit would jeopardize Wayne Wain's efforts and so, with a brisk step, he made his way towards the bridge which crossed Thordale Gill on the road to Thorncroft.

Rowan Cottage was in fact a large stone-built house and Pluke felt it would have been better named as Rowan House or Bridge View. It was very spacious with a red pantile roof and squatted on its beckside site as if it had been there for generations. It looked very much a part of the landscape due to its design and the age of the stones from which it was constructed. The architect had emulated the design of similar moorland houses, sturdy, spacious and comfortable with plenty of room both inside and out, all enhanced by pleasing views from an elevated site.

There was a large farm-style gate and a smaller garden gate, both leading into the gravelled drive which swept in a large half-circle towards the main entrance. Pluke pushed open the smaller gate and strode purposefully along the drive, and then, as he was able to see past the corner of the building, he spotted the trough. A magnificent double-header, it was standing on a stone base at the far end of the lawn, beyond which was a ha-ha separating a field from the garden. The trough occupied a vantage point – as Pluke approached, he realized that, by standing close to the trough, he had open views down the dale towards the sea.

Wonderful . . . this trough must have the best view in Yorkshire, or even England! A brass tap had been fitted above the western end, and a small drain to the east, but this was indeed the trough which had appeared in the painting. When he inspected it, he saw the name 'Trough House' carved in the front, overlooking the open field, and this had been picked out with white paint.

But he must not allow his delight to overshadow his real purpose; he was supposed to be investigating a murder and so he turned towards the house, making for the front door. To one side, on the wall, was a sign announcing that this was Rowan Cottage, and planted a few feet from the front door was a rowan tree, rich in its autumn colours and heavy with fruit. In former times, these were planted near houses and other buildings to ward off witches, evil spirits and disease, and even now some people believed they brought good luck.

Then he pressed the door bell and waited.

Chapter Seven

There was no reply so Pluke pressed the bell button again; it was working, he could hear it ringing deep inside the house. As he waited, he peeped through the glass panels of the upper door and saw a pile of mail scattered across the hall floor, most of which looked like circulars. But a good police officer is never satisfied with a lack of response at one door – he tries all the doors and even peeps through the windows, and so Pluke decided to check the rear. He walked around the side of the house, using a concrete footpath, and on the way checked the interior through open curtains without seeing signs of anyone at home. The rooms into which he could clearly see – the lounge and the dining room – were both deserted, and both tidily kept. It was a nice-looking house inside, handsomely furnished and well maintained with pictures on the walls. Then he found himself at the kitchen door. There was no bell and no door knocker, so he rapped the wood with his fist. The resultant noise was very feeble, not enough to penetrate the furthest corners of the house. As he waited, he peered through the window into the kitchen. The table was set with pots, not breakfast or dinner pots but two mugs and two plates beside a tin of biscuits whose lid was lying on the table. There was a glass jug of milk beside a half-emptied coffee percolator. Morning coffee for two, he smiled. So did it mean the house was occupied this weekend?

He repeated his knocking with no response, and then, in the manner of a determined police officer, tried the door handle. The door opened; it was not locked. Some country people, even in the twenty-first century, never lock their doors, especially if they merely pop next door, or go for a short walk. Considering that the unlocked door was not particularly odd, he pushed it wider and shouted.

'Hello, anyone in?'

There was no sound within the house, no hissing water as one hears when a bath is being run or a toilet cistern is refilling, no radio playing or television broadcasting, no vacuum cleaner at work, no sounds of feet on floorboards upstairs, no one talking on the telephone or conversing with a visitor or friend. Nothing. He waited, ears alert for sounds of occupancy, then shouted again, several times, in his loudest voice. There was no response. He was sorely tempted to venture inside, at least into the kitchen, and to shout again, hoping his voice would carry upstairs. Police officers often did this – they entered houses under such circumstances, shouting to announce their presence and sometimes they saved lives by finding sick or injured people . . . in that way, such an intrusion could be justified. Sometimes they even caught intruders. And, he told himself, he was currently engaged upon a murder enquiry even if his interest in the horse trough had brought him to this place.

As he pondered his next move, he realized something was wrong. The house had an air of desertion, almost as if the occupants had left suddenly to go about some urgent business. Or was there another reason? He began to sense that this house had not been occupied for some time. Even from the scanty evidence, it seemed the departure of its residents had been so swift they'd not had time to clear their dirty pots. And they'd left an open biscuit tin on the table in an otherwise tidy house – and why was there so much mail in the porch? That mail had not been delivered today – it was Sunday. Indeed, the sheer volume suggested an accumulation over a period. How long a period, he wondered? Then other worries came to mind. Why was the back door unlocked, for example?

Standing on the doorstep, he shouted several times but before entering the house, he decided to examine the outbuildings and garden. After all, the occupant or occupants might be in the garden . . . it was just possible they'd rushed outside without bothering to collect their mail. They might have just arrived, of course; could they have returned moments ago after that sudden departure, and gone out to check something? But the exterior was just as deserted. There was no one in the garden and no sign of recent activity – indeed, cutting of the lawn was overdue and the borders were producing substantial weeds, indicating a distinct lack of recent attention. There was no one in the greenhouse or any of the outbuildings, but there was a car in the garage. It was a large garage, easily big enough to accommodate a pair of medium-sized cars, but he could see only one. It was a small black open-top with a black canvas hood, a Volkswagen by the look of it, although he could not get a very good view through the dusty small windows of the door. He could not see the registration plates. He toured the whole exterior, calling when he was among buildings and noting that the house had no close neighbour. There was no one to oversee the house and its garden, no one to show interest from behind lace curtains. For all its splendid views and position, it was a very private place.

He returned to the house, shouted his presence several times, then entered the kitchen, still calling and still getting no reply. Now, though, he could see that the milk in the jug was practically solid, the dregs in the mugs had been there long enough to evaporate into mere stains and the biscuits in the open tin were showing signs of mouldiness. There was a fridge, he saw, and it was functioning, he could now hear its motor running quietly; he opened it and saw it was almost bare. A few items of food remained – mushrooms, tomatoes and a lettuce, all looking distinctly past their best, cheese in an unopened plastic wrapper, a carton of milk with a use-by date which had expired nine weeks ago, some yoghurts with a similar expiry date. He closed the fridge and felt the kettle: it was cold but contained water. He moved into the centre of the house, heading for the front door, calling out from time to time. When he reached the pile of mail, he found some letters – a telephone bill, a brown envelope with 'Daleside Garage' printed on it, a picture postcard from Spain signed by Sally and Jack, a bill from Yorkshire Water – and all were addressed to Susan Featherstone at Rowan Cottage, Gunnerthwaite. Much of the remainder comprised circulars of various kinds, some addressed to the occupier of the house, some to Susan Featherstone and some without a name or address. The postmarks indicated the mail had been despatched at various dates between early July and today. He decided to leave the mail where it was for the time being – but he did sneak a look into the little brown envelope from the garage because it was not sealed. It was a bill for petrol and oil, along with some minor work to a Volkswagen car during June. That was more than three months ago. It contained the registration number of the Volkswagen. The work included adjustment of the handbrake along with attention to the car's carburettor and timing. Pluke noted the date of the bill – 30th June – and the name and address of the garage. He also recorded the name of Susan Featherstone, but decided to leave the mail where it was – after all, he had no cause to remove any of it, although he was vaguely aware that his teams might have occasion to examine it. It was now late September: it seemed no one had collected the mail for several weeks and, in his opinion, the garden had been neglected for a similar period. So had that coffee session also occurred so long ago?

Pluke's brief examination of the ground floor did not reveal anything of immediate or evident significance – the house was very tidy if a little dusty and although the furnishings were of good quality second-hand style, they were fairly sparse, as one might expect in a house used only for occasional holidays and weekends. In the lounge, though, he found a watercolour painting of Trough House – the original of his print! Much larger than his version, it occupied a central position over the fireplace and it was signed by the artist. Susan Miller. So Miller did sell her originals! He'd love this one . . . Pleased at this further link with Trough House, he decided to go upstairs to check that the occupant was not lying injured or dead. He'd done this sort of thing earlier in his career – on one occasion, neighbours had called the police to a house because the occupant had not been seen for four days. The young Pluke had entered to find the elderly male owner dead in bed – from natural causes. On another occasion, he'd had to search for a suspected burglar but instead had found a cat shut in a bedroom – and an elderly woman dead in bed, also from natural causes. It was with some trepidation, therefore, that Montague Pluke climbed the open staircase, shouting with each step while listening and looking for indications of any occupant.

The landing doors were closed, all five of them. He knocked on each in turn, calling 'Hello' and shouting his name, but there was no response. He opened the first and found it was the bathroom; the glass shelves above the washbasin were full of feminine things – lotions, perfumes and bath salts – and there was a single toothbrush in a glass, beside which was a tube of toothpaste, little used. There were towels on the rail, a bath-mat on the floor, two yellow plastic ducks sitting on the side of the bath and a shower head above the bath with a plastic shower cap lodged behind a handrail near the shower unit. A woman's bathroom albeit with the air of not having been used for some time, like a disused house almost. Then a bedroom, a large room with fitted units, containing a double bed, neatly made with a teddy bear lying near the pillow, a dressing table covered with jars and bottles, a hairdryer on the top of some drawers, a silk dressing-gown behind the door and pictures on the walls, five pictures, all abstract paintings in oil. A real contrast to the traditional appearance of the room. The third door was the airing cupboard full of towels, sheets and bedclothes, the fourth was a smaller bedroom with a single bed, neatly made, wallpapered as if for a child.

The fifth door led into a second large double room fitted with a washbasin and an en-suite shower unit. It contained an iron bedstead, an antique walnut wardrobe and a matching chest of drawers, with some Victorian-style country scenes around the walls. The guest room, Pluke wondered? But there was no sign of any current occupant. He did search the wardrobes – they contained only women's clothes – and then beneath the beds, all traditional hiding places, but he found no one. In his notebook – now his official police notebook – he wrote details of his search with an impression of each room, then decided he must leave. A call at Daleside Garage might reveal more about the owner of the black Volkswagen. As he walked back through the deserted house, he was tempted to drop the Yale latch on the kitchen door as he left, but decided against it. After all, in spite of the deserted atmosphere of the place, the door had probably intentionally been left unlocked. And so he returned to the exterior, stood awhile to gaze around the house in the hope it might reveal further secrets or provide some inspiration, and then, after a final look at the magnificent trough, he decided to return to the incident room.

'We thought you'd got lost!' was the first thing Inspector Horsley said as he walked in. 'It's nearly lunchtime!'

'Has there been a development?' replied Pluke.

'No, nothing. But as we'd heard nothing from you for ages we were beginning to wonder whether somebody had knocked you on the head. You didn't answer your mobile when we did a routine check.'

Pluke had forgotten to switch it on, he realized, but muttered something about probably being out of reception range and then explained how he had spent his time, both at the church and in his limited exploration of Rowan Cottage, adding that he was now very keen to trace any member of the Featherstone family who might have recently used the cottage, Susan in particular.

'Are you suggesting she has killed our victim and done a runner?' Horsley put to him.

'No, but it is significant, I feel, that the house has all the appearances of having recently been occupied by a woman, a lone woman I might add, and that she left hurriedly, possibly with another person but without her car . . .'

'You mean she could be our victim?' Realization now dawned on Horsley's face.

'In any murder investigation – in fact in any crime investigation – coincidences need to be treated with the utmost caution, true coincidences in such circumstances are extremely rare,' Pluke reminded Horsley. 'Here we have a dead woman whose name we do not know, and we have a house, within easy reach of the dead woman's last resting place, which has obviously been occupied recently by a woman. And she is a woman who has apparently – and I emphasize apparently – disappeared, perhaps with another person. We need to establish whether or not these occurrences are connected.'

'You have been busy, Montague,' Horsley acknowledged with more than a hint of admiration in his voice. 'What with this and the likely grave site, you've turned up more than the rest of us put together. This could be the break-through we need.'

'Progress is slow, is it?' Pluke asked.

'It is,' Horsley sighed. 'We're not getting much feedback from the residents. I'm not saying there is a conspiracy of silence, but they're not telling us much. So how do you want us to tackle the enquiry into Susan Featherstone's absence? It could be genuine, you realize, she might not be the victim.'

'Then all we have to do is find her alive,' Pluke said. 'She has a black Volkswagen with a soft top, it's still in the garage, and here is the registration number.'

'You managed to get that? I thought you couldn't get into the garage?'

'It was on an invoice I found in the mail,' smiled Pluke. 'I conducted a brief examination of her correspondence, leaving it intact for our SOCOs in case our interest reaches that stage. Can you circulate the car's registration number and description to our teams, they might find someone who has noticed it or its owner around the village or elsewhere in the moors – with or without a passenger.'

'Will do. So what does she look like, this Susan Featherstone? How old is she, for example?'

'I have no idea,' Pluke admitted. 'I did not notice any photographs which might have been of her, but I must admit I did not search the house that thoroughly. After all, I had no reason nor, I suspect, any authority. I was merely checking to see whether or not anyone inside needed help of any kind.'

'I understand, but even your limited search could prove very useful. Right, Montague, I will contact the police in West Yorkshire to see if they can trace the Featherstone family who used the cottage. They're from Wakefield, you think?'

'According to Miss Pyke, yes.'

'Right, it shouldn't take long for that enquiry to be completed. So what will you be doing in the meantime?'

'I want to visit Daleside Garage in Granthorpe – they sent the bill to Rowan Cottage, in Susan Featherstone's name. They must have seen, or been in touch with, the car owner. I hope I can get a description of her.'

'Right, but will they be open? It's only a small village and this is Sunday, remember.'

'I will ring first,' smiled Pluke. 'And if they are open, I shall require a driver.'

'Wayne Wain is busy with house-to-house,' Horsley reminded him.

'There must be someone who is not engaged on particularly urgent enquiries. Some young detective who might benefit from the wisdom of an experienced senior police officer like myself.'

Horsley smiled at Pluke's opinion of himself, and said, 'Well, yes, there's Detective Constable Waring, Anna Waring. Her colleague is busy filing their statements and she's hanging about, waiting. How long will it take, this trip to Granthorpe?'

'It's only two miles away – allowing for my enquiries, an hour at the most,' Pluke estimated. 'And it is a tourist village, retailers will surely be open at weekends.'

He rang to check. The garage was open but Pluke did

not state the reason for his enquiry nor did he identify himself as a police officer. He liked to surprise those he interviewed so as to gauge their instinctive reaction.

And so, sitting beside a beautiful red-headed young woman who was at the wheel of the plain police car, Pluke was driven across the moors to the pretty village of Granthorpe. Noted for its undulating village greens tended by sheep, its watersplashes, the walks along its gills and its open moorland charm, Granthorpe was a honeypot for tourists. Daleside Garage was tucked away behind the main street, almost opposite the Crown Inn, with a discreet sign announcing its whereabouts. Its presence did not spoil the village in any sense and Pluke guided his chauffeuse down the short lane and into the spacious yard where she parked.

'You must join me.' Pluke realized the girl was thinking of herself as merely his driver, not a partner in this investigation. 'I want you to be part of this enquiry, Detective Constable Waring.'

'Thank you, sir, I was hoping you'd include me,' and so she followed him into the bowels of the garage where an overalled man was lying beneath a Ford and doing something to its exhaust pipe.

'If it's a breakdown, no chance,' came the voice from beneath the car. 'I've enough to keep me going till ten tonight!'

'I do hope you have time to help the police with a murder enquiry,' Pluke said, stooping low to peer into the man's eyes. 'I am Detective Inspector Pluke and this is Detective Constable Waring.'

'Detectives? Murder, did you say?'

'We did,' retorted Pluke.

'Oh, right, well, yes, I could do with a break anyway, my back catches it if I lie under here too long,' and he slid from beneath on a lowslung metal trolley on wheels. 'I thought it was another tourist who'd forgotten to top up his radiator or hadn't made sure his spare tyre was blown up. We get 'em all in here, urgent jobs on Sundays, always urgent, it's always clowns who cause their own problems. Makes you wonder how they get anywhere safely. I charge 'em all treble rates on Sundays, mind. So, what can I do for you, Inspector?'

'The body of a woman has been found in a stream in Thordale,' he began. 'We are treating the death as suspicious, and we are making enquiries to establish her identity as well as her recent movements and contacts.'

'I can't see how I can help with that.' The garage man scratched his head. 'I don't know any woman who's missing and I haven't been up Thordale since I was a lad courting.'

'I had reason to attempt to contact a lady in Gunnerthwaite an hour or so ago,' Pluke went on. 'A Susan Featherstone at Rowan Cottage. I believe she comes here from time to time, with her car.'

'Oh, well, yes, I know Susan. I see to her car when she's over here, routine services, MOT, tyre checks, that kind of thing. Nice woman. It's not her, is it?' and the shock showed on the man's grease-stained face.

'I have no reason to think it is.' Pluke tried to calm the situation as the man wiped his hands on an oily rag. 'But we must eliminate all possibilities, and that is why I am here.'

'So why ask about her?'

'She is not at home, the door of her house was open and I sense she had not been in it for some time. Then I found one of your invoices and thought you might know something about her, or her whereabouts.'

'I don't know her all that well, and have no idea what she does with herself when she's not here. She only comes to Rowan Cottage once in a while, sometimes just for a weekend, sometimes for a bit longer. Sorry, but I've no idea where she might be, except she's from West Yorkshire, the Wakefield area.'

'We are making enquiries in that area. What does she look like?' Pluke continued. 'Age, colour of hair?'

'Bonny woman, Inspector, quite tall and slender with it, a good-looker. Black hair, long. Age? I'm no good with women's ages, but she'll be younger than me and I'm forty-six. Not much younger, though. In her thirties mebbe.'

'Black hair?' It was Anna's turn to venture a contribution to the discussion. 'What kind of style?'

'Long and straight.' He frowned. 'Aye, long and straight, down to her shoulders. And a fringe, like them Beatle singers used to have.'

'Any sign of grey?' Anna asked a woman's question.

'If there is, I've never noticed it,' the garage man said. 'It's always black and shiny, very smart. And she wears red clothes, a lot of the time. I've seen her in a red jacket and black skirt, looking like a Spanish senorita or summat. Nice-looking though, very nice-looking, nice skin, white and smooth.'

'What about ear-rings?' asked Anna.

'No idea, her hair always covers her ears,' said the garage man.

'She doesn't sound like the woman in the pool.' Anna looked at Pluke. 'She has light fair hair, worn short, sir.'

'True, but if Miss, Ms or Mrs Featherstone is missing, we need to find her – not that I am suggesting she is guilty of anything, but if one woman has gone missing then we may find ourselves having to consider others who have vanished. It's important that we trace her. Does she ever have anyone with her?' Pluke pressed the man.

'I've never seen her with anybody, Inspector, not when she comes here or when she's at the Gunnerthwaite house. I do deliver the car to her house sometimes, after a long job, I've never seen anyone about the place, other than her. I've never heard her mention a man, she doesn't strike me as the marrying kind, too businesslike if you know what I mean.'

'Too businesslike?' smiled Anna.

'Well, she takes control of things, not like some women who don't know one end of a car from another. She knows what she's talking about, knows what she wants. I can imagine her breezing into a car showroom and letting the salesman know she knows more about cars than him. She's that sort of woman. And she keeps her little Volkswagen in good condition. She loves it, she says she likes a country garage to look after it because they're more trustworthy.'

'I believe her car is still in her garage,' Pluke said. 'That adds to my concern about her. It's a soft-top, in black. It seems she's gone away without it.'

'If she's gone without her car, she must have got a lift somewhere, eh? She goes everywhere in that little car.'

'I do know there is no regular bus service in Gunner-thwaite and no trains, so her car was obviously of impor-tance to her. We'll keep asking in this area and we'll check at local hospitals. I hope you will think about this, then perhaps if you do remember anything else . . .'

'Well, I will, of course, but I don't think I can help you any more, I've told you all I know and that's not a lot.' He shook his head. 'She never talks about her family or any-thing, she's not very chatty. More businesslike than chatty as I said, but she's a nice woman, always pays her bills, never complains about things. But that house in Gunner-thwaite is just a holiday home, you know that? I mean, she's in business so she could be anywhere, off somewhere doing a deal, attending a conference, anything.'

'So what is her business?' asked Pluke.

'Summat to do with selling paintings,' he said. 'There's times she has a car full of 'em to hawk around the tourist shops.'

'Does the name of an artist called Susan Miller mean anything to you?' Pluke then asked. 'Her work is sold in local tourist shops.'

'No, never heard of her, I'm not very arty-crafty but Susan Featherstone would know, you could ask her – if you can find her.'

'I appreciate your help,' Pluke acknowledged. 'And thank you. I do hope she isn't missing and hasn't come to any harm. Can I ask you to call our incident room if you do recall anything that might help us?'

Pluke wrote the telephone number on a pad supplied by the garage man and noted that the name on the headed paper was George Linfield.

'Are you George Linfield?' Pluke asked, indicating the name.

'Aye, that's me. I'm usually here, I never seem to get closed at six like I should, it's usually ten or later. The wife plays hell, but my greasy hands help keep her in nice clothes. Oh – you could ask at the tea shop just down the road. Sometimes if I have to do a job for Susan while she waits, like adjusting her brakes or changing a tyre, she'll pop in there for summat to eat and drink instead of hanging around the garage.'

'You call her by her first name, do you?' asked Anna.

'Oh, aye, she says I can call her Susan. Not Sue, she doesn't like Sue, doesn't like her name being shortened and prefers Susan to Miss Featherstone.'

'It is Miss, is it?' asked Pluke.

'She never contradicted me when I used to call her Miss Featherstone.'

'Thank you, Mr Linfield.' Pluke realized he had exhausted his enquiries at the garage. 'You have been most helpful.'

They departed as George Linfield lay on his trolley and steered himself into position beneath the waiting car, then Pluke said, 'I do believe it is getting on for lunchtime, Detective Constable Waring. What are the teams doing for lunch?'

'Well, sir, there is no pub in the village, so most have brought their own. I couldn't believe there'd be no pub nearby . . .'

'So you've not brought your lunch here?'

'No, sir, it slipped my mind.'

'Me too, so we must eat at the tea shop,' he said. 'It will be a good reason for studying the place as we eat. And we can claim expenses too, modest I admit, but sufficient to ensure we are not out of pocket if we enjoy ourselves modestly. So come along, let us continue our enquiries at the tea shop.'

Granthorpe Tea Shop was fashioned from a lovely bow-fronted cottage on the green, and it boasted blue and white chintz curtains, beamed ceilings, stone floors and a renowned collection of teapots and tea strainers. In spite of its old-fashioned appearance, it had the wisdom and grace not to advertise itself as Ye Olde Tea Shoppe. For all its quaintness, it was mentioned in most tourist guides to the moors and had a reputation for its afternoon teas with hot scones, brown bread sandwiches with ham fillings and thick chunks of fruit cake made on the premises. Pluke led his attractive young companion inside. A bell rang as the door opened and he found himself in a spacious room, the two front parts of the cottage having been knocked into one to accommodate the customers. It was filled with tables draped with blue and white cloths, each with a vase of fresh flowers in the centre and each bearing a neat wooden teapot-shaped device which held the menu. There were around a dozen customers. A plump and grey-haired lady materialized through an open door behind the glass counter of sweet cakes and buns.

'For two, is it?' she asked with a large smile glowing between her red cheeks. 'Over there, in the window. A table for two. No smoking. And we've no prawns. There's been a run on prawns ever since that food column in the *Evening Press* said they were good for easing stress. Now everybody wants them, we haven't any and I'm feeling very stressed about it. And I haven't a licence for liquor, so I can't do wines, spirits or beers. The bread's fresh today and the menu's on the table.'

Pluke led the way and soon they were settled and examining the menu as their hostess busied herself with other customers. Pluke explained that as Millicent would be preparing an evening meal, he was content to have a sandwich of some kind, but said he did not wish to restrict the choice of his companion. She said the same – she lived with her boyfriend and tonight he was preparing a nice meal for her, a treat after work – and so they settled for a sandwich apiece, a sweet cake of some kind, tea and a drink of orange juice. As the hostess turned her attention to them, however, the door opened to the tinkling of the bell and in walked Millicent Pluke.

For a brief moment, she did not notice her husband at

the window table with a young woman at his side, but as she cast her eyes around the establishment to locate a suitable seat, she spotted him. She happened to notice him just as he was peering earnestly into the eyes of his colleague to explain the stress-beating claims of prawns, but he did not notice Millicent's unexpected presence.

'Montague! You cheat . . . you scoundrel . . . how dare you meet a younger woman in secret . . . and I thought you loved me . . .'

And with that, she stormed out and slammed the door.

Chapter Eight

Montague Pluke, with coat tails flying while holding his panama on to his head, hurtled from the tea shop in hot pursuit of Millicent. She was moving swiftly in the manner of a woman who felt she had been wronged, her feet thudding on to the ground like pile drivers, but Pluke was surprisingly fit and agile. He caught her as she was trying to unlock the car door. His private car door.

'Millicent!' he shouted. 'Millicent, it's not what you think!'

'They all say that!' she shouted. 'All double-crossing men with mistresses say that . . . I've seen them in the films, you know. Montague, I am surprised at you and most upset too . . . You did it while I was doing my best to trace the artist of that horse trough painting . . . You deceived me, you were meeting another woman, a red-head no less, and you took advantage of my absence. How could you?'

In her haste, she was not having much success with the car door and her futile attempt to open it allowed Pluke to put his hand on the door frame above the window to hold it firmly shut in the event of her unlocking it. His stance produced a most effective kind of imprisonment with her positioned between him and the door. Now that she was temporarily immobilized, he could speak to her.

'Millicent . . .' He spoke with a firmness which surprised even himself. 'Millicent, you are being silly. Just stop and listen. That young lady is my driver, she is Detective Constable Waring and we are about to question that tea shop lady about the murder in Thordale. As there is no

111

police canteen on site, mobile or otherwise, and no public house in Gunnerthwaite, we have to make other meal arrangements.'

She sniffed and raised her head in the air, aloof from such a silly, hollow explanation.

He ploughed on. 'As I did not have a packed lunch with me, it makes sense for me to eat in that tea shop, and for the detective constable to join me. I shall not pay for her meal, she will claim the regulation subsistence allowance and so shall I. I cannot understand why you have to behave like this every time you see me in the company of another woman, and to suggest I have ulterior or romantic notions is outrageous. I am not the romantic type, and I do not cavort with mistresses and other women, red-heads, blondes or otherwise. That person is a colleague!'

'I've done it again, haven't I?' she whispered after a suitably long pause. 'Oh, Montague, why do I love you so much, why do I react like a love-sick teenager when I see you with another woman? I am no oil painting, am I? Not beautiful like the young women of today and I do try desperately hard not to be jealous, but you are a man of such a high profile, so well known and respected, such a target for lustful and unscrupulous women . . . I do not want to see you hurt or compromised . . .'

'Just calm down, my dear,' he said. 'You are as beautiful as ever, I want no one else. Take a deep breath, gather yourself together and then come and join us . . .'

'I'm not going back in there!' she snapped. 'I am not going to embarrass myself any further . . . no, you go and have your lunch, finish your enquiries without me. I will see you at home tonight.'

'Why did you come to Granthorpe? I never expected to see you here.' Now that her temper had evaporated, he could ponder her presence.

'You said that if I wanted to find that artist today, being Sunday, I had to visit places which are popular with tourists. I did go to the framing place in Crickledale first, but they are closed and then I saw Mr Griffiths cutting his lawn. He told me about this craft shop so I drove out here.

The arts and craft shop is just along the street, two or three doors away from this tea shop you see, and they sell paintings like those I saw in Gunnerthwaite post office, so I thought I would check. I thought I'd treat myself to lunch before I went to the art shop but it was such a surprise seeing you in there, it really was. A shock really. Yes, a shock.'

'I am sorry if I caused you to have a shock, my dear, but much as I would like to join your search for the artist, I cannot compromise my murder investigation. I have certain enquiries to make in that tea shop and then I hope to return to the incident room in Gunnerthwaite.'

'I don't want to get in your way, Montague, so you must continue your work and I shall see you at home tonight. I shall prepare a special meal, my way of apologizing for embarrassing you in the tea room, and I hope I shall then have good news about your trough artist.'

'That is very noble of you,' he told her with sincerity. 'Now, I must return to my duties. I shall see you tonight – remember we close the incident room early on Sundays. I should be home by eight, all being well.'

And so, suitably calm and dignified, they parted and Montague watched Millicent walk, with head held high, along the street towards the craft and arts shop. He was pleased to see that it bore a sign saying 'Light snacks available'. At least Millicent would not go hungry.

Montague apologized in whisper to Detective Constable Waring, saying that Mrs Pluke, who didn't get out much, was most unaccustomed to seeing him in the company of other women, especially those who were young and attractive, adding that she had now calmed down after gaining a genuine understanding of the situation. Anna Waring blushed, partly because she was pleased to hear Pluke describe her as young and attractive and partly because her presence had caused some embarrassment to the officer in charge of the investigation. The tea shop lady did not appear to have reacted to the drama, probably having experienced similar fracas in the past, for she took their order without commenting on the flying departure of the funny man in the big coat, and within minutes, Pluke and Anna were enjoying a calm and leisurely lunch. From time to time, Pluke caught sight of customers looking at them quizzically, but he ignored their lack of manners as he ploughed through his thick and juicy sandwich followed by a large slice of fruit cake and cup of tea. When the lady came with their bill, Pluke spoke to her in what he thought were confidential tones, but which most of the assembled diners could hear.

He said, 'I am Detective Inspector Pluke and this is Detective Constable Waring. We would like to speak to you, please, briefly, on a matter of some importance, preferably in a quiet room away from the public.'

'Well, you couldn't have picked a worse time, Mr Pluke, right in the middle of lunch, it is my busiest period and I do have customers to consider . . .' Her voice was loud enough and sharp enough to jolt even the sleepiest of diners into a state of fresh curiosity.

'It will take a mere minute of your time,' persisted Pluke. 'And as it is a murder enquiry, we should be most –'

'A murder?' she shrilled. 'I know nothing about a murder . . .'

By this stage, she and Pluke had attracted the undivided attention of all the diners; every one of them stopped eating, and so, to avoid further embarrassment, the tea lady said, 'Follow me, I will give you one minute, just one minute.'

Striding away to the rear of the room she opened a door and led them into a small cosy parlour furnished with a round table in the centre. Ten chairs were arranged around it.

'We use this for small meetings,' she said. 'So, what is it you want?'

'Might I enquire after your name first?' Pluke hoped that his smile of friendliness would not be misinterpreted.

'Morris,' she said. 'Mrs. Mrs Josephine Morris if that's what you need.'

He had now produced his notebook and jotted down her

name, along with that of the tea shop. He explained the thrust of his enquiries, completing his introduction by saying he had reason to believe that Susan Featherstone, whom he described in the terms offered by George Linfield, was an occasional customer at the tea shop.

'I do know the woman you mean, she's very smart with jet black hair.' Mrs Morris had now considerably lowered the tone of her voice. 'Yes, she did come in here when her car was being serviced but it wasn't the only place she went. She spent a lot of time at the arts and craft shop just along the road, she was a dealer in paintings. But you said murder? I hope nothing's happened to her, she was a very nice woman.'

'We have an open mind.' Pluke tried to placate Mrs Morris's obvious concern. 'All I can say is that Miss Featherstone is not at her cottage in Gunnerthwaite and does not appear to have been there for some time. Her car is there, however, and so we are trying to trace her. Would you know anything about her whereabouts? Her home address? Any friends and contacts she had in the district?'

'Sorry, no, Inspector Pluke. But you could ask at the arts and crafts, my daughter runs it. Helen. Helen Morris. Miss Featherstone spent more time there than here, Helen told me once when I was wondering who she was and where she came from.'

'Thank you, I'll go there immediately. And thank you for giving us some of your time. I do hope your customers do not complain.'

'Some complain about anything and some even grumble about nothing, but I'll cope,' and she smiled at the detectives. 'At least you've given them something to talk about, I bet most have forgotten what they ordered anyway!'

Pluke was not sure whether she was referring to Millicent's visit or his enquiry, but, with Millicent's car still on the road outside, he sailed from the tea shop.

Anna hurried behind as they made for the arts and crafts emporium just along the street. It was readily identifiable with its range of handmade baskets, walking-sticks and garden-sized pottery on display on the footpath outside; when they entered, they found themselves inside a series of small ancient rooms, each full to its beamed ceiling with knick-knacks, art work, hand-crafted goods, wooden toys and almost anything a tourist would take home – and then wonder why they'd done so!

Among the treasures, Pluke noted prints of the kind he'd seen in the post office at Gunnerthwaite, all framed and clearly the work of the artist who'd produced his Trough House picture. All were signed by Susan Miller. With Anna at his heels, he pushed through the galaxy of assorted goods, sometimes having to duck through a doorway due to things hanging from the beams or the ceilings, and sometimes squeezing past three-legged stools or rocking horses. He spotted a sign indicating the refreshment area up a flight of stairs – Millicent would be there – but for the moment decided not to venture into that department. He wanted to have words with Helen Morris and, in a back room full of handmade cushions and colourful blankets, he found a woman who was a younger version of the tea shop lady – same size and shape but with a younger face and brown hair. Happily, there was no one with her and then he spotted the till among the adornments.

'Excuse me,' Pluke began as he edged into the limited floor space. 'Are you Helen Morris?'

'Yes, that's me. Can I help you?' She sounded just like her mother.

He introduced himself and Anna Waring, then explained the reason for their presence with due reference to Mrs Morris in the tea shop and Mr Linfield in the garage. He did emphasize that there was no reason to believe that the victim was Susan Featherstone, but stressed they were anxious to trace her, to eliminate her from their enquiries.

'It's funny you should mention Miss Featherstone,' smiled Helen Morris. 'I've just had a lady in asking about her – she's upstairs now, in the tea room. A small lady, grey hair, spectacles . . .'

'Really? Then I must speak to her. Might I ask what is her interest in Susan Featherstone?'

'She noticed some prints in the front of the shop, scenes from the moors, and she was asking about them. I told her they were not originals, they're prints, some in limited editions, and when she asked where I got them from, I told her that Susan Featherstone acts as agent for the artist. Whenever we want new stocks, we contact Susan and she arranges delivery – and gets them framed for us. At Crickledale.'

'Ah!' The identity of the grey-haired lady with spectacles now dawned on Pluke. 'And is the lady with spectacles still in your tea room?'

'Yes, she has to pay her bill in here, so she's still there.'

'I need to talk to you some more, about a means of contacting Susan Featherstone, but first I must speak to that lady in your tea room. I suspect it is my wife . . .'

'Your wife? Is she a detective as well?'

'There are times I wonder about that,' smiled Pluke. 'Come along, Detective Constable Waring, let us see what my wife has been up to.'

'Sir,' said Anna Waring, following him to the staircase up to the tea room. 'I am still not sure whether you think Susan Featherstone is the victim.'

'We must establish, from Helen Morris, how she makes contact with her, to order new stocks of prints. But first, I must catch Mrs Pluke before she heads back to Crickledale. Then I might have a clearer understanding of whether Susan Featherstone *could* – and I stress *could* – be our victim.'

'The descriptions don't match, sir. Well, I suppose they do, except for the hair. Susan has black hair worn long with a fringe, while the victim's hair was light brown and short.'

'Women are somewhat prone to changing their hairstyle, and that can alter their entire appearance,' Pluke said.

'And some wear wigs, sir,' she added as the climbed the stairs. 'I did wonder if that jet black hair was a wig.'

'And why did you think that?' he asked.

'Well, the garage man didn't mention any grey hairs. I've noticed that, even in young women with jet black hair, there is often a grey strand or two, especially if the woman is in her thirties or older.'

'So why would a smart businesslike woman like Susan Featherstone wear a wig?' Pluke was now nearing the top of the staircase. It opened on to a wide landing with the tea room ahead and toilets at either side. He could see Millicent sitting at a table with her back to him, and there were others in the room.

'To match her overall appearance, to cover up some problem with her hair, even as a mere fashion accessory . . .'

'So our victim could be Susan Featherstone without her wig?' Pluke was now crossing the landing with Anna trotting at his side.

'Yes, sir, it could.'

Pluke padded across the carpet and arrived at Millicent's table without her being aware of his approach or presence, and then he said, 'Ah, Millicent, glad I caught you.'

She jumped out of her seat, startled at the sound of his voice, and her cup crashed into its saucer, spilling tea and rattling the crockery. Everyone turned to stare at her and she blushed crimson.

'Montague!' she cried. 'What on earth do you think you're doing, frightening me like that! Creeping up behind like some furtive creature of the night . . . You are the limit, Montague, you really are.'

'I'm sorry, my dear, but I do need to talk to you before you leave. It is very important.' Everyone was watching them closely, wondering if the odd man in his funny coat and panama was a pest or a stalker or something equally nasty. He lowered his voice. 'I'll see you downstairs in the owner's back room, the one with cushions and blankets in, it's where you pay. We will wait there.'

'What's it about this time, Montague?'

'You've been asking about the paintings downstairs, well, prints to be more precise.'

'Yes, they are from originals done by the artist who painted your Trough House picture.'

'Then let us continue this conversation in private,' he said. 'I don't want to rush your meal and meanwhile I have further enquiries to make downstairs. Join me there when you can.'

'I won't be long,' she assured him, returning to her seat with a big sigh as she noticed a blob of spilt tea on her skirt. She sat for a long time, wondering if the people around her had stopped staring, and in the meantime Montague and Anna returned to the room stuffed with cushions. Helen Morris was still beside her till.

'You found her?' she asked.

'I did, thank you, and it is indeed my wife, Mrs Millicent Pluke. She will join us when she has finished her meal. Now, Miss Morris, you said that Susan Featherstone arranges delivery of your prints, already framed.'

'Yes, she does.'

'So when did you last see her?'

'I can't give you a precise date, Mr Pluke, but it would be during the early summer, when I placed my order for coming autumn. Those prints you've seen are the last of that order. She delivered them soon afterwards, early in July I'd guess. I've not been in touch with her since then.'

'And how do you contact her?'

'I have a telephone number, I ring when I want to replenish stocks.'

'I'd like that number, please, I need to ring to see if she answers. Is it a local number?'

'Oh, no. It's 01924 code, that's Wakefield. I know that because I had another business contact there. But she's never left any business card or given me an address. I do all my business with her by telephone. I must admit there were times I couldn't make contact but she does have an answerphone, I left messages.'

'Well, we can trace the address of the number if we have

119

to, but at this stage I need to be very discreet. I must not give cause for undue concern. Now, if all your business is done over the telephone, how do you pay her?'

'Cash, Mr Pluke. She insists on cash, not even a cheque. It's not unknown, in some businesses. I place an order over the phone – I take whatever is available, any moorland scene appeals to tourists – and she delivers the prints after she gets them framed, that's when I pay her in cash. On the spot, right here. She always rings in advance, so I have the money ready. Most of our income is cash anyway, that method doesn't really cause any problems. And, I might say, she's always very reliable.'

'Does she give receipts?'

'Yes, I need them for my accounts. They're the sort you can get from any stationery shop, not specially printed. And she just signs them – Susan Featherstone.'

'So you do not deal directly with the artist?'

'No, according to Susan she doesn't like the hassle of dealing with customers and can't spare the time for travelling around to sell her stuff, she prefers to spend her time painting and gives Susan a percentage of the sales. A good one, I think, she's always smartly dressed . . . Ah, this must be Mrs Pluke.'

Somewhat self-consciously, Millicent entered the little room and smiled at Anna Waring, then Montague took over and introduced her, explaining to both Anna and Helen the role currently played by Millicent.

'My wife's enquiries are not connected to my murder investigation,' he felt obliged to tell them. 'She was merely helping me trace the whereabouts of a horse trough depicted in one of Susan Miller's paintings. I was hoping to do this by making contact with the artist but in fact have found the trough in question – it is in the garden of Rowan Cottage, Gunnerthwaite, the holiday home of Susan Featherstone.' He added the last piece of information for the benefit of Millicent.

'You've found your trough?' She sounded so pleased for him, if a little surprised. 'So I needn't have gone to all this trouble! I thought you didn't mix your leisure interest with your police work, Montague!'

'The two are now intertwined to a considerable degree, I fear,' he told her. 'The fate of our deceased lady on the moors may somehow be mixed with that of Susan Featherstone. And it seems she acted as agent for Susan Miller. So what have you discovered in your travels?'

'I went to the framers as you wanted me to, Crickledale Framers, but they were closed all day, being a Sunday, but as I was walking away after checking in the window, Mr Browning, you know, from Browning's Electricals, happened to be passing and told me that the owner of the framers, Mr Owen Griffiths, was cutting his lawn just round the corner. I did not wish to disturb him on a Sunday, Montague, but I knew how important this was and, well, I stopped for a chat. Mr Griffiths doesn't know Susan Miller but says her work is very popular throughout the moors and along the Yorkshire coast. He told me about this shop and says her prints sell in thousands, people collect them because she always paints a shepherd in the background. But Mr Griffiths did tell me that he deals with Susan Featherstone who acts as an agent for Miss Miller. She brings in a whole lot of prints – hundreds in some cases prior to the summer season, and sometimes an original or two – and he frames in accordance with her instructions, then she collects them at a later date and distributes them around the retail outlets. He did say she always paid cash for the work, so he had no idea where she lived or whether or not she had an office. I have visited several outlets too, in shops and places on my way here, and they support that. None of them have ever seen Susan Miller, Miss Featherstone always does the deals by telephone, and always insists on cash.'

'You have done well, and so a picture is now emerging,' said Pluke, oblivious to his unintended pun. 'And did you ask where I might find Susan Miller?'

'I did ask, Montague, but Mr Griffiths has no idea, nor have any of the others I talked to. Among the art world of this region, she is something of a mystery woman. She produces very popular images of the moors, but is never seen at work, she never gives public appearances and never turns up at her own exhibitions.'

'So . . .' Pluke rested his chin in the cup of his hand as he pondered aloud. 'So, bearing in mind Susan Miller produced an accurate painting of that trough, albeit not in its original setting, she and Susan Featherstone must know each other very well. Indeed, the original Susan Miller painting is in Rowan Cottage and there were two coffee mugs at the cottage . . . a business meeting perhaps, between them? Interrupted for some reason? It could explain why the car was left behind . . . the artist might have had her own transport, they might have gone off together to sort out some problem.'

'Sir,' said Detective Constable Waring. 'There is another possibility.'

'Which is?' invited Pluke.

'That Susan Miller and Susan Featherstone are one and the same person.'

'Why on earth would she pretend to be someone else?' asked Helen Morris.

'Authors use pen-names as a means of gaining privacy, actors make use of stage names and some artists use names which are not their true ones,' Anna pointed out. 'And I must admit I wondered if that black hair was a wig, it sounded rather too perfect the way the garage man described it.'

'My sentiments exactly!' cried Helen. 'I've always thought it was a wig, part of her power-dressing style . . . it's very black and smooth, not a hair out of place . . . yes, Mr Pluke, speaking as a woman, I agree. I'd say Susan Featherstone's hair is a wig.'

'Does she wear ear-rings?' asked Anna.

'I think so.' Helen's brow creased in thought. 'Yes, I'd say she does, jet ones quite often. I'm sure I've seen them.'

'And pierced ears?'

'I'd say so, although I can't be sure.'

'So if she has adopted a dual identity – why would she do so?' pondered Pluke.

'It's an acceptable part of her work.' Millicent decided to express her views. 'I agree with your friend, the detective lady, that she probably uses her alias to visit customers in the hope she'll discover exactly what the customers are buying or wanting. It's hard telling an artist that his or her work is not wanted, or that it's not depicting the right moods in the right places, but to tell a third person . . .'

'And,' smiled Helen, 'if she does act as her own agent, she'll keep all the income, she'll not be paying expenses and commission to another person. One of the chaps who calls at our shop with booklets about the moors both writes them and publishes them, so he gets all the profits. That kind of thing is not all that unusual.'

'I doubt if that author disguises himself to do so,' put in Pluke. 'But yes, I agree with Detective Constable Waring. It is possible that our two ladies are one and the same person, but it could still be she who is in our mortuary. If so, why? Now, I must get back to the incident room to establish some more focused identification procedures. Millicent, Miss Morris, thank you both, you have been most useful.'

'Shall I go home now, Montague?' asked Millicent.

'You may wish to visit some more retail outlets,' Montague smiled. 'Now, we need to learn as much as we can about Susan Miller and her work, as well as Susan Featherstone.'

'It is quite exciting.' Millicent blushed again. 'Now I feel like a real detective!'

And so they parted, with Pluke rejoining his official police vehicle and being driven back to Gunnerthwaite by Anna Waring. As she drove him carefully across the open moorland, he said, 'Thank you for your contribution to that investigation, Detective Constable Waring. There are times a woman's intuition and knowledge are vital, as they were today. I do appreciate your help. We did achieve rather a lot, I am pleased to report.'

'How will you link the two women, sir, with so little to go on? Really, we still know almost nothing.'

'We can trace the address of the telephone number – I did consider ringing it from the shop but decided against it. Perhaps you could do that from the incident room while British Telecom is telling us the name of the subscriber. I feel we might be able to make a more detailed search of Rowan Cottage, first to obtain fingerprints from some object within the house for comparison with the finger-prints of the dead woman. There will be DNA evidence too – and we might be able to isolate some from that original painting – and we might learn that it matches that of the woman calling herself Susan Featherstone. So, I now feel confident that we shall soon know if Susan Featherstone is Susan Miller, and whether she is lying in our mortuary. And if she is, why was she killed? And by whom? There is a long way to go yet, Detective Constable Waring.'

'This is better than the long slog of unproductive house-to-house enquiries, sir,' she smiled. 'I enjoyed those enquiries, it felt as if we were getting somewhere.'

'And so we are,' he smiled. 'So, let us get back to the incident room and you can begin by tracing that Wakefield telephone number. And then I think you could try to find out more about the dress worn by the deceased. Where has it come from? How old is it? Has either of the Susans been seen wearing it? For all this kind of thing, I feel a woman's knowledge could be very useful.'

'Yes, sir, I'd like that. And please tell Mrs Pluke that I fully understand her actions . . . I hope she was not too embarrassed, she seems such a nice lady.'

'She is, she is very nice,' smiled Pluke with pride. 'Even if she does sometimes misinterpret things. So, incident room, here we come. Let's see what the rest of them have discovered.'

Chapter Nine

Inspector Dick Horsley was delighted with Pluke's news. In response, he said he would select experienced teams to visit all stockists of Susan Miller prints or originals while an attempt was made to discover as much as possible about the reclusive artist. He was hopeful of tracing her home address or current whereabouts.

So far as Susan Featherstone was concerned, Horsley would arrange checks at every hospital to see if she had been admitted and, if necessary, enquiries could be made at air and sea ports to establish whether she had gone overseas. A check on the registration number of the Volkswagen had shown it was registered in her name at the Gunnerthwaite address but Pluke stressed the need to ascertain whether or not the two Susans were one and the same person. Even though there was no evidence to suggest that, the possibility could not be ignored.

West Yorkshire Police at Wakefield were still trying to trace Susan Featherstone – they had apologized for the lack of a rapid result but said there were hundreds of Featherstones in their area and it would take a considerable time to check them all, even by telephone.

Exercising his usual caution, Pluke felt that it was too early to arrange a full-scale scientific search of Rowan Cottage. He had no authority to do so and it was doubtful if the magistrates would issue a warrant simply because the police were worried about the occupier's absence. After all, they'd only been searching for her for a few hours and he'd already conducted one search of the house.

For anything more detailed, there had to be a substantial reason.

Nonetheless, Pluke tried to be practical. 'We need fingerprints from the house, Mr Horsley, and DNA samples if we can find any. Shall we apply for a warrant, quoting our worries about the identity of the unknown woman?'

'I don't think that's necessary – and it takes time. We can enter Rowan Cottage on the grounds that we're worried about the safety of the occupants as you did. We may still suspect she is ill or concealed on the premises, tied up in the loft or held hostage in the cellar, hit on the head and stuffed in a wardrobe, locked in the toilet even – there's plenty of valid reasons for searching without a warrant. I'll get Scenes of Crime to do it the minute they're free,' Horsley assured him.

'Remember we've no power to search for evidence, and it's evidence we need. Evidence that she may be the victim of a crime, or even its perpetrator. I have already established the occupant is not dead in bed or in need of urgent medical attention.'

'Don't let it worry you, Montague. Let SOCO do their stuff – it's amazing what can be found while checking for the safety of the occupant. I am aware we are trying to find a killer and to identify a dead woman. Common sense, or even Common Law, must be on our side.'

'So long as you remember that Miss Featherstone may be alive and away on business, or even at home in Wakefield, so we must not take it for granted that she is either a victim or perpetrator.'

'Diplomacy is my middle name!'

'If Susan Miller is a reclusive artist, she might be working quietly in some remote place this very minute,' Pluke said. 'Utterly unaware of our interest in her and away from any form of contact, telephone, television, radio, newspapers.'

'Even so, publicity must encourage them to come forward,' suggested Horsley. 'If they know each other, one will tell the other.'

'Or they might retreat into further obscurity,' Pluke said.

'If I was a recluse and saw my name in the paper, especially if it was linked to a murder investigation, I might be tempted to lie low and conceal my whereabouts even further.'

'All right, I hear you. Let's take things one step at a time,' concluded Horsley. 'We'll go for a simple identification by fingerprints for starters. It does mean getting into Rowan Cottage, though, even if it's just to remove something we can examine for fingerprints. We need an object which is sure to bear Susan Featherstone's prints – those coffee mugs could have anyone's prints on them. I want an object we can be sure she's handled – like the car's interior mirror or something from the bathroom such as a tooth mug or can of hair spray.'

'You've made your point very clearly, Mr Horsley, I will leave the arrangements to you,' and Pluke now turned to Anna Waring. 'Now, Detective Constable Waring, what progress are you making with that telephone number?'

'Not a lot, sir. I've rung it several times and all I get is an answerphone without a name. "Leave your message after the tone," it says, and "Please give your own contact number." It is a woman's voice though.'

'And have you tried British Telecom? To get an address for the number?'

'They wouldn't give it, not without going through normal procedures. I don't know what those procedures are, and the woman at the other end wouldn't tell me, except to say they have to be followed if we are police officers on a murder enquiry.'

'Inspector Horsley will have words with them on your behalf, won't you, Mr Horsley?'

'No problem. Give me the phone.'

Minutes later, Anna was holding the handset, now with a very co-operative BT person at the other end, and when she explained her requirements, he said, 'Yes, the subscriber is S. Featherstone of Thordale House, Calderton near Wakefield.'

'Thanks,' said Anna, then turning to Horsley, added,

'I've got her address, sir. All we have to do now is find her.'

'I'll get Wakefield Police to visit that house,' Horsley said. 'At least we can tell them something they should have discovered for themselves!'

'The address does have a ring of truth about it,' Pluke observed. 'The Thordale reference, I mean.'

And so Inspector Horsley rang Wakefield Divisional Police Office and asked for Inspector Sam Brownlow, the man with whom he had earlier been speaking, and provided him with the Calderton address.

'Ah,' said Brownlow. 'Odd that you should call just now, Dick. We've been working through the Featherstones by telephone and personal visits, and our man in Calderton has just radioed in. Literally a couple of minutes ago. He's been to Thordale House, he's confirmed it's owned by Susan Featherstone – Miss Susan Featherstone – and it is locked. There's no sign of any occupant, but the house is secure, no break-ins or anything like that. He's spoken to the neighbour. Susan has not been seen for several weeks, but the neighbour doesn't think it unusual because she regularly goes away, often to spend time in Thordale. It's her favourite place in the world, so he said.'

'She lives alone, does she?'

'She does. Thordale House was owned by her parents, and by her father's parents before that. Her parents are dead and she inherited the family home, a very old and substantial stone house. She's an only child, very much a maiden lady, according to the neighbour, and something of a loner. She works in the art world, self-employed, but has no need to work, she has money so she does it as an interest. Her father was in the textile business, quite a noted businessman, and he left a lot of money and property. She's very comfortably off. She's not known to us, Dick, but we'll try to trace her for you, we'll check likely places in this area.'

'Thanks, it's important we locate her,' said Horsley, who then added, 'Look, Sam, that neighbour, how well does he know her?'

'He's a retired gardener and sees to Susan's lawns and borders while she's away, waters the plants and so on. In view of what you told me earlier, I did ask him for a description of her.'

Inspector Brownlow then provided a description which matched that given by George Linfield at Daleside Garage and by Josephine and Helen Morris.

'It's her all right,' Horsley said. 'It matches the woman known here as Susan Featherstone, but it doesn't match the woman in our morgue. She's got light brown hair which is cut short but the age and height are about right. I can't see any point in that chap looking at the body, it's in poor condition and besides, it doesn't match his description. We must get something from the house in Wakefield as well – something bearing her fingerprints or even DNA, then we can match it with stuff from Rowan House and check it with the body.'

'We'll have to get into the house – the neighbour has a key because he waters her indoor plants. Leave it with me, Dick, I'll obtain something then call you.'

'One other thing, Sam,' Horsley said before terminating his call. 'Our body was wearing a very old dress, a full-length dark brown one, pre-First World War by the look of it. If you get into the house, have a look in her wardrobe and see if she kept any such things about the place. She might have had a penchant for historic clothes or dressing up as someone from a bygone era – that's if our victim is your Susan Featherstone. And wigs. See if she had any wigs in the house. Women's wigs.'

'Leave it with me, and if your teams want a look around the Calderton house, let me know.'

'We might have to do that. Thanks, Sam.'

Pluke agreed with Horsley's response and added that if the Wakefield Police managed to procure something bearing Featherstone's fingerprints, then a motor cyclist could be despatched to collect it for the necessary scientific examination.

Now that the Wakefield address had been confirmed, Detective Constable Waring turned her attention to tracing the origin of the long brown dress while Pluke wondered about progress in the house-to-house enquiries conducted during his absence.

'So, Mr Horsley,' he said. 'Have the teams interviewed those young men from Thordale?'

'That was our first job today, Montague!' beamed Horsley. 'I sent our most experienced detectives. I have in mind that these are young men and our deceased is a young woman, the sexual element must be considered.'

'Nothing of that nature was revealed in the post-mortem,' Pluke reminded him. 'So have you a result?'

Horsley admitted that the great problem with this enquiry was that the time and place of death were unknown. That created enormous difficulties in checking the movements and timings of potential suspects, although it also meant that alibis were hard to establish.

He said, 'The twin musicians from Throstle Nest – Alec and Patrick Hall – are the most active in spending time away from the village. They're twenty-seven and work away, but return home each evening. Sadly, neither can suggest an identity and to their knowledge the victim's never been part of their social circle. They haven't been up to the moors since they played there as children, and couldn't help at all, Montague. We tried to talk to Winston Livingstone at length; he's single, thirty-two years old and lives with his mother in Gunnerthwaite, Mountain Ash Cottage. He's deaf and dumb. We caught up with him at Cragside. He cycles to work at seven and finishes around five but rarely has a day off. Reuben and the farm are his life, he doesn't want to do anything else although he'll take an occasional Saturday afternoon off to watch the local cricket. He's rather simple, I must add, not just deaf and dumb. He's not certifiable, just slow. There's not a lot he can do apart from farm work and even then he has to be given specific instructions. He'll copy anything Reuben does and can work alone if he's shown what to do. Reuben can cope with him, he hasn't the initiative to find his own work though, even if he's been doing the same thing year in, year out. He's been there since he was sixteen – muck-ing out the pigs, tending sheep, leading hay, spreading manure, harvesting potatoes and wheat, hedging and ditching, doing odd jobs like hoeing or cleaning machinery, killing and plucking geese and turkeys for Christmas, feeding the hens . . . he does the lot. He couldn't tell us anything, he just kept shaking his head when Reuben tried to interpret for us.'

'He does go up to those moors,' Pluke reminded Horsley. 'Tending the sheep, rounding them up for counting or clipping once a year, taking nutrients up to them every day, as he was doing when we saw Reuben. He knows his way around up there and, from what I've seen, he'd have no trouble wielding a spade and digging a grave.'

'Yes but he always goes with Reuben,' Horsley said. 'I don't think Reuben trusts him to do much on his own although he is very capable at doing what he's told. Reuben said he can show Winston how to build a haystack, he'll do it on his own and make a real good job of it, but he'll never think of collecting the eggs or feeding the pigs unless he's told to.'

'There must be something he does without Reuben's knowledge!' cried Pluke.

'Maybe so, but Reuben says he's totally unable to use his own initiative. When they go to the moors, they take the tractor past Devil's Dump and Trough House. Reuben remembers that cloudburst in July – the water rose and fell extremely quickly. He said the deluge washed half the moor down the gill and a lot of sheep were lost, none of them his. He did say stuff often gets washed into that cavern on Devil's Dump, then washed out again next time there's high water, sheep carcasses especially. There's times they can't be seen at the back of the cavern, even with their white fleeces, but they get washed out and caught in those roots. Sometimes, they get washed out of the roots entirely and finish up a long way downstream, usually in small pieces.'

'That backs up Mr Fairweather's theory,' agreed Pluke.

'Now, in the opinion of your teams, is either of those men a suspect?'

'No more than anyone else,' Horsley admitted. 'But with lads like Winston, you can never tell. You never know what's goes on in his head and he's as strong as an ox, with all that manual work.'

'We must examine their movements with great care even if we can't pin them down to a particular time and place,' Pluke said. 'Remember they know when tourists can be expected on the moors, they are familiar with the movements of other sheep farmers. When no one's around, that could be the time the murderer was committing his crime or digging his victim's grave. Either then, or late at night when everyone had gone home. I am sure the killer knows the routine of the locals and visitors alike.'

'I'm coming round to your idea that a local man is responsible, Montague, and we can't ignore the fact that the dead woman would be lying there as those men passed by every day but, if they're innocent, they had no reason to stop and search. Our team quizzed them both about possible sightings of the woman on the moor while she was alive, walking perhaps or having a picnic, and they were asked about suspects with or without vehicles. But they've noticed nothing out of the ordinary during the past year or so, and a detailed check of the dead woman's description means nothing to them. Reuben is a single man too, he never married, so we can't ask his wife or family. He lives alone, the farm belonged to his parents and he worked for them; when they died, he just took over where they left off. He does have domestic help – Winston's mother who does his washing, cleaning and a spot of cooking, going to the farm three times a week, or more if necessary.'

'So when he dies, who gets the property?' asked Pluke.

'Our men didn't go into that kind of detail, although Reuben told us he'd promised to care for Winston, giving him work and helping him grow up. He didn't say why he was doing this, and never said anything about disposal of the farm when he dies or retires. To be honest, Montague, I wonder why Reuben bothers to work all day and every day when he could sell up and live on the profits.'

'He'll know no other life,' Pluke smiled. 'I'm sure he enjoys what he's doing. He's the sort who'd fade away and die of boredom if he had nothing to do. Now, there is another young man in Thordale, is there not?'

'Yes, Michael Booth. He works for his parents at Ling Garth. He's twenty-two, much younger than our lady in Devil's Dump. Michael came home at lunchtime today after helping a friend move house but he couldn't help us. He works for his parents – they're more modern than the other moor farmers around here and have holiday cottages as well as livestock, but although their sheep run on the moors, they're in a different part from Reuben's. They run to the south of Ling Garth, about two miles from the peat bogs, so neither Michael nor his parents have cause to visit the area around the peat bogs and couldn't help. We did quiz them about any young woman who might have used their cottages, but none matched our description. They did provide a list of people who've used the cottages over the past couple of years so I'll have them all checked – some are regular visitors. I have no reason to disbelieve any of the accounts given by any of those witnesses, young or not-so-young. After discussing this with the teams, I don't consider them prime suspects.'

'Thank you,' said Pluke. 'So that means everyone living in Thordale has been interviewed, so what about the village? Have house-to-house enquiries in Gunnerthwaite produced anything?'

'Still nothing. Our teams have done some good work. We've checked the postman, the farm milk collection driver, the local milk lady, travelling butcher, early morning commuters, everyone who comes and goes from Gunnerthwaite in fact, but all without result. One Gunnerthwaite resident pointed out the obvious – that the road up the dale is not one which the local people use to go to work or for shopping or for any regular purpose. It means there is very little regular traffic along that road, the only constant users being the farmers who run sheep on Rockdale Moor, although visitors do sometimes find themselves driving down past Trough House and through Thordale to Gunnerthwaite. We did find one man who drives up to the peat bogs to walk his dogs once in a while but in the three times he's been up there this year, he's seen nothing untoward. We've talked to a young woman who works as the receptionist in the surgery but she doesn't know either of the Susans and, like Dr Ingram, knows of no local woman who is missing. Another check we did was with Thordale Estate. Their estate manager is Hamish McGregor and we asked him about shooting parties using the moors but as he pointed out, the grouse season doesn't start until 12th August and so there'd be no group activities by shooting parties until that time – in fact, as it fell on a Sunday this year, the shooting didn't begin until 13th August. Our woman could have been dead and buried a month by that time so the chances of someone in a shooting party spotting someone behaving oddly are remote – unless the killer returned to the scene. We can trace most of those parties and the beaters and loaders, although McGregor himself can't help us. He is out and about on the moors throughout the year, at all hours, coping with everything from heather burning to peregrine falcons by way of protecting ground nesting birds, coping with stray hikers, litter louts, poachers and thieves who steal stones from dry-stone walls, but he's not seen anything that caused him concern. And he is a very observant man, his job demands it.'

'He didn't spot the grave!' smiled Pluke. 'So it's all negative information?'

'I'm afraid so, Montague. Mind you, we've more villagers to talk to and your news conference tomorrow which should generate some interest. We've reached the stage where we need something to lift the spirits of the teams.'

'I remain convinced a local person can enlighten us.' Pluke was emphatic. 'The entire scenario has all the hallmarks of a local person making use of local knowledge. That is something the teams must consider in depth.'

'You're not saying you know the killer, are you?'

'No, I'm not. All I am saying is that I am increasingly convinced a local person is responsible.'

'Montague, if you have any reason to believe you do know the killer, you would tell us, wouldn't you? You'd make sure the teams were aware of your suspicions?'

'All I know at the moment is that my head is full with a combination of threads which are currently a hopeless tangle of thought with no end in sight . . . I need to sort them out, Mr Horsley, I need to find the end to my tangle of thread, to unravel my confused strands. The answer is in there somewhere. When I have it, I shall let you know.'

'Don't keep us in the dark too long! We're all in this together, remember.'

Pluke smiled. 'For the moment, Mr Horsley, I'd like to keep my thoughts to myself, I need more supportive information before I extend any one of those threads. In spite of what I have just said, it is very important that our officers continue to comb the area and ask questions of everyone in the dale and village.'

'Talking of combing the area, Montague, here comes Inspector Theaker with what looks like bin bags full of rubbish. I think it might be for you!'

As Horsley left Pluke, Montague turned to see Theaker heading his way with two large black plastic bags in his hands, followed by two detectives each carrying a further two black bags. They deposited them near the stage of the church hall whereupon Theaker said, 'Well, Montague, here we are. Our lads have done their litter-collecting stint. Here it is, the result of our search of Thordale Gill from the peat bogs right down to Devil's Dump and beyond – we searched further downstream to make sure we found everything that might have been carried past Devil's Dump. And thanks for finding the grave, we checked it but found nothing of evidential value. As you said, it does have a covering of silt in the bottom and that makes it hard

135

to identify as a grave. Like you, I am convinced it is a grave. It's man-made, the marks of the spade can just be seen in one corner and it's of the right size to accommodate the dead woman. But although we went through the silt with a fine tooth comb, we found nothing. It's as clean as a bath that just's been wiped by a houseproud lady. So the question is – what do you want us to do with all this litter? Do you want to go through it or is that a job for our forensic friends?'

'Much as I dislike wading through mountains of other people's litter, I fear it will have to be examined, every bit of it,' Pluke sighed. 'So what have we? Anything that stands out in your mind?'

'Not particularly. Most of it looks like normal tourist litter,' Theaker said. 'Sandwich wrappers, sweet papers, cigarette packets, indigestion tablet boxes, drinks containers – cans and plastic bottles, dozens of them, an old T-shirt, several old newspapers and magazines, assorted bits of paper of the kind you'd use to wrap food in or even use as toilet paper, in fact one piece looked like a Christmas decoration. There was an empty camera film carton – all stuff that tourists have discarded rather than take home. We did find some old used cartridge shells, twelve-bores, evidence of shooting on the moors, grouse shooting I hasten to add – last year that would be – a pair of very old hob-nailed boots size eleven, an old dining chair, an old mattress, an electric oven, an electric toaster and a car radiator, all in very bad condition. Somebody's been disposing of their household rubbish up there.'

'The human race enjoying the countryside!' laughed Horsley.

'You've recorded where it was all found?' asked Pluke.

'We have. Every piece has been recorded. We have drawn up a scale drawing showing where every item was found.'

'No sign of a pair of women's shoes? Sandals?'

'Sorry, Montague, no. We did make a special search for those – I don't think those old boots are hers. They are very old. No sign of any jewellery or underwear. And there's nothing that might be the murder weapon. We searched meticulously around the grave too, and among those broken rowans.'

'Well done. And any conclusions of your own?'

'Just that this all seems to be either tourist litter or household junk that's been disposed of. Most of it was found along the route of the gill, washed into corners or lodged behind rocks, along with broken twigs and heather debris, including some sheep wool. There's nothing here I can relate to our dead woman, Montague.'

'Not even the Christmas decoration?' Pluke smiled. 'I can imagine those other items being tossed away by tourists or disposed of by householders, but why would anyone get rid of a paper Christmas decoration on those moors? It's an odd thing to find up there.'

'Well, I'm not sure it was a decoration . . .'

'Can you retrieve it for me?'

'Well, yes, everything's been tagged and wrapped in individual exhibit bags . . .'

It didn't take long for one of Theaker's Task Force officers, under the eyes of everyone in the room, to ferret inside one of the bags and find a transparent plastic exhibit bag containing the decoration. He passed it to Theaker who nodded and then handed it to Pluke.

'And where was this found?' Pluke asked, looking at the wet and dirty piece of folded white tissue paper.

'About half-way down the gill,' Theaker said. 'Washed into the roots of a stunted hawthorn along with umpteen pieces of broken twig, some sheep's wool and roots of heather. It was lucky we found it. I'd be careful how you handle it because it looks like toilet paper to me, Montague.'

'Yes, it does,' agreed Montague, twisting and turning the plastic package to examine the contents from every angle. 'But it is not. This is the remains of a maiden's garland.'

Chapter Ten

'Pardon my ignorance, Montague, but what is a maiden's garland?' asked Theaker.

Pluke explained to them all, adding that the parish church at Gunnerthwaite was noted throughout England, especially among folklorists and travel writers, for its collection of such garlands. He acquainted them with their purpose, adding that one of the collection had been stolen or removed while confessing that he had not pursued its disappearance because there was no reason to think it had any relevance to his enquiries. Now things had changed – the missing garland must be linked to the woman's death.

'Because she was a virgin, you mean?' suggested Horsley.

'That may be relevant,' Pluke mused. 'I can think of no other reason why a maiden's garland should be found in the proximity of this woman's final resting place. Maybe it is nothing more than coincidence, but as I have already affirmed, in crime enquiries one tends to treat coincidences with great respect and some suspicion.'

'But if the thing was hanging in the church and some dishonest tourist went inside, he or she could have nicked the garland as a laugh or even found it on the floor, taken it away, realized it was worthless and falling to bits in his hand, then tossed it away. More tourist litter.'

'I agree,' Pluke said, 'except that the church is kept locked. Access is granted upon request, visitors have to ask for the key.'

'Just the one key?'

'I'm not sure if there is a spare. The keyholder is a Miss Weston who lives in the village, she's also clerk of the parish council. She'll know who's been into the church in recent weeks.'

'I'll see if she's been visited by our teams,' and Horsley went across to the computer, entered the name of Weston, scanned the list of those already interviewed and shook his head. 'No, she's not been interviewed. She's all yours, Montague. Now, before you talk to her, one point does occur to me – about this garland.'

'Yes?'

'If – and I stress if – the killer did place such an old-fashioned thing on the woman's grave, he must have known she was a virgin.'

'That seems very likely,' Pluke nodded.

'Which in turn suggests he knew her very well indeed – or even that she had rejected his advances. A facetious gesture by a spurned suitor? It means there *could* be a sexual motive behind this death.'

'That likelihood must now be considered,' Pluke agreed. 'And there is another factor – the old-fashioned dress. It would not surprise me if the dress and garland are somehow associated.'

'But if the custom was to hang garlands in church after a funeral, or place them on the coffin,' queried Theaker, 'why would it be thrown away after this burial?'

'I do not think it was thrown away,' Pluke told them. 'I think it was buried with the woman and cast out of the ground by the floodwater at the same time as the body. Once out of the grave, it would be separated from the body.'

'That would make some sense,' agreed Theaker. 'It was certainly along the route of the floodwater.'

'And,' Pluke reminded them, 'whilst it might be a simple matter to remove the garland from the church, it might not be quite so simple to return it. Besides, this would not be a real funeral, it would be a secret burial. The killer was operating without anyone knowing what he was doing – so although he may have had a good reason for adding the garland to his burial arrangements, a display of his love for the woman perhaps, he could not afford to let anyone else know. So he got rid of the garland in the most logical place. The grave.'

'Well, you know more about these things than most of us,' Horsley acknowledged. 'I've not come across any of this background stuff filed in the computer . . .'

'Until now, there was no reason to think this was relevant,' Pluke said. 'I had words with the vicar only this morning – he comes only on Sundays – and he told me, *en passant*, about the loss of the garland. I must now pursue the matter. I shall speak to Miss Weston without delay.'

'Time's pressing on, Montague.' Horsley checked his watch. 'It's nearly six. Can we close the incident room at seven?'

'I think so. I shall conclude my interview before then and I am sure the others will want an early finish.'

'There are no matters of urgency,' Horsley said. 'I'll have Rowan Cottage searched tomorrow, but we've still no positive leads.'

'Then go off duty as planned. I shall see Miss Weston immediately,' Pluke said. 'And I shall return before seven. Don't let Detective Sergeant Wain leave without me.'

Hilda Weston lived at Greenside Cottage, which occupied a pleasing site on the northern slopes of the valley in which Gunnerthwaite was located. A detached double-fronted house built of moorland stone, it had a green gate, a small drive at the eastern side with a garage at the end, and a neat garden in front. The front door, with a horseshoe-shaped door knocker, was painted green too. Green was not the luckiest of colours, he knew, except for those born under the sign of Cancer, Leo or Sagittarius, so perhaps she was such a person? Nonetheless, he rang the door bell, quickly producing a response from a dark-haired lady wearing heavy spectacles. She was sturdy, and wore black low-heeled shoes, a navy skirt and a blue cardigan over a white blouse. There was no green in her clothing, he observed. She looked like a retired matron, which in fact she was.

140

'Yes?' she smiled.

'Miss Weston?' Pluke raised his hat in greeting. 'I am Detective Inspector Pluke and I am engaged on enquiries into the death of a young woman.'

'I'd heard about it, yes, word gets around. Miss Pyke told me. How dreadful. It's awful, the things young people get up to these days . . . So how can I help, Inspector? From what Miss Pyke told me, I feel quite sure I do not know the unfortunate young lady.'

'I believe you hold the key to the parish church?'

'I do, so if you wait a second, I'll go and get it for you.'

'Er, no, I don't want to visit the church, not at this point anyway. But I need to discuss a little matter with you.'

'Oh, well, you'd better come in. The kettle is on, Inspector, I was just starting to get my tea ready. Can I get you a cup? And a bun perhaps, or piece of apple pie?'

'That would be most welcome.' He was feeling rather peckish and did not regard such an offering as an attempted bribe. After all, Miss Weston could not be considered a suspect – or could she? She had access to the garlands, but was hardly the sort of person to kill another woman . . . but in this moorland village, it would be impolite to reject her offer. And he tried never to be impolite. As he removed his hat, she led him into her lounge, a warm room with an open fire. There was a *Mail on Sunday* on the circular table and a pair of comfortable easy chairs beside the hearth. She pointed to one and invited him to read the paper while she organized the refreshments. He placed his hat on the arm of the chair.

As he read a piece about a politician misbehaving with women, she returned with a tray which she placed on the table. Moments later, she settled in the chair opposite and invited him to explain his presence. Putting aside the paper, he decided not to mention the discovery of the garland at this point, but to approach his enquiries from the angle of thieves preying on rural churches. He wanted to see if she made any reference to the garlands as he opened with a brief account of the discovery of the

141

deceased in Devil's Dump. He provided a description of the woman in case it revived memories in Miss Weston and also introduced the absence of Susan Featherstone from Rowan Cottage, but Miss Weston listened carefully while offering no enlightenment. Then Pluke turned to the question of access to the church.

'Miss Weston,' he tried to sound very authoritative, 'in every murder investigation, we have to consider local criminal acts which have occurred in the past, eliminating those which are not relevant. I have spoken to the vicar and understand the church is kept locked due to some past incident?'

'A thief stole some valuable antique chairs, Mr Pluke, and so the vicar of the time decided we should keep the church locked. But that was years ago, I can't see it would have any bearing on that poor girl's death.'

'Had the chairs been taken by a local person, it would show that there was a person with criminal tendencies living nearby.' He thought he sounded very knowledgeable. 'And we do need to know about the activities of such people. But since that time, there have been no criminal acts, I believe? Not even minor acts of vandalism or attempts to steal from the offertory boxes?'

'No, nothing. I keep the key and if people want to look around the church, then I will hand it over to them – against signature, I might add. I do take their names and addresses in a little book I keep – just in case someone forgets to return the key. That has happened on occasions – but not with criminal intent I am sure, Mr Pluke, just forgetfulness.'

'And is there just the one key?'

'No, I had a duplicate made for myself, just in case the original is mislaid or lost, and I believe the vicar also has one. I keep mine in my bureau.'

'So what about people who need regular access? I don't know the routine of your church, but I would imagine it has an organist or choir who need to practise, cleaners who need to be in and so forth.'

'They all come to me, Mr Pluke. I'm always in the

village, and I do make alternative arrangements if I have to go to the dentist or something like that. The cleaners go in every Wednesday morning, for example, flower arrangers on Fridays, and after I've handed over the key I've a couple of hours to myself before they finish. That's when I do my bits of shopping, visit friends or go to the hair-dresser – she lives in the village, you see, so we are well catered for in Gunnerthwaite.'

'And your system has never allowed any problems to develop? No more thefts, no vandalism . . .'

'If you're thinking about the missing garland, Mr Pluke, I should forget it. The vicar goes on about it every time he meets a new person. I'm sure he would have told you, he's very proud of our collection, but one of them vanished a few weeks ago. I reckon a bird flew into it, a robin or something trapped in the church, and it got knocked to the floor. It would fall to pieces, Mr Pluke, they're so old and very fragile, and the cleaners would think it was bits of waste paper and it would get swept up. I have mentioned it to our cleaners, but they can't remember sweeping up anything like that. I don't think it would be stolen, do you? I mean, the garlands are not worth anything, they're just bits of paper made to look nice, not worth any money.'

'The vicar did mention it in passing, Miss Weston. He is as puzzled as anyone, but he has no idea when the garland vanished.'

'Well, it wasn't very long ago, I can tell you that. A couple of months or so, even less. One of the cleaners noticed it had gone, she told me and I told the vicar, but there's others left. We've still got a good collection, they still draw tourists who want to look at them and that's good for the church, they donate money for the upkeep and so on.'

'The garlands are not used any more in the district, are they?' he put to her. 'Old traditions do carry on in some places, you know.'

'Yes, we still have Blessing of the Sheep here, that's centuries old, but no, those garlands aren't used, they've not been used for more than a hundred years.'

Pluke took a long drink from his cup of tea. He was struggling to decide whether or not to inform Miss Weston that part of a garland had been discovered near the body's final resting place, his worry being that if he did disclose this, word of the discovery might reach the ears of the culprit. That being so, he would be pre-warned of its discovery and thus concoct some kind of denial, should he ever be asked. On the other hand, reasoned Pluke, knowledge that the garland was featuring in the enquiries might prompt the killer to panic, to try and cover up his crime and perhaps make mistakes . . . and then, bearing in mind advice received years ago, Pluke knew that, when in doubt, you tell the truth.

'Miss Weston,' he said at length, 'my interest in the garland stems from the fact that we believe remnants of it, or perhaps remnants of a similar one, have been found close to where the body was discovered.'

'Goodness me!' she cried. 'How on earth could that happen?'

'That is what we have to determine, Miss Weston. I am working on the theory – and it is only a theory – that the killer placed the garland with the body when it was buried. Now why would a killer place a maiden's garland on the body of a person he had just murdered?'

'He must have loved her,' said Miss Weston. 'I can't think of any other reason and, of course, if he was following the tradition then she must have been a maiden. And he must have known that as well.'

'Exactly. Now, to be somewhat vulgar, Miss Weston, I am not sure whether "maiden" in this context means an unmarried woman or a woman who is a virgin. In modern-day England, there is no guarantee an unmarried woman is a virgin, if you follow my logic.'

'I do indeed, Mr Pluke, and I am not the innocent and unworldly maiden lady you might think I am, after all, I was a hospital matron until my retirement, and what with nurses and young female patients . . . but you have no need to hear all that. But if the killer did place our garland in that woman's grave, how did he manage to steal it from the church?'

'My question precisely, Miss Weston. And that is why I am here. No one can get inside that church without your knowledge –'

'They can, the vicar has a key,' she reminded him.

'But he comes only on Sundays, I am assured,' countered Pluke.

'Yes, but the garland could have been taken on a Sunday. I mean, if he was in the church, talking to someone after the service in the vestry, anyone could walk in, the door would be open. And it's only a moment's job to lift down one of those garlands, those chapel roofs are not very high.'

'Is it? I'd have thought a stepladder would be required.'

'You can use one of those long tools we keep for opening high windows,' she told him. 'They've a brass hook on the end, you hook them into the window latch and lift it – they're about eight feet long, Mr Pluke, long enough to hook one of those garlands from the chapel ceiling. I know because we had a photographer in some years back, he wanted a close-up for a travel article and I hooked it down for him. It was covered in dust which I blew off and it was very fragile, made of tissue paper, but he got a picture of it. It was the last one to be put there, the one that's missing. So there's a photo of it somewhere, Mr Pluke, if you can trace it.'

'Thanks, I'll consider that. So if the vicar was otherwise engaged, out of sight in the vestry, you think one of those garlands could be removed very quickly without him being aware of it?'

'Without doubt, Mr Pluke.'

'And what about mid-week? Do you accompany visitors to the church?'

'No, I don't. I record their names in my book and tick them off when they bring the key back. I don't go in with them, that would suggest I didn't trust them and I believe that if they've decided to ask for a key, then they are honest and trustworthy. And we've had nothing stolen since we started this system.'

'Except a maiden's garland,' he said.

'Most odd, Mr Pluke. I wonder if he used it instead of flowers?' she mused. 'I mean, I wonder if he wanted a proper funeral for her but couldn't do so, for obvious reasons. So he did what he thought was best.'

'But he knew where to find a garland, Miss Weston, he knew what to do with it and he knew she was qualified for it. An odd gesture by a murderer, nonetheless.'

'But thousands of people know about these garlands, Mr Pluke, they're very famous, they're often photographed and articles are written about them. And I'd say most of the local people are familiar with them.'

'I agree, but who knew the victim, and who knew she was a virgin? I think a local man knew they were here and what they were for, and it is therefore very important that I discover when the garland was removed. You say you noticed it missing and told the vicar?'

'I did, yes. It was while I was away, Mr Pluke, I went to Norfolk to look after my sister when she was ill . . . now, let me see. It'll be in my book because all issues will be in Mrs Braithwaite's writing, she looked after the key while I was away . . .'

She went to a bureau in the corner of the room and produced a lined register bearing the title 'Church Key Book' and turned the pages.

'I do like to keep neat records, Mr Pluke, something I learned in the hospital, you can't keep too many records especially when members of the public are involved. Ah, here we are.'

She had found the relevant entries and came to his side with the book open. 'Now, I issued it to the cleaner on 13th June, that's a Wednesday as I said, and then a chap called Williams collected it on the Friday afterwards. Then it's Mrs Braithwaite's writing, Mr Pluke. Yes, I went off to Norfolk that Saturday, the 16th, and I was away a fortnight. I came back that Saturday, it would be 30th June. You see, I issued the key again on the Wednesday following, 4th July – to the cleaner – and then it went out on the Friday, to the flower ladies, and again on 11th July. The cleaner again. No visitors. Now, I did go to church for several Sundays after I got back, to pray for my sister's improvement, and that's when I saw the garland was missing. It might have been the middle of July, the 15th or so. I mentioned it to the vicar, the flower ladies and the cleaner and others who come to church regularly, but no one had noticed it had gone. We all thought it must have fallen to bits and the scraps got blown away if the door was open, or swept up without the cleaners realizing what they were. But why are these dates important, Mr Pluke?'

'If the killer took the garland before he killed his victim, Miss Weston, it implies foreknowledge, it may even show he intended to kill and bury her. That is clear evidence of premeditation. If he came into the church *after* killing her, however, it may suggest regret or deep emotion. I must be precise, for I do believe the girl was buried before 20th July – the date of those dreadful floods in Thordale Gill.'

'Oh dear, I see . . .'

'So, from your book, who has been into the church since, say, 1st June? I need names.'

There were lists in both her writing and that of Mrs Braithwaite, but the addresses were too imprecise for immediate checking. They said simply names and towns, like 'Simpkins, Middlesbrough; Wardle, Leeds; Ironside, Ripon; G. Wilson, Thirsk; Thompson, Guisborough; Willoughby, Brighton; John and Mary Preston, Newcastle.'

'We can check these, but it will take time,' Pluke said. 'But I note you have not included the names of local people in the book?'

'No, I know them, like the cleaners, flower arrangers and so on. There's no need to book the key out to them, it goes out every Wednesday and Friday and if they forget to fetch it back, I know where they are. It's strangers and tourists I have to be careful with.'

'And, I suppose,' he brooded, 'that if one of your visitors was actually inside the church, having unlocked the door, someone else could come along and join him or her, without booking out the key. So any record of yours will be incomplete.'

'Oh, yes, Mr Pluke, that happens sometimes. I've had one lot book the key out and another book it back in. And folks often pay visits while the cleaner and flower ladies are there . . . it's not a totally secure system, but it has stopped thieving.'

'That all seems very feasible. Now, in Mrs Braithwaite's writing, I see there were quite a number of visitors during her stewardship, other than cleaners and flower ladies. So where can I find her, Miss Weston? I'd like a chat with her.'

'She's dead, Mr Pluke. She died a month ago, she got pneumonia after breaking a hip, poor old thing. She's buried away from here, near her sister in Scarborough. But you can see the names she put in.'

Pluke's spirits slumped at this news, but as Miss Weston passed him the book and he began to jot down the scanty details, he reacted to one name: Susan Miller. She had been into the church on 21st June.

'Do you know Susan Miller?' he asked Miss Weston, more out of hope than expectation.

'I've never met her, Mr Pluke, but she's that artist who does all those nice pictures of the moors. Mrs Braithwaite did say she'd asked to look inside the church and she wondered if she was wanting to do a painting of it, but that's all she said. She didn't go with her, if that's what you're wondering, but did say Miss Miller spent about two hours there.'

'And has there been a painting of the church, inside or out, by Susan Miller since that time?'

'If there has, I haven't seen it.'

'I am very interested in her work,' Pluke said. 'I am trying to trace both her and that agent of hers, the lady I mentioned earlier, the one called Susan Featherstone who owns Rowan Cottage.'

'I've heard Miss Pyke at the post office talk about them, Mr Pluke, she stocks Susan Miller prints and sometimes an original or two. She always paints a shepherd in the back-ground, probably you know that.'

'I have recently discovered that trait,' he nodded.

'It makes people want to collect her works although some believe there's a few early Millers without the shep-herd. Not that I'm an art collector, I'm not. My salary and now my pension didn't permit any kind of extravagance. But I've never come across either of them although the Featherstone woman stays in the village quite often. I believe Miss Miller is very reclusive.'

'And do you know where I can find her?'

'Sorry, no. I've no idea. I don't think anyone knows where she lives.'

Having jotted down her list of names to be checked by his teams, Pluke then quizzed Miss Weston, in her capacity as clerk to the parish council, about events in the village which might have sparked off some kind of confrontation between residents and visitors, or which might have pro-duced local enmity, but she had no recollection of any such source of trouble or conflict.

Pluke left with a feeling that this had been a productive meeting – if nothing else it had provided a rough idea of when the garland had been stolen even though there was no obvious suspect. It did seem, however, that the timing of that theft could be linked with the death of the woman – both had apparently occurred during the recent summer.

It had also established that Susan Miller had been in the village around that time and earlier enquiries had estab-lished that Susan Featherstone had also been in the vicinity – the invoice for work on her car had established that. So could all these isolated events be links in one puzzling chain? They all served to further tangle Pluke's web of theories while confirming his view that the answer to his riddle lay in this isolated dale and village. So what had he overlooked?

When he entered the incident room, it was twenty min-utes to seven, and the place was humming with activity as the detectives assembled to enter their statements, file their reports and discuss the day's events over a final cup of tea and biscuits. Soon, they would depart for home and leave a solitary night duty detective in the incident room. His overnight task would be to abstract salient details from the statements and double-check that they had been entered into HOLMES, the computer system designed, among other things, to aid the detection of murders.

As he sipped a cup of tea, Pluke moved among the detectives, praising them for their dedication and hard work, asking if anything interesting had been discovered and exhorting them to continue their fine work tomorrow morning. Detective Constable Waring said she had an appointment with a costume specialist and that looked promising; she now had photographs of the dress. All too soon, it was time to leave with little positive news, other than his own, being forthcoming. Wayne Wain was anxious to be off because he had a date – he'd been captivated by a woman he'd met on an activities weekend in the Lake District and she was now staying with relations near Crickledale.

'Come along then, Wayne, I don't want to be the cause of angst in your search for true love,' smiled Pluke. 'And besides, Millicent will have a nice meal awaiting.'

As they left Gunnerthwaite, Wayne was in chatty mood, saying, 'Sir, how was your day? Ours was a long slog, I'm afraid, with little to show for it.'

As Wayne drove along Thordale towards Devil's Dump, taking the shortest route back to Crickledale, Pluke provided a factual account of his own endeavours, with due emphasis on the garland, but as he spoke to Wayne he sounded frustrated. 'I am frustrated, Wayne,' he admitted. 'There is something I have missed. It worries me, knowing there is something I should have taken into consideration during my investigations, something that has slipped through my fingers. Yet I cannot bring it to mind, that is most frustrating.'

'We're all like that, sir, it happens in every investigation. That elusive link we need, that flash of inspiration, that one link in the chain which makes everything add up to something sensible. We always know it's there and we can't find it . . . but it will come, mark my words. You'll be doing something totally unconnected with this enquiry when the inspiration strikes you.'

'You are right, of course,' Pluke said. 'It is early days, as I believe the saying goes, but this is day two and we don't yet have a name for the deceased. Unless I get a break-through very soon, I fear we are in for an extended inves-tigation, Wayne.'

As they drove homewards, they approached Devil's Dump with the hill past Trough House rising ahead like a dull grey ribbon as it wound its way through the heather. Evening shadows were darkening the area of the trees which concealed the sinister pool and Pluke felt a shiver ripple down his spine.

'If I was a young constable, I'd say this place gives me the creeps!' he laughed at Wayne Wain. 'But I am a senior police officer and so perhaps I should say that it makes me feel in awe of the location, in fear even. There is something rather unsettling about this area, Wayne, in addition to its sinister reputation.'

'It's all in the mind, sir. You are very sensitive to such things, more sensitive than most. I'm not. It's just a pretty part of the moors so far as I'm concerned, although I must say that it does mean more now it's the focus of a murder enquiry.'

'But it does have a sinister past, Wayne. Two deaths in that pool. And now our lady. And why has Trough House been allowed to fall into such dereliction, why does this corner, this beautiful corner of the moors, have such a sense of evil about it, foreboding even?'

'Because that shepherd and the young girl drowned here,' Wayne said. 'When I was talking to one of the men this afternoon, asking if he could help us, he said when he was a lad no one would venture into this place at night. It was supposed to be haunted, he said, because the shep-herd was found drowned. Some said he'd been murdered and others said he'd done it himself. The girl's death was an accident, no one doubts that. I know these things happened a long time ago but people still talk about them, it's part of local folklore.'

'That's it, Wayne, thank you,' Pluke said. 'That is what was niggling at me all the time . . . the shepherd.'

'The shepherd? You can't link that death with this one, surely?'

'I don't know the precise date of his death, but why does Susan Miller include a shepherd in all her paintings, Wayne? And why include one in the picture of Trough House?'

Wayne did not reply for a while, and then, as they were driving past Trough House, he glanced towards the ruin and said, 'You mean it's her way of depicting a ghost?'

'Not so much a ghost, more a memorial to a real person. So what is the relevance of that shepherd? Why does she include him in all her works? I think Susan Miller knows who he was, and what happened to him.' Pluke spoke softly now. 'And she has painted Trough House complete with its trough.'

'I still can't see what stories of a ghostly shepherd have to do with our murder investigation,' Wayne said. 'And we don't really think Miller's in our morgue, do we? We think it's Susan Featherstone even if she doesn't look like her. I'm not sold on the idea they're one and the same person, you know.'

'Nonetheless, I think they could be, Wayne, and what about the maiden's garland? And that dress worn by our unfortunate young lady? Like the shepherd, they're all from a bygone era.'

'Do you know something I don't?' asked Wayne.

'I very much doubt it, but a new thought is now forming in my mind. Come along, Wayne, let's get home. It's been a long day,' smiled Detective Inspector Pluke with more than an air of mystery in his voice.

Chapter Eleven

Over a relaxing dinner with Millicent, Pluke recounted his adventures. Although it was not his normal practice to discuss police work with his wife or anyone else outside the service, he felt that, on this occasion, his trough work and his police duties had become so inextricably intertwined as to be almost inseparable. As Millicent was steadfastly assisting him in the former – and doing some good work – he felt he should keep her informed.

She listened with dutiful interest, expressing her astonishment at some of his revelations such as the theft of the maiden's garland and his opinion that there might be a link between the dead shepherd of Devil's Dump and those in Susan Miller's paintings. Then there was the fact that Rowan Cottage, the holiday home of Susan Featherstone, was constructed with stones removed from Trough House and that it now hosted the actual horse trough from the latter. He told her about the ongoing enquiries – his discovery of the hilltop grave near the rowan patch, the fruitless investigations of the house-to-house teams in Gunnerthwaite, the efforts by Wakefield Police to trace Susan Featherstone, the work of Detective Constable Waring in determining the history and origin of the long dress worn by the deceased and the continuing mystery of Susan Miller. Millicent, still embarrassed by her behaviour in the tea room at Granthorpe, expressed her wifely amazement at the complexities now confronting her hard-working husband and praised him for intellectual prowess in assessing the case.

In return, she told Pluke about her day, or to be precise,

that part of it which followed her departure from the Granthorpe craft shop. Using information gleaned from Helen Morris, Millicent had visited several other outlets for Susan's prints and watercolours, these ranging from several cafés to a museum of rural life by way of a glass-blowing gallery, a pottery, a garage and a shop selling hiking equipment and maps. During the afternoon, Millicent had inspected the works on display in all those places, pretending to be a potential buyer whenever an assistant had approached her, but in all cases, she told Pluke, ordering and delivery of the works had been completed through an agent – Susan Featherstone. The system she used was the same as that deployed in the Granthorpe craft shop, and all those in charge of those outlets had said how popular and collectable were her paintings – and all depicted the now familiar figure of a shepherd.

Millicent did appreciate that none of this increased Pluke's knowledge nor did it contribute anything towards his investigation, except to confirm what he had already discovered about the Susan Miller paintings. But then Millicent added a little more.

'One thing did emerge,' she said as she sipped her coffee. 'It was when I was talking to the man in the glass-blowing gallery, you know the place, Montague. We once went and saw a man blowing glass and making things for sale, coloured glassware of all kinds . . .'

'At Haggington, if my memory serves me correctly,' he said.

'Yes, that's the one. A nice place with a nice young couple running it, man and wife, and I bought a lovely blue swan with a yellow beak . . .'

'I remember it well,' Pluke nodded, recalling that it is unlucky to kill a swan because it was once thought they embodied human souls. It was always said that anyone who killed a swan would die within a year. That old belief concerned real swans, of course, not artificial ones made from blue glass for ornamental purposes. Nonetheless, he did feel that an image of a swan in the house was a good omen. Then there was the well-known story of a swan-maiden who became the wife of a human man. The legend told of a flock of swan-maidens which descended to the shores of a lake and there divested themselves of their feathery robes to bathe as women in the nude. A man secretly watched them and stole the robe of one of them, thus gaining power over her and so, somewhat reluctantly, she became his wife. He kept the robe, concealing it from her and so, it seems, they lived as man and wife until one day she discovered the hidden robe, put it on and changed back into a swan. Then she flew away and was never seen again. Pluke saw parallels between that story and the deceased woman of Devil's Dump: both were maidens, water featured in both stories and the Thordale maiden had worn a robe – in her case a long brown dress over an almost naked body – and now she had gone. Or her life had gone. The same thing, really. So where had that brown dress been hidden? And by whom? A man wanting control over her?

'Montague?' Millicent was calling to him and he jerked himself back into attentiveness. 'Are you listening?'

'Oh, sorry.' He blushed just a little at his unintentional rudeness in ignoring her. 'My mind was on our crime . . . I'm sorry, do go on. You were telling me about the glass blower of Haggington.'

'Yes.' She sounded rather upset at his lapse. 'As I was saying, Montague, before you drifted into one of your fantasies and shut me out of your mind, I was talking to the man in the glass gallery and expressed my interest in Susan Miller's work. I turned the conversation around to Susan Miller and the man said, "Well, I've never met her, I believe she's very reclusive but that agent of hers did once tell me she used a place similar to this near Gunnerthwaite – and this studio is a converted barn." That is what the man said, Montague.'

'Near Gunnerthwaite?' He was alert now. 'How near Gunnerthwaite?'

'He didn't know, I asked him. He couldn't help any more, it was just something let slip by Susan Featherstone. He said she tried to correct herself immediately, saying she shouldn't have told him that, it was breaking a confidence. It's intrigued him ever since but he did not follow it up and he has no idea where her studio is – and he's never met Susan Miller.'

'Millicent, you've done it again! My word, this could be just the lead we want. I shall take steps tomorrow to have every converted barn searched and examined to see if it contains her studio. Wonderful, my dear.'

'If she is so secretive, Montague, she could have died in her barn, couldn't she? And be lying there now, undiscovered? Without anyone knowing where she is.'

'Anything is possible, Millicent, but I shall do my best to find her. If we find her, or her place of work, then we are half-way to discovering whether or not she is our mystery victim. Wonderful, Millicent. I am really proud of you.'

'Oh, you say the nicest things, Montague, it was nothing.'

And so, once they had cleared the table and washed the pots, they settled down to a quiet evening before the fire, Millicent reading her Joanna Trollope while Montague began to search his bookshelves.

'What are you looking for?' Millicent asked eventually, when it was evident he couldn't find what he wanted.

'That book about murders and mysteries from the North York Moors,' he said. 'There's bits of folklore in it, an account of witches and unsolved murders. I thought it might contain something about the shepherd or that young girl.'

'It's in the car,' she told him. 'You put it in the glove compartment months ago, you wanted it readily available during your research into troughs. There's some others with it, one especially about ghosts and another about historical mysteries.'

'Thank you, Millicent, you do look after me. I'll go and get them.'

For the next hour or so, Pluke studied the books, checking and rechecking, looking up stories of ghosts, murders and folk tales and then, more by good fortune than by careful research, he found what he sought. The area upon which he was concentrating was not referred to as Devil's Dump or Thordale – which was why he didn't find it in the index. Instead, the story was titled 'The Spectre of Pyman Gill'. Pyman Gill was the name in the index.

When he turned to the story, he found it had occurred in the early years of the nineteenth century – and, as he knew, a man called Pyman continued to live in the vicinity. He wondered if the location was named after one of Reuben's ancestors. How long had Pymans lived in Thordale, he wondered? With a thumping heart and a sense of great anticipation, Pluke settled down to read the old story.

He learned that stories of a ghost had begun to circulate in and around Thordale during the mid-1800s and early 1900s, and such was the strength of the tales that experts began to examine the history of the area then known as Pyman Gill. Pluke was in no doubt that Thordale Gill was the beck in question, but at the time of the tale the hill was a mere unsurfaced track, rough and uneven but used by carters, horsemen, panniermen and other traders who trekked across the moors towards York via this direct route. The building now known as Trough House was then called the Pyman Inn and it was a stopping place for these traders – horses could be hired, food and accommodation obtained for both horses and men, and water taken from the splendid trough. It was a thriving place with lots of rooms, but with the increase of rail traffic in the mid- and late 1800s the need for horse-drawn freight vehicles gradually subsided and the Pyman ceased to operate as an inn. For a time it functioned as a farmhouse, but around the arrival of the twentieth century it was abandoned completely and left to fall into a ruinous condition. No one has lived there since that time. Sometime prior to its demise, however, the first tragedy occurred in the gill and some said it was this which led, perhaps directly or perhaps indirectly, to the eventual decline of the Pyman Inn.

For one thing, it generated the stories of hauntings around the old house and the gill which flowed nearby. Few, if any, dared venture along the dale towards the old inn, neither did they proceed up the hill and over the moors towards York – as a trading route, therefore, their regular passage through Thordale came to an end. The tragedy, which according to the author of Pluke's book had been authenticated from contemporary records, involved the death of a shepherd. His name was Joshua Featherstone and he was found drowned in the pool now called Devil's Dump. Joshua, who was twenty-six at the time of his death in 1821, worked for the farmer who ran the Pyman Inn – as well as being an inn, the enterprise was also a farm with extensive grazing rights for sheep on the moors above, plus a herd of milking cows, horses for sale or rent, as well as poultry and dogs. The reason for his drowning had never been determined – there were rumours of suicide, murder and accident, the former being eventually discounted because Joshua was known to be a powerful swimmer with no black moods or signs of depression. He was a cheerful, capable and popular young man who, in 1820, had married a local girl called Hilda Marshall. An accident was also considered most unlikely, bearing in mind Joshua's knowledge of the terrain, his swimming ability and the fact that he regularly walked up the route of the beck to check his sheep. And the water, for most of its route, was far too shallow for a strong grown man to drown accidentally within it. That left the possibility of murder but with no formal police service at the time and no modern investigative techniques, murder was never proved although the finger of suspicion did point to a young blacksmith/farrier called Henry Livingstone who also worked at the Pyman Inn.

No evidence for that suspicion was given in the account studied by Pluke, other than to say that Livingstone did show more than a normal interest in the shepherd's beautiful young wife. Down the years, though, those rumours grew into something stronger, until everyone living nearby believed that Henry Livingstone had murdered Joshua Featherstone to make the way clear for him to have Hilda. But, although she later bore a son called Reuben Featherstone, she never did marry Henry Livingstone and he left the area. No one was ever tried for the supposed crime –

if indeed it had been a crime – but soon rumours of the ghostly shepherd began to manifest themselves.

There was also a brief record of the second tragedy, the accidential drowning of a six-year-old girl in 1872. Pluke recalled that this was the last recorded use of a maiden's garland but the death had not exercised the imagination of the public in the way of the shepherd's death. The girl's death was a pure accident with no overtones of a mystery – but her name was given. Cissie Featherstone. It meant two Featherstones had been found dead in Devil's Dump.

There was nothing of further value in that book and although Pluke searched his moorland reference library, no other volume contained any reference to the deaths. And now, thanks to an artist's work, the stories had been revived – but how many people knew those tales? Had there been interest in the shepherd other than by Pluke? And was that the reason Susan Miller had included the shepherd in all her works – to revive interest in the figure, a kind of ongoing puzzle for her devoted followers?

Pluke put down the volume and sighed. 'Well, Millicent, this has proved most fascinating. On the moors above Thordale only yesterday I spoke to a man called Pyman and his farmhand called Livingstone while seeking a woman called Featherstone – and all those names feature in the mystery of the ghost of the Pyman Inn. Most curious, Millicent, most curious indeed,' and he provided her with a full account of the tales.

'But all this happened such a long time ago, Montague, surely there cannot be a link with your current investigation?'

'There may be a distant link,' he mused. 'Especially if that shepherd was an ancestor of the artist.'

'But her name is Miller,' Millicent reminded him. 'Susan Miller, it's her agent who is called Featherstone.'

'I am still half convinced it is one and the same person,' Pluke said. 'And if that is the case, then it is quite feasible that an ancestor of the drowned shepherd would wish to perpetuate his memory, and in this case, she's chosen to include him in *all* her paintings – not just those depicting this part of the dale.'

'But if she includes the shepherd, why not the girl?' asked Millicent.

'A very good question,' he nodded. 'And I don't know that answer yet.'

'But if the artist is another person entirely, not connected with the Featherstone family, why would she include the shepherd? Is it coincidence, Montague, that she has chosen a shepherd for her trademark? After all, she could have selected a skylark or a peewit or a grouse or, well, anything associated with the moors.'

'She could, but she hasn't,' Pluke said. 'She has chosen a shepherd who might be the one who died mysteriously all those years ago in the very pool that a child died in and where a mystery woman has also been found dead, a woman who might be Susan Miller or Susan Featherstone. I find that most intriguing, Millicent. Most intriguing. I need to sleep on this one to digest the whole scenario to see if I can link the past with the present.'

'It is getting late, Montague, I think we should go to bed, you need to be fresh for tomorrow's enquiries.'

And so, after their nightly cocoa, Pluke and Millicent went to bed, each harbouring a feeling of great achievement and contentment; Pluke, of course, had looked under the bed before climbing in, just to ensure that nothing of a nasty nature was lurking there – it was something he'd done since childhood – and he likewise entered the sheets at the side from which he would emerge in the morning. He had no desire to get out of the wrong side of the bed, especially on a Monday morning with his first news conference looming. He knew that Monday was a bad day to meet anyone with flat feet, especially when starting a new journey, but it was a good day for getting a haircut. But, with tomorrow promising to be a very important Monday, he felt he had no time for haircuts, and he knew Millicent would not turn the mattress tomorrow either. Monday was a very bad day for turning mattresses. And so, having completed his nightly rituals, Detective Inspector

Montague Pluke fell into a refreshing sleep and dreamt about finding a golden horse trough.

At eight the following morning, Detective Sergeant Wayne Wain collected Pluke in the official police car and drove him to the incident room, a journey of almost an hour. Millicent would not be venturing into the moors today – Monday was washing day when she had to deal with dirty clothes accumulated during the week and then, that afternoon, there was the flower arranging club with all the excitement of having to decide who should be the next President. There was a distinct possibility that Millicent might be elected, chiefly because she bore the name of Pluke; the association between the Pluke family and the history of Crickledale – a most honourable and long-standing association – dated into the mists of time. Being a servant to others was a cross Millicent would have to bear – but she did rather enjoy the notion of being President of Crickledale Flower Arranging Club.

Montague, on the other hand, had equally serious matters on his mind as he was driven towards the lofty moors. For a time, he settled in his seat and said nothing to Wayne as he mulled over the tangled web of information in his head, leaving Wayne to listen to some ghastly loud and tuneless music on a local radio station. But after half an hour or so, Wayne said, 'Sir, what's on the cards for today?'

'Cards, Wayne?' Pluke was momentarily puzzled.

'Programme, our programme, sir. What are our plans for today?'

'Ah, yes, I was going through that in my mind, Wayne. It is going to be a busy day and, I trust, a fruitful one. I have several positive leads to follow.'

'Well, I'm all ears, sir.'

Pluke told him all about his discoveries, and about the likelihood of finding a barn containing Susan Miller's studio, and then said, 'I am of the inclination, Wayne, that we should not make too much fuss about these revelations. I do not want to alert any likely suspects to the fact I may be getting close to them, and so I feel it might be wise for us to say nothing of this to our colleagues, not at this stage.'

'So you'll let them continue with their house-to-house enquiries without knowing what you know?'

'Yes, Wayne, for the time being. Now, as you know, we have a news conference at half-past ten and for that, I shall concentrate upon trying to get our victim identified. I shall make no mention to the press of the shepherd in the pictures, the old dress, the grave, the maiden's garland or my hunt for Susan Featherstone and Susan Miller. And I shall not refer to our hunt for her studio, not yet.'

'Softly, softly catchee monkee, eh, sir?'

'Yes, Wayne, I think that is the best approach. You and I will deal with these aspects for I am even more convinced the solution to this enquiry lies in those few farms at the head of Thordale.'

Soon they were driving along the heights, picking their way along the unmade road which led towards the peat bogs, and Pluke lapsed into another silence as he studied the landscape. Now, in the fresh light of morning, the waters in the old peat bogs looked serene and blue, but when one studied the landscape in the sun's light, it was far from flat. There were deep undulating sections of ground, evidence of ancient earthworks and of more recent ravages by flood. He saw the broken remains of the rowan patch on the edge of the moor, an eternal marker for the grave of the unknown woman. A mixture of charm and savagery.

'You know, Wayne,' said Pluke, 'a man could dig a grave up here without anyone seeing him, couldn't he? And working alone up here, he'd have a wide view of anyone's approach, either on foot or in a vehicle, from any direction, so he could take the necessary avoiding action. Here we are now, completely alone, just as Pyman and Winston were when we encountered them.'

'But if a visitor saw what looked like a local man digging, he'd think it was for peat and that's not unusual, is it? If we asked for tourists to report suspicious sightings, I doubt if such information would include a local moorland farmer digging on a peat moor. People have always dug on peat moors, and still do. I know a pub whose fire is made up of peat and the landlord digs it from the moor – not here, but the point is that peat is still used.'

'Exactly, Wayne. So if a local person saw another local person digging on the peat moor, that, likewise, would not be unusual?'

'Probably not, sir.'

'So whoever dug that grave up here might have been spotted without anyone realizing he was doing anything sinister?'

'Right, sir.'

'Then I think we must revisit the grave now, for a quick examination of its site, and later revisit all the farms in Thordale, Wayne.'

'As you say, sir.'

They parked and walked past the devastated rowan clump, a strange sentinel above the site of the grave. Now, though, a small bunch of chrysanthemums had been laid upon it.

'Someone's tribute,' said Wayne. 'They do this at the scenes of road fatalities, don't they?'

'Indeed they do, Wayne, but who has been to do this? Who knew the site of the grave, apart from a few police officers? Let us keep this development to ourselves for the time being. Now, look at the view from here. What do you see?'

'The dale below?'

'And?'

'Well, nothing else.' The detective sergeant shrugged his shoulders.

'The farms? All the farms in the dale? Gunnerthwaite in the distance? And Trough House just below, you can just see the site, it's tucked well into the base of the hill, Wayne.'

'Right, yes, I can see all those.'

'Good,' said Pluke. 'It's time to go.'

As they descended the steepest gradient of the track down to Trough House and Devil's Dump, Pluke was recreating in his own mind the events of 1821 and 1872, and trying to link them to the events of 2001. Was there a link, he pondered, or was he chasing shadows?

Then he was aware of a tractor and trailer heading towards their car; Wayne spotted it and drew to a halt, but the road was too narrow for the two vehicles to pass. Wayne, reacting swiftly, slammed the police car into reverse and roared backwards up the hill until he found a small area on which to park. He waited as Reuben Pyman's tractor approached, driven by Winston, then Wayne eased down his window as the unit halted at his side.

'Thanks,' shouted Pyman. 'Easier for you to back up than us to back down.'

'Off to see to your sheep, are you?' Wayne asked.

'Aye, daily trip. Any luck with that enquiry of yours?'

'Not yet.' Pluke now joined the conversation. 'But we are continuing our enquiries. We shall be revisiting everyone in the dale. You'll be in today?'

'Aye, we're never far away, me and Winston. Sylvia's not in today, Tuesday's her next day, so if you can't get a reply from the house, we'll either be in the outbuildings or down the fields. Come and find us.'

'Thank you,' and so the tractor unit continued its slow way to the top of the lane as Pluke and Wayne continued their journey.

'You know, Wayne, this is our lucky day. I've just seen a wagtail.'

'A wagtail, sir?'

'Yes, a pied wagtail, or a water wagtail as some people call them. If you see a wagtail on the road, you make a wish, and that wish will be granted.'

'Really? So what is your wish, sir?'

'That we reach a satisfactory conclusion to this case, Wayne. What else?'

Chapter Twelve

When Pluke and Wayne arrived at the incident room, Inspector Dick Horsley had already received a call from Wakefield Police to say that two officers had entered Susan Featherstone's house at Calderton yesterday evening, ostensibly to make sure she wasn't lying dead or injured. They had acquired a glass tumbler from her bedside – it bore a good set of fingerprints, almost surely Susan's – and while in the house they had searched thoroughly for her or her remains. Nothing was found although they did discover several wigs, all female and all with long black hair. They had not removed any, but had left them on their stands in her dressing room. There were no period clothes, however – her wardrobes (three of them) were full of expensive modern clothing of the kind used for both social and business functions. Wakefield Police had expressed a view that the house did bear signs of a planned absence – no milk or papers had been delivered, the refrigerator was empty and the water turned off.

Miss Featherstone's gardener could only confirm her habit of going away for days or even weeks on end, usually without telling him where she was heading or how long she would be away. He knew when she'd gone – the doors were locked, there was a lack of lights in the evening and her Volkswagen was absent. When she was away, he would tend her plants, both indoors and outdoors, without being asked – he did have a key to the house and he was not worried by her current absence. In his view, it was utterly normal. That search, undertaken by officers knowing nothing of the intricacies of Pluke's investigation, produced no clues to Susan's present whereabouts – no contact telephone numbers or addresses were found.

'They've some other stuff to go to Wetherby, unconnected with our enquiry, so they'll take the glass direct to the lab,' the Wakefield officer had told Horsley. 'It'll save you time, rather than have it sent to you first.'

Horsley had been most grateful for that welcome cooperation and had despatched a SOCO to Wetherby to liaise with the forensic scientists and Dr Meredith. The result of that exercise – comparison of the prints from the glass with those of the body – should be known before lunchtime today. Then they'd know, with reasonable certainty, whether the dead woman was Susan Featherstone.

When Montague Pluke mounted the stage to address his officers, he explained that Wakefield Police had now provided what might be a breakthrough. In anticipation of the victim being confirmed as Susan Featherstone, however, his teams should make every effort to trace her movements and contacts since the probable time of her death, i.e. during the recent summer. Yet more efforts were needed to trace people and vehicles visiting Rockdale Moor near the peat bogs and the site of the grave and, in addition, he exhorted the teams to continue their enquiries to trace the mysterious artist, Susan Miller.

'Is she a suspect, sir?' asked a detective. 'Or is Featherstone?'

'Neither possibility can be ignored,' Pluke confirmed, 'although I must remind you there is a possibility that Susan Miller and Susan Featherstone are one and the same person. Bear that in mind during your enquiries and remember that Miss Featherstone might have worn a wig. If you ask me why either woman should adopt this sort of masquerade, then I do not know. That is something else to determine.'

'We have saturated the village already, sir, without gaining any worthwhile information, the people don't know anything,' remarked a detective sergeant.

'Then we must keep trying. There's no harm returning

to houses after the residents have had time to reconsider their own knowledge. They might have talked things over with neighbours and friends and realized they do know something useful after all. We need to gain access to any clue, however small. Now, Detective Constable Waring, you are concentrating on the dress worn by our victim. Any developments to date?'

'I'm collecting a specialist in period theatrical costumes at eleven this morning, sir, and I've arranged to take her to the forensic lab. The forensic people don't want the dress to leave the premises due to the risk of damage or contamination, but they don't mind this lady looking at it there. I do have photographs as well.'

'Good, keep me informed. In view of that development I will not inform the press about the dress just yet. We need to keep a few tricks up our sleeves, in a manner of speaking. Now, any sign of the victim's footwear?' he asked the general audience.

Inspector Theaker responded. 'No, Montague, not a sign. We did a second sweep of the entire route of Thordale Gill and the grave site, but there's nothing.'

'That is something we must also keep in our minds,' Pluke said. 'I shall not inform the press about that either, it is something to keep back should I find myself interviewing a serious suspect.'

Satisfied he had provided sufficient background, Pluke despatched his teams to their duties and prepared for the news conference at ten thirty. The force press officer, Inspector Paul Russell, had already attended the conference of detectives and was aware of all facets of the investigation.

'My priority is to identify our victim,' Pluke stressed. 'But I don't want the press to publish the names of either Susan Miller or Susan Featherstone just yet. We don't want anxious relatives learning of their possible murder through the newspapers, we want them to suggest those names to us. And I don't want the press to mention the dress – get them to concentrate on a physical description of the victim, Inspector.'

167

'What about your theory that the body was washed out of a peat grave?'

'I don't want to dwell on that at this stage either. Just say she was found in Devil's Dump, say we are still investigating the cause of death and we are treating the death as suspicious. Make a mystery out of it, Inspector, and let us keep a few pieces of information in reserve.'

'So the cause of death? The head injury? Are we revealing that?'

'No, not yet. Say it is still being investigated.'

'Talking of news conferences, Montague,' chuckled Horsley, 'the morning papers have arrived and I see you are splashed all over them.'

'But we've not talked to the press yet,' Pluke said.

'It's not about the murder,' grinned Horsley. 'It's about your appointment as the County Horse Trough Liaison Officer. Here, look at some of these headlines.'

Horsley showed a selection of papers to Pluke with these headlines: *Police Horse Trough Supremo; Water Wonderful Appointment; Top Dick Lands Trough Job; Tough Trough Task for Pluke; Top Cop Pluke Harnessed for Trough Search* and *CID Troughs – Copper Investigates Drinking Troughs*. Pluke blushed as he read the headlines and blushed even more crimson when he realized that some of the papers had unearthed ancient photographs of him during a long-ago investigation into a confidence trickster who was visiting dog owners and selling them a little battery-operated machine which he claimed was guaranteed to rid their pets of fleas. *Pluke's Flea Success* was one headline at the time, but none had seen fit to resurrect that item even if his photographs reminded him that he was more handsome and debonair now than in his youth.

There was no time to dwell on that publicity because Inspector Russell ushered the small party of news reporters and photographers into one of the ante-rooms and then called Pluke to address them. Montague outlined the case and provided a summary of the information he wished to impart, then handed over to Russell for the details. At the end of the conference, Inspector Russell asked, 'Any questions? Detective Inspector Pluke and I will be pleased to answer them.'

'Yes,' called a radio journalist. 'How was the body discovered, Mr Pluke?'

'My wife found her,' Pluke said. 'She was walking near Thordale Gill and noticed the woman at the side of Devil's Dump. She called me.'

'Your wife! So where were you?'

'I was examining Trough House,' said Pluke in all innocence. 'I was off duty at the time and was keen to seek the trough after which the house is named. But my wife interrupted my work with her discovery, and I then alerted the police.'

'You are the Horse Trough Pluke of this morning's papers?' grinned a seasoned reporter. 'She wasn't drowned in a horse trough, was she? Your victim?'

The reporter in question was already sensing his own paper's headlines – *Trough Boss Finds Drown Victim* or *Top Cop in Trough Drama* or *Horse Trough Detective Saddled with Murder Case.*

'I do hope you will respect the dignity of the deceased,' Pluke admonished them. 'Whilst I can understand you wishing to jest at my trough links, I would ask you to consider the victim and her family, whoever she is. And, I might add, I do not engage in my trough activities whilst investigating crime.'

There was a moment of silence as they digested and understood Pluke's rebuke, then a young girl reporter asked, 'Mr Pluke, might I ask this – did you find the missing horse trough?'

'I abandoned my hunt for it the moment my wife made her dreadful discovery,' was Pluke's textbook response. 'And now, I am not concerned with horse troughs, I have a murder victim to identify and a killer to find. Those are my priorities.'

There were a few more innocuous questions and then they departed to file their stories; some would appear in this evening's papers, some in tomorrow's dailies, some in weeklies and others on radio or regional television. Pluke felt sure his case would receive good coverage, and that identification of the deceased would quickly result.

'I wished they hadn't asked that question about finding the body, Montague,' said Paul Russell.

'Why? We have nothing to hide!' stressed Pluke.

'No, but they might go to town on your horse trough hobby and that could trivialize our enquiries . . . or, of course, some of them might take it into their heads to go and find the lost trough! If that happens, they'll get on to the story of Susan Featherstone and it won't take many questions around the village for them to discover our interest in her . . . I just hope they don't ruin our investigation. But if we know they're likely to follow that line, we can be prepared, we need to find some logical response to cope with such questions, Montague, if they are asked.'

'With your experience of dealing with the media, Mr Russell, I am sure you can find something suitable to say.'

But Pluke then wondered if some reporters would find Rowan Cottage and take photographs of the trough or try to talk to the owner – if they found the trough, they might claim they'd found it right under the eyes of a senior detective who was trying vainly to find a killer, the same detective who couldn't find a trough . . . Have I done the wrong thing? wondered Pluke.

'So what are you going to do now, Montague?' Paul Russell interrupted his musings. 'I must be able to contact you if there's a major development.'

'Detective Sergeant Wain and I have some very important enquiries to make in the dale,' Pluke told him. 'But my mobile telephone will be switched on, my number is on the noticeboard behind you.'

Pluke and Wayne prepared to embark on their barn-finding mission in Thordale. It was eleven o'clock and with only four farms to visit, they felt confident they would complete this section of their enquiries before lunchtime. If this did not reveal what they sought, they'd tour all the farms around the extremities of Gunnerthwaite. Every barn within miles would be visited but their first call was at Throstle Nest, the home of Eric and Sally Hall and their musical twins. Eric Hall, cutting the verges of his drive with a large sit-upon grass cutter, greeted them by switching off the engine but remaining on board.

'Back again, Inspector Pluke, eh?'

'You know Detective Sergeant Wain,' Pluke reminded the farmer. 'We have received further information about a lady who cannot be traced, one we are anxious to find,' he continued. 'My sources tell me that she may have rented a barn in this area, probably around Gunnerthwaite. She is an artist and I understand she uses the barn as a studio. Our information is rather limited and I do not know whether the barn has been fully converted into living accommodation or merely a place of work, or whether it is used in its original form. We are asking at every farm whether such an arrangement has been made.'

'Not here, Mr Pluke. I'm all for diversification and making full use of my premises but she's not come to me. Have a look around if you want but all my barns and other outbuildings are used for farm work. If it's converted barns you're after, the only ones I know are those at Ling Garth. Steve Booth's turned his into holiday cottages. I haven't the capital to do that sort of thing.'

'I think we'd better have a quick look, sir,' said Wayne Wain. 'Just in case our bosses put us on the spot!'

And so Eric Hall gave them a guided tour of his farm, taking them into every barn, cattle shed, stable, pigsty, machinery store, garage and outbuilding, but there was no sign of an artist's studio. They thanked Hall for his trouble and moved on. Ling Garth was next. When they arrived, they were greeted by the dark-haired twenty-two-year-old son of the owners – Michael Booth. Pluke had not met Michael, but he had already been interviewed during routine house-to-house enquiries.

'Dad's gone over to Pickering,' he said after Pluke had announced himself, 'to look at a new tractor, and Mam's gone with him to do some shopping.'

171

'Well, it's not a complicated enquiry,' and Pluke explained their presence.

'Sure, I'll show you round. We've two converted barns, Mr Pluke, those cottages you can see across that field. Numbers 1 and 2, Ling Garth Barn, but neither's let to an artist. Both are used as holiday cottages. It's not often we get anybody wanting them for more than a couple of weeks at a time, we've none on a long let, and they're empty now. Come along, I'll show you round, you might be able to put in a good word or two about them. All publicity helps.'

Michael, tall, slender, chatty and polite, took them around the converted barns, both very well equipped, and then he led them into all the other outbuildings, and even the farmhouse. It was evident no artist was using any of these premises but when Pluke asked if Michael knew whether Dale Head or Cragside let any of their barns, Michael said, 'Well, I do know Dale Head haven't anything of that kind. With their kind of farming, Mr and Mrs Hepworth need all the space they can find. I'm not sure about old Reuben, though, he runs sheep on the moor so he doesn't need a lot of space around the farmhouse. You could ask him but I've no idea, I never go up there. He's not my type – and neither is that daft hand of his, Winston.'

'Daft?' asked Pluke.

'Well, he's a bit slow, Mr Pluke. I mean, I sometimes go out with the twins from Throstle Nest or lads from the village, but you'd never get Winston going anywhere. I know he can't communicate but he should go out more. We'd help him if he'd let us. I think his mother keeps him tucked away from the rest of us, a bit over-protective she is. It would do him good to get out a bit more.'

'Reuben seems to cope with him,' said Pluke.

'Oh, aye, but he has to show him how to do everything, then he'll work all day at it, but he won't look for work. He can't think for himself. Anyway, sorry I can't help more and sorry about that woman in the gill.'

They thanked the cheery youngster and headed for Dale

Head, home of the uncommunicative Frank Hepworth and his fierce wife. As before, she emerged from the kitchen at the arrival of the car, this time carrying a mop and bucket.

'Nothing today, thank you,' she bellowed before recognizing Pluke. 'Oh, it's you again, Mr Pluke. Sorry. Shall I get Frank? He is very busy, you know . . .'

'No need to interrupt him,' Pluke said, then he explained the purpose of his visit.

'Oh, well, no, not us, Mr Pluke. We don't like strangers wandering about the place so we'd never turn a barn into something like a studio or a cottage. Mind you, we have a barn in the top corner of our ten acre, up against the moor edge, and on occasions hikers spend the night there. Sometimes they ask and sometimes they can't be bothered, they seem to think it's open house if there's no door on the place. But it's full of hay and very cosy – I don't mind, of course, except that some of 'em leave their rubbish behind. No manners, brought up like louts, they are.'

'But it's not let to an artist? Or never has been?'

'No, not it. You can have a look if you want, but I was up there yesterday and it's empty. Just hay and straw, the sheep use it sometimes, when it rains or snows.'

'All right, thanks, Mrs Hepworth.'

'You might find that old Reuben has a barn to let,' she said as they returned to the car. 'He has a lot of space he never uses, in the house as well as on the farm.'

And so it was that they drove to Cragside. Reuben was in one of his outbuildings and emerged with his hands covered in oil, closely followed by Winston, similarly oiled.

'Just changing t'oil in my car,' he said. 'Mucky job, Mr Pluke, but necessary.'

Winston did not come close but lingered in the background.

'Winston's helping,' Reuben added, almost as an afterthought. 'So what can I do for you fellers?'

'We're looking for a barn which has been rented to an

artist,' Pluke began. 'We can't find her and need to ascertain whether she's still alive. We understand she might have rented a local barn as her studio.'

'Oh aye, it's here at the back of my farm. Susan Miller's her name,' said Reuben.

Chapter Thirteen

'Susan Miller?' Pluke repeated the name to be sure he'd heard it correctly.

'Aye,' nodded Reuben. 'Yon lass that paints them pictures of the moors and spots around here. Nice lass. Comes here when she can, she doesn't like folks knowing about this spot, but she won't mind me telling you fellers, not under the circumstances.'

'So is she here now?'

'Oh, no, she said she was going up the Yorkshire Dales to do some exploring, she wants to paint pictures of that part of Yorkshire as well as these moors. Wensleydale, I think she said. Somewhere up Hawes way for a start and then she was talking about doing the remains of some old lead mines up near Grassington.'

'When was this? When did she head for the dales?'

'Oh, it'll be a month or two back, before t'All-Yorkshire Agricultural Show at Harrogate. I allus take two days off for t'show, I go for t' first two days, the Tuesday and Wednesday. Thursday's never a good day, it's allus full of parties of schoolkids collecting brochures and busloads of old folks. Anyroad, I allus take a couple of my best sows, done it for years and won a few prizes in my time. I've a truck to ferry 'em over to Harrogate and it's got a sleeping section. I stay there, in my truck – it's my annual holiday, Mr Pluke. Sylvia comes to live in while I'm away, seeing to things and helping Winston. I didn't take my pigs this time, all livestock was banned due to foot-and-mouth, but I went anyway. I like seeing new machinery and stuff, and meeting my pals. I remember talking to Susan a day or two

175

before t'show- she allus wanted to be called Susan, not Sue, by the way – and I told her I was getting ready for Harrogate and she said she was heading that way an' all, not that Harrogate's anywhere near Hawes.'

'And is that the last time you saw her?'

'Aye, it was. By t'time I got back that Thursday morning, she'd gone. I've never seen her since.'

'Has she been in touch?'

'No, not a word, Mr Pluke. Mind you, she's like that. She goes off and you never hear a word from her until she turns up next time. I've got used to her now.'

'So how long has she been renting your barn?'

'Dunno, I can't be exact but I'd say summat like ten or twelve years, mebbe longer. Time flies. She likes to get away from folks and things, so she comes here for a bit of peace and quiet, somewhere she can paint without folks bothering her. There's times she's here and I never set eyes on her. She comes in by that back road, gets cracking with her work and never comes out till she's finished whatever she's doing, and then she goes away. There's times I'll never know she's there, unless she comes over to buy some eggs or milk, or borrow summat.'

'I need to trace her, Mr Pyman,' Pluke said. 'Have you an address or telephone number?'

'No, nowt like that, Mr Pluke. I've no idea where she comes from. She never talks about her home or family or owt like that.'

'Does she ever bring friends, then? Or a companion?'

'Nobody, Mr Pluke, not even a dog. She's allus alone. She likes it that way.'

'So what about paying her rent? Doesn't she give you a cheque?'

'Cheque, Mr Pluke? We try to keep away from cheques then we don't have to worry too much about the tax man. No, she pays cash. I only charge her a fiver a week, two hundred and fifty a year. It's an old barn I wouldn't be using for owt else so it's a bit of pocket money for me and it's hers to come and go as she pleases. It suits us both.'

'Has it been converted for living, then? If she stays a

while, I was thinking of cooking facilities and bathroom and so on.'

'Oh, aye, she fitted it out, just enough for her. Not a kitchen exactly but a corner with a Calor gas oven and a little fridge, and some cupboards and a table and chairs, but she uses my toilet and bathroom, I've had one fitted in an outside shed, handy for when I'm up to the backside in muck and want to go in a rush, for a sitting down job I mean, otherwise we make do with hedgebacks and bushes. And Winston, he gets taken short now and then, so he uses it. Do you want to have a look at it? She won't mind, I've a key.'

And so Reuben excused himself to go into the house to collect the key, told Winston through a system of hand-waving to busy himself cleaning out the interior of the car and then led Pluke and Wain through his farm buildings. They were clustered around the farmhouse like chickens around a broody hen, sheltering the house from the moorland storms which were a continuing feature of this rugged landscape.

They walked across a concrete farmyard, kept surprisingly clean by regular swillings of cold water, and then they could see the barn. It was about quarter of a mile away from the complex of other buildings, sitting in the corner of a field like a sturdy stone cottage; there was an unmade lane leading from it, away from the farm.

'I had that lane put in ten year back,' Reuben told them. 'The estate built a new road round the dale and that track connects with it. It means I can reach places at that side of the dale without going half-way round the world to get there. Susan uses that track most times when she comes and goes, it means she doesn't come through my yard, she's got her own entrance.'

'So when are you expecting her again?' Wayne asked.

'Search me.' Reuben spread his hands. 'She never says.'

By now, they were approaching the isolated barn. Pluke noticed that while it looked untouched – no extra windows had been added, the sole entrance was the original wide double door – it was tidily kept and well maintained with a rose climbing around the doors and a few flowers growing in the earth by the walls. Someone had created a small border along the southerly wall. A woman's touch.

Reuben made for the entrance. The two large wooden doors were padlocked together – there was no sophisticated security system here – and he unlocked them, allowing the chain to dangle noisily from one of the handles. He led the way inside, the light from the two windows being quite adequate. Hanging from the centre of the roof was a single unshaded bulb for the living area, which comprised a single room with an earthen floor, dry and as hard as iron.

Primitive though it was, the place did feel very cosy and dry. At the far end was a balcony, formerly used for storing hay but now containing a single bed and an old wardrobe. Access was by a steep, narrow ladder and Pluke saw that the area had its own light bulb, although it was also lit by a window set in the sloping roof.

The centre of the floor and the walls, however, were littered with trophies from the countryside and moorland – an old scythe, a turf cutter, two miniature stone troughs, several chunks of dressed stone, a straw bee skip, a cast-iron cauldron, a range of thatching tools, a peat cutter, a complete plough, two merrills boards, umpteen horse-shoes and brasses, various tools and kitchen utensils. These objects, doubtless used in Susan's paintings, made the place look like a rural museum. Among all this clutter, there were several easels – some empty but three bearing half-completed watercolours. Stacked around the walls or leaning against the artefacts were dozens of completed works, some half-completed ones and some which appeared to have been either rejected by the artist or awaiting further attention. Almost all were of the local moors – and all those had the familiar shepherd figure somewhere in the background; pictures of scenes away from the moors, like a couple of coastal areas, lacked the shepherd. A trestle table erected near the wall bore her pots of paints and umpteen mugs containing brushes, all cleaned.

'She turns up with all kinds of things, Mr Pluke,' Reuben explained. 'Mostly stuff you and me would chuck out. She wants it for atmosphere, she says, to put in her paintings, backgrounds and so on.'

'It does look like a museum,' smiled Pluke. 'And I see she's got a couple of little troughs!'

'We had to help her with those,' he said. 'Not long before she went away. We helped to lift 'em out of her car, me and Winston. A present from somebody, she said. They're very heavy, well, they would be, eh, being of stone.'

'I don't think they are horse troughs.' Pluke was examining the two objects which had been placed near the foot of the ladder. 'They are too small and there are no drainage holes. I'd say they are ornamental troughs, probably used as plant containers or for garden decoration.'

Identical in size and shape, each was a shade over two feet long by fifteen inches wide and eight inches high. Always fascinated by troughs, Pluke squatted on his haunches for a closer look, testing the weight of each. Each was fashioned from heavy sandstone and it would be a two-person task to lift just one. If these were modern reproductions, they were very skilfully made, he realized; this was real stone, carved by a proficient stonemason to produce a very natural appearance, even down to some discolouring as one might expect through age and external elements. Old stone, new troughs, he felt, but too small and unlikely to have come from Trough House – and just for a moment, he forgot he was investigating a crime. His keen eyes were scanning every mark and in one corner of one trough he found some rust marks. The sort of marks made by a tap dripping on to metal; they had affected both the base inside and the stonework of the corner and he could see that some effort had been made to remove the marks. The stone was cleaner where it had been scrubbed but some of the marks had stubbornly resisted any attempts to move them. The marks did look as if rusty water had dripped or run down the stonework, or, he

179

realized, it might be paint splashed from her brush. One of her easels was standing nearby.

'She likes 'em at the bottom of that ladder, for effect,' said Reuben. 'I was all for putting 'em outside the door, one at each side, so she could put plants in, but she wouldn't have it. Mind you, she's not done a thing with 'em since we put 'em there.'

'A true artist, I am sure,' smiled Pluke. 'Anxious to get exactly the right atmosphere in her work.'

Tucked into a corner at the far end, beneath the balcony, was the Calor gas cooker, fridge, cupboards, table and chairs. There was an old easy chair too. Her kitchen and lounge were separated from her working area by a tiny wooden fence, the sort you'd find in furniture stores or cafés. Pluke decided he should have a closer look at the kitchen, for kitchens often reveal signs of recent presence or a long absence as do bathrooms and bedrooms. He strode through the collected pieces, being careful where he placed his feet, and arrived at the little fence, only eighteen inches high. He stepped over it followed by both Wayne and Reuben. The formica-topped kitchen table was clean, he noted, with no sign of being hurriedly abandoned – no crumbs or dirty pots littered it. When he peered into the cupboards, he noted they contained crockery and other domestic objects such as a box of matches, cleaning materials, paper, pen and pencil and other necessities. There was no fresh food anywhere although he did find some tins of soup, beans and fruit. The fridge was empty too and switched off, but it was plugged into a socket which appeared to be a recent addition.

'I fitted that power supply for her.' Reuben had noted their interest. 'It's modern, we've had power in the barn for years but with modern stuff like kitchen equipment I thought it wanted modernizing, new sockets, modern switches upstairs and downstairs, and some rewiring. I never charged her for it nor put her rent up.'

'It seems she's not prepared for a rapid return visit,' Pluke said. 'The power's off, she's cleared everything out.'

'Aye, well, she did tell me she was going up the dales,'

Reuben reminded them. 'And if she was going for a long time, she'd not want to leave food about the place. Rats and mice can smell it wherever it is.'

'Mr Pyman.' Pluke now turned to the farmer. 'I'm not sure whether you appreciate why we are here. We are trying to find Susan Miller –'

'Aye, I know.'

'And we have a dead woman to identify –'

'Her that was found in Devil's Dump, aye, I know.'

And then it dawned on Reuben that his visitors might be talking about the same person. The look of horror and shock on his face was combined with disbelief and even fear as Pluke continued.

'We have to explore every possibility, Mr Pyman,' he said gently. 'You can see why we are anxious to find Susan Miller.'

'Aye, but it can't be her, can it? I mean to say, I never thought that when you asked me the other day, you said it was a fair-haired lass, short hair you said, but Susan's a red-head, Mr Pluke, a real good looker, curly auburn hair, and you asked if I knew if anybody was missing, well, Susan's not missing, she's gone up the dales to paint, so she told me.'

'We have to eliminate her from our enquiries,' Wayne told the farmer. 'We have to be sure the lady who died is not this artist. Now, if she was heading for the dales, how would she travel? Did she rely on taxis and public transport, or did she own a car? It is very important that we find her.'

'Oh, she has a car, Mr Pluke, a little red one. A Fiat, I think. A nice little car, four or five years old. She uses it a lot, fetches all those bits and pieces in it.'

'It's not around here, is it?' Pluke asked.

'No, but it wouldn't be, would it, if she's gone off in it.'

'We'll look for it. Would you know its registration number?' asked Wayne.

'Not me, no. I never bothered looking at it as close as that.'

'A pity, otherwise we could have asked our colleagues to keep their eyes open for it, in places she might be likely to visit in the dales. Car parks and so on.'

'Sorry, Mr Pluke. It's a little Fiat, a red one, that's all I know.'

'Is there a garage for it here?'

'No, not at the barn, she usually leaves it outside. If the weather's bad, I've said she can put it in one of my implement sheds. More often than not, though, it stands outside the barn, she likes to keep it handy.'

'Mind if we look around?'

'No, feel free!'

'We'll do it before we leave. Now, we need to remove something from here, Mr Pyman, something bearing Susan's fingerprints. Then we can compare them with those of that dead woman. I just hope it proves not to be her.'

Wayne butted in. 'Sir, perhaps Mr Pyman would look at the body for us?'

'I think not, Wayne. I doubt if anyone could state categorically that those remains were or were not a particular person. And, remember, Mr Pyman has said Susan Miller is a red-head whereas our corpse has light brown hair, almost fair. I am aware that wigs can transform a person's appearance and so I think we should test our fingerprint method first.'

'That'll suit me.' Pyman spoke nervously now. 'I mean, I've never seen a dead body, not even my old mum or dad when they passed on, and if this one's been in t'water for any length of time, well, I know what a sheep looks like after getting drowned and can't say I'd relish that sort of job . . .'

'You're the only person we've talked to who has seen Susan Miller,' Wayne said. 'It means you are important to our enquiries, Mr Pyman. So, how old is she, do you think? And what does she look like? You said she has red hair?'

'Aye, auburn-coloured, very shiny and well kept, curly.

182

Tallish, she is, about as tall as you, Mr Pluke, and slim with it. Nice friendly face, good teeth . . .'

'Eyes? Can you remember the colour of her eyes?'

'Aye, dark brown. Very big and friendly, they are. I know that because one of my cows has big brown eyes just like her . . . beautiful.'

'And what does she wear?'

'Nothing very smart,' he smiled. 'She never likes dressing up, Mr Pluke, she goes for jeans and T-shirts, sweaters if it's chilly. And sandals. She allus wears sandals, brown leather ones.'

'And brightly coloured clothes, would you say?' asked Wayne.

'Not really, no. More the sort of stuff suited for the countryside, greens and browns, so she'll not stand out like a sore thumb if she's painting, she once said to me. She likes to merge with the background, that's one of her phrases.'

'Now, Mr Pyman, what about her background? Has she ever said anything about a husband or parents or children? Where she lives? That sort of thing.'

'Not a word, Mr Pluke. Like I said, she never speaks about her family and I never ask. I don't like to pry, you see. I take her on face value.'

'Well,' said Pluke, 'as I said, I need something for finger-print testing. If Miss Miller does return before we can talk to her, perhaps you'd mention this and ask her to get in touch as soon as possible. We're in the church hall at Gunnerthwaite, and of course, we'll keep in touch with you about developments. You've been most helpful. Now, if there is no bathroom here, I need something from her bedroom. I hope she's left something behind, a bedside glass would be ideal.'

Leaving Wayne to chat with Reuben, Pluke climbed the ladder up to the bedroom area. It was not easy, the ladder was steep and narrow with no handrail and he found it rather precarious. When he reached the top, he saw that the bed-space was about fifteen feet by twenty, the edge protected by a series of wooden bars, formerly holding the fodder in place but now a decorative feature as well as a means of preventing people falling over the side. Against the far wall was a single bed covered with a colourful duvet, slightly rumpled but with the appearance of having been straightened in something of a hurry. Against the wall was a single wardrobe while beside the bed was a small cabinet and a dressing table covered with perfume bottles, shampoos, a hair spray and other feminine accoutrements. Pluke looked for any sign of a wig but found none, not even an empty stand.

On the bedside cabinet was a glass tumbler, empty, and lying beside it a toothbrush and tube of paste, partially used. Pluke now had to retrieve the glass without obliterating any prints it might bear and he used a trick taught on his detective training course. He took one of the Bic ballpoint pens from his jacket pocket, inserted it top first into the glass until it touched the bottom and then, with a fingernail of his other hand, flipped it over and at the same time, lifted his pen. Now the glass was upside down and borne on the tip of his upright ballpoint, tilting sideways like a wilting daffodil trumpet and with no hands touching it. Pluke returned to the ladder for his descent. Holding on with one hand while balancing the glass with the other did call for some skill, but as he began his descent he felt confident to continue, even if Wayne had now arrived at the foot of the ladder to catch whatever fell down.

As Pluke eased himself backwards and somewhat precariously down the steep rungs, he found himself looking under the bed – he'd not noticed that part of the room during his ascent as he'd been looking up for most of the time, but now that his eyes were level with the floor, he spotted a pair of brown leather sandals. But, because Reuben Pyman was still below, he said nothing of the thoughts which now flooded into his mind. He realized, as he continued to the ground, still with the glass tinkling on the end of his ballpoint, that he might have to resort to just a little subterfuge and so he said, 'We shall be taking this away for examination, Mr Pyman. It is sure to have Miss Miller's prints upon it and we shall compare them with our deceased lady. I shall return the exhibit once we have concluded our investigation.'

'Oh, well, I'll tell her and she'll not object, not under the circumstances, I'm sure.'

'There's some exhibit bags in the car, sir,' Wayne told him. 'We needn't drive back to the incident room with that tumbler sitting on the end of your pen.'

'Good. Well, Mr Pyman, I think that concludes this part of our business for the time being. Thank you for your co-operation. I hope to return before long, to bring back this glass. A week or so perhaps.'

'Aye, well, that's fine by me. So shall I lock up or will you want to come back in here?'

'I will want to come back, Mr Pyman, but not today. It all depends upon the outcome of our tests for finger-prints.'

'You'd better have this key then.' Pyman passed it to him. 'I shan't need it and she's got one of her own, not that she bothers to use it. She regularly goes off and leaves the place open. Winston pops in to see her when he's working nearby but now she's away, he doesn't bother. Me and Winston's usually about the place to keep an eye on things but we do go up to the moors every day, seeing to the sheep, and we can be away for a couple of hours or more at a time. So if you have this key, Mr Pluke, you can come and go as you please, either using the road through my farm or going round the other way.'

'A very sensible suggestion,' smiled Pluke, his ploy hav-ing been successful. They left the old barn with Wayne securing the padlock and chain, and they walked back to their car, Pluke bearing aloft the tumbler on its ballpoint support. After depositing it in the car, they examined all likely garaging places on the farm, such as sheds and outbuildings, but there was no sign of a little red Fiat. As they boarded their vehicle, Pluke noticed Winston peeping at them from the security of the shed in which he had been working and then, moments later, they were driving away and heading back for the road which took them down the dale. Sitting in the front passenger seat, Pluke was smiling

185

with an unusual show of confidence. Wayne wondered if it was because it was lunchtime.

'You look pleased with yourself, sir,' he ventured.

'That was a most fruitful operation,' Pluke said. 'Most fruitful.'

'We're one step closer to knowing if the artist is our casualty, sir,' offered Wayne.

'Right, but there's more, Wayne. Beside that glass tumbler, on the bedside cabinet, there was a toothbrush and tube of paste.'

'She keeps them there because she has no bathroom of her own,' suggested Wayne.

'I am sure you are right, Wayne, but wouldn't she have taken them with her, if she's gone up to the Yorkshire Dales for an extended visit?'

'Yes, unless she keeps a spare.'

'Right – and under the bed, there was a pair of sandals. Brown leather. I appreciate that if she always wears sandals, she'll have several pairs, but I did not want to make a detailed search with that farmer watching every step, nor did I want to ask him directly for the key –'

'Why not, for heaven's sake?' demanded Wayne. 'If we want to do a thorough search, we can seal the barn.'

'That takes time, Wayne, and I am not sure whether there may be another key somewhere on that farm. If a suspect thought we were interested in the old barn, he could enter and remove anything . . . there's that back road in, Wayne, anyone could reach the barn without Mr Pyman knowing about it. I had to pretend our only interest was identification of the girl, because that is what Mr Pyman will now relay to anyone who shows interest in our presence.'

'Well, it is, isn't it? Our reason for going there.'

'It was then, Wayne, but I do fear that that barn might be the scene of our crime.'

'Scene of the crime, sir?'

'There are some very puzzling elements to all this, but I have also noted marks on one of those miniature troughs,

Wayne. Dark stains – mud, rusty-coloured water, paint. Or blood.'

'Blood? Her blood?'

'That is something we must determine.' The car was speeding down the dale as Pluke continued. 'Let us assume, for the sake of argument, that our deceased is the artist, Susan Miller, and that she was murdered. Imagine the scene. She was at home, in that barn, when her assailant entered – there is no sign of a break-in and so one must assume that whoever entered did so with permission of some kind, either implied or specific. But suppose she was in bed, Wayne. Might she sleep naked? A temptation for a virile young man? Or might she have been caught partially dressed after having a wash in the farm bathroom? Suppose she tripped as she was trying to avoid him? Overbalanced – it would be easy to fall headlong down that ladder. If she did, she could have struck her head on the corner of that trough. It would be enough to fracture her skull. And there would be blood, lots of it. There has been an attempt to wash away the stains, Wayne. Whatever happened, her sandals were left under the bed . . . and our victim has no footwear, Wayne. And she did not take her toothbrush . . . small indicators, I know, but enough to make me wonder if she died in that room – it would explain a lot.'

'And the killer straightened her bed? So what about that red hair?'

'If it was a wig, someone could have removed it, it would be on show, surely, if the woman had gone to bed. Her body was then removed without her shoes . . . but it was covered up for the journey to the peat bog, Wayne, with an ancient dress. So where did that come from?'

'I have no idea at this stage. I agree that all you say is feasible, sir, but how did the body get to the peat bog?'

'In her own car, perhaps?' suggested Pluke. 'It's not around the barn, but it could be hidden somewhere else. The snag is we don't know much about it nor do we know its number. A red Fiat. Not much to go on. There must be thousands of them.'

187

'Let's put an All-Stations out for any red Fiat that appears to be abandoned. And if she is the victim, sir, and if she was killed as you say, she must have died just before her intended trip to the Dales.'

'Because she'd cleared her fridge in preparation, you mean?'

'Yes, sir.'

'Unless someone was trying to make it look as if she'd intended to leave.'

'You don't mean old Reuben, surely?'

'He's got to be top of our list of suspects, Wayne, and then there's Winston. He's always around the place, although don't forget that back road to the studio. Anyone could visit her without Mr Pyman knowing. I know Reuben didn't respond to our initial enquiries about a local woman being missing, but Susan Miller hadn't then entered the equation. But first, before we go arresting people or calling suspects into the police station for interrogation, we need to find a motive.'

'And for that, we need to have our victim identified?' smiled Wayne.

'And don't forget we have no motive yet. She wasn't raped, remember, if we're thinking of an attack by a young man. So why would a young man attack her? I don't think that studio has been searched during a burglary or raid of any kind. All very curious. So it's back to square one, isn't that what they say, Wayne?'

'It is indeed, sir, it is indeed. So what's next on our agenda?'

'If that barn is the scene of the crime, we need to have it thoroughly examined by forensic scientists and Scenes of Crime Officers, and that trough tested for bloodstains, but we can afford to wait until we have more news about the identification. So it's back to the incident room to see what has developed and then we must get this tumbler to the Scenes of Crime Department as soon as possible.'

And the car bore them safely down the dale and into Gunnerthwaite where they eased to a halt outside the church hall, now awash with police vehicles. Pluke had left his lunchpack here before departing and so he proposed to spend a quiet half-hour or so over his sandwiches and cake while assessing the situation which had now developed. Inspector Horsley was already tucking into his packed meal when Pluke and Wayne entered.

'Ah,' he said as the cheerful duo returned. 'Batman and Robin in person. So how did it go, Montague?'

'We might have discovered the scene of the crime,' Pluke announced with the intention of gaining immediate and concentrated attention from Horsley. 'But that depends upon what is revealed by this glass we've recovered.'

'Scene of the crime? Really?'

'We have found a studio used by the missing artist, Susan Miller,' said Pluke with some pride. 'She is not there and has not been seen for several weeks – since the middle of July in fact. I have recovered this tumbler from her bedside with the intention of comparing her prints with those of the deceased lady of Devil's Dump.'

'Well, I don't want to disappoint you, Montague, but I've had word from the forensic lab. They've compared fingerprints from the exhibit sent along by West Yorkshire Police with those of the dead woman. They're identical, Montague. In my book, that means the dead woman is Susan Featherstone. I know it's not absolute proof but I'd say, on the balance of probabilities, it is she who is lying in the morgue. I've already set in motion, through Wakefield Police, enquiries to trace any known relatives because we do need a positive identification. I reckon that's a good morning's work.'

'Nonetheless, Mr Horsley, I want my tumbler examined.'

'Well, the way I see it, Montague, is that your artist lady has done a runner from her studio barn, taken her car and vanished. If you think that barn is the scene of our crime, then it might that she – Miller – killed Featherstone. They were business associates – a motive there perhaps? At this moment in time, it seems to me we should be looking for Susan Miller as a murderer, not a victim.'

'I still believe Susan Miller and Susan Featherstone are

one and the same person, Mr Horsley. I am more convinced than ever – little clues have come my way.'

'What sort of clues?'

'Well, for one thing Susan Featherstone always insisted
on being called Susan, not Sue,' Pluke said. 'We learned
that from our enquiries yesterday, in Granthorpe, and this
morning farmer Pyman told me that Susan Miller also insisted on being called Susan. I regard that as significant.'

'So what? They knew each other, it might have been
something they agreed to between them, artist and agent.
I know umpteen Peters who insist they should not be
called Pete, and I know Roberts who don't want to be
known as Bob and Reginalds who don't mind being called
Reg. I'm sure lots of Susans don't want to be called Sue. In
this case, I'd say it's irrelevant, Pluke, old son.'

'It is far from irrelevant, Mr Horsley, nothing is irrelevant in a murder investigation. I have also learned that
Susan Miller has a habit of going away for long periods
without telling anyone and not giving a date of return –
and Susan Featherstone also does that, according to her
neighbour at Calderton. Little clues, but relevant. So have
we anyone who can safely convey this tumbler to Headquarters for the Scenes of Crime Department to work on it?
I need an answer quickly, I need to know whether any
prints on it match those of our deceased lady, or indeed
those of Susan Featherstone. And, Mr Horsley, we need to
find Susan Miller's car, a small red Fiat by all accounts,
although I do not have its registration number or model.
Can you issue an All Stations message to search for it? In
the Yorkshire Dales especially. I suggest that detectives on
house-to-house enquiries make local enquiries about it too
and that anyone visiting farms should ask to inspect all
outbuildings in case it is hidden there.'

'No problem,' said Horsley. 'I'll check the PNC and
DVLC to see if we can link her name with ownership of
any motor vehicle, Fiat or otherwise. Now sit down,
Montague, and relax. Enjoy your snack. Your little friend
Anna Waring radioed in, she is on her way back here,
I think she has some news about that dress.'

190

Chapter Fourteen

After arranging the widespread search for the red Fiat and initiating the necessary computer checks for car owner-ship, Horsley despatched a detective to Headquarters with the tumbler. Not long afterwards, Detective Constable Anna Waring returned, her face revealing her delight at the success of her trip. She found Pluke ensconced in his office in the ante-room where he was wading through a pile of statements, the result of house-to-house enquiries. He invited her to sit down.

'You seem elated?' He could sense the joy in the young detective's demeanour.

'It was fascinating, sir,' she smiled. 'As you know, I took Joyce Burrows with me, she's the theatrical costumier, and she has no doubt the dress dates from around 1910 – certainly prior to the First World War. She's had to produce lots of dresses complementary to that period and this one is mainly made from wool – hand-sewn, she believes, rather than machine-manufactured. She says it is not the sort to have been worn by a well-to-do or upper-crust lady. It's a working dress, sir, with a narrow skirt to keep it out of trouble. It's not a glamorous gown, and that is con-firmed by forensic tests. The fabric has been damaged, probably through age, fair wear and tear, but also by being battered against rocks in the flood. Forensics say it contains peat deposits and particles left by the floodwater but they've also found hay seeds, a couple of pieces of corn lodged in the hem and other indications of it being used around a farm, both for outdoor work and in the kitchen. Some specks of flour were found on it, and some spilt egg-white. The dress was well cared for and was cleaned prior to the burial, but it seems to have been hung for a long time in a clean condition – there are long-term coat hanger marks on the shoulders – although there is some evidence of attack by moth larvae and the presence of moth balls. And, due to its age, it is very fragile.'

'And who might have worn this dress?' asked Pluke.

'A countrywoman, sir, almost certainly a farmer's wife, sir, or someone who worked on a farm, a farmer's daughter perhaps or even the wife of a farmhand – some woman helping with the haytime, feeding the hens. Outdoor and indoor work. Miss Burrows and the forensic scientist were both agreed on that, a written report will follow.'

'So the question to which we must now address our minds, Detective Constable Waring, is whether the dress belonged to the deceased, to be worn by her on certain occasions, or whether it belonged to someone else who dressed her in it prior to burial. Was she wearing the dress at the time of her death? Was that point discussed?'

'Dr Meredith felt not, sir. It wasn't her size for one thing, it was too large. It was made for a bigger woman, broader across the shoulders and back, and with a bigger bust. Our victim is very slim. Joyce thought it had been handmade by the woman who owned it way back in 1910, made to fit her own measurements. The general feeling of both Joyce and Dr Meredith was that the original owner was as tall as our victim or perhaps a fraction taller, but far sturdier, needing clothes of a generous fit. She might have worn a chemise with sleeves under the dress, to absorb sweat while working, and she'd probably have used an apron over the lower half. The owner may have been a little older than our victim but they felt she was not much her senior – the dress is right for the period, not high fashion nor the sort worn by an elderly lady. Not a child or a teenager either. They feel the dress was well made and a good fit for its original owner – probably a woman in her late thirties or early forties.'

'Whoever she was, she'll be long gone so I am afraid she cannot help us with our enquiries,' mused Pluke. 'All we have to do now is to find out where that dress came from! Who keeps such old dresses? And why? Could it have come from a museum or theatrical stock perhaps? Or even a child's dressing-up box?'

'Well, actually, sir, Joyce did have a suggestion. She said that many of the older country people tended to keep – and use – clothes worn by their parents. Even in fairly recent times, it wasn't unknown for a young man to get married in his father's suit, or even his grandfather's. Suits, jackets, trousers, overcoat, hats and even shoes were handed down, especially among the poorer people or those who might wear a suit just occasionally – weddings and funerals for example. Clothes often survived for years because they were used only for Sunday best or on special occasions. That culture was perhaps more common among the men because countrymen weren't – aren't – particularly fashion conscious, but some women would also wear old clothes, coats and hats especially, although most women were capable of making their own dresses and skirts, especially for work. They'd use an old dress for remodelling, they'd adapt it themselves for its new purpose. Good rural prudence, sir, by all accounts.'

'I can vouch for that,' said Pluke. 'The clothes in which I am now sitting belonged to my grandfather and my overcoat is an old coaching coat, dating well into the mid-1800s. I do opt for comfort rather than being a slave to fashion.'

'Joyce did mention your coat, sir, she's seen you in it, on television and around Crickledale . . . She suspects it might not be an original, she thinks it could be a copy of a coaching coat. It seems the original fabric would not have survived all this time.'

'A copy? I beg to differ, Detective Constable Waring! This is an original, a rare item of clothing, a Pluke family heirloom! It was handed down to me by an uncle and he told me –'

'Joyce is willing to have a look at it, sir, she'd be delighted to advise you.'

'I have no time for such things at the moment. Now, what did she say about that dress?'

'She said that theatrical and film costumiers depended heavily on people who have retained old clothes as family keepsakes. They either borrow them or buy them in house sales or even merely copy them. But she did tell me about some help she got from a Thordale farmer, sir, a few years ago when she was seeking clothes for a play set in the 1920s. She wanted some women's clothes for the period and got talking to Miss Pyke who said she should have a word with Reuben Pyman. Reuben never married so he never had a wife to clear out his cupboards and things, and it seems his own parents never threw out any of their own parents' or even grandparents' things. Neither has Reuben, so she said.'

'So the finger of suspicion turns back to Reuben Pyman!' sighed Pluke.

'Well, sir, Joyce said she'd once been invited to see the stuff he's got in his spare rooms, for one of her productions, and she said it was like a museum. Dozens of dresses, skirts, men's suits and jackets – all from a bygone time. His parents wouldn't part with anything and neither will Reuben, so it seems.'

'We have photographs of that dress, haven't we?'

'Yes, sir, the Photographic Department took a selection in case we wanted to issue them to the press.'

'The evidential value of the dress is something I want to keep out of the press, unless we fail to trace its origins, of course. However, in view of what you've said, I think we must show a sample of those photographs to Mr Pyman. Not with any suggestion he's guilty of killing the woman and dressing her in one of his family heirlooms, but rather to pick his brains, to ask him to help us identify the source of the dress. I wonder if he'd know if it had come from his stock?'

'I've no idea how much stuff he's got in his house, sir, or whether he could recognize something removed from there, but if it has come from his farm, how can that be explained? Does it put him in the frame, sir, as our prime suspect?'

'I think it is fair to say that he is a suspect, Detective Constable Waring, but I would not go so far as to confirm that he is a prime suspect. He is no more a suspect than any of those other farmers who live in Thordale, or their family members, or those who work for them. However, you have just talked yourself into another investigation. Can you cope with a trip to Cragside Farm?'

'Yes, sir,' she beamed. 'I'm not afraid, if that's what you mean.'

'No, I am sure you are not, and, if I need to set your mind at rest, I do not think Reuben is the killer, his reactions when I called to look at the studio were not those of a man with a secret or any guilt to hide. So I am not in the least concerned about you going there alone, and in this case I think you would be better than me – a woman's touch, in matters of fashion and style, is much more sensitive than mine.'

'I'll go now, sir.'

'Good, and I shall now pay another visit to Rowan Cottage.'

As Anna prepared for her trip to Cragside Farm, Pluke entered the body of the hall where Horsley was sitting among a sea of statement forms and computer printouts.

'A bright young lady, that Anna,' said Horsley as the youngster disappeared about her task.

'We need young blood and young minds in the Criminal Investigation Department,' said Pluke. 'But we need experience too – a combination of both is the ideal, of course. Now, Mr Horsley, I have despatched Detective Constable Waring to see Pyman of Cragside Farm about that dress. It seems he has a collection of old clothes, family keepsakes, and the dress might have come from there.'

'Do you want us to bring him in then, Montague? For interrogation? His name's already in the frame! Pretty high in the frame now, I'd say. Probably at the top if my instinct's anything to go by.'

Pluke glanced at the mock-up of the runners' frame which appeared on racecourses – Reuben Pyman was the favourite, Winston Livingtone was second favourite, with the Hall twins close behind and Michael Booth fifth at twenty-to-one. Several other names, farmers and young men, were all listed at a hundred-to-one.

'I'm not sure how anyone could produce that kind of list,' he smiled. 'I do not think Mr Pyman is guilty, and I have no reason to think any of the others are guilty, we have no evidence to sustain those beliefs.'

'Gut feelings, Montague. Nothing more than that, with good old-fashioned police experience. Now, if that dress has come from Cragside, then it's another notch in favour of Reuben being the killer. Anyway, what are you doing next?'

'You've not had Rowan Cottage examined yet?' Pluke put to him.

'No, I was waiting until we'd got confirmation about Susan Featherstone, and happily there is a team of Scenes of Crime Officers in the village. I've asked them to give it a thorough examination the moment they've completed their current task.'

'I'd like a look at it first,' Pluke told him. 'If Susan Featherstone is the deceased owner, then we have a right and a duty to search the house for evidence of a motive, or indication of the perpetrator of the crime. But I would like to have a look around alone before we begin our detailed examination.'

'What will you be looking for?'

'I'm not really sure. My main concern is to find a motive, we have no idea why anyone would want to murder Miss Featherstone. She seems to have been a quiet, self-assured young woman from a good background who did nothing but act as agent for a successful local artist, probably more out of interest than a means of earning lots of money. We have not found anything to hint at problems caused by her – blackmail, an affair with someone else's husband, marital strife, jealousy, some form of criminal activity . . . there's none of this, Mr Horsley. I do find it most odd that anyone would wish to kill Susan Featherstone. Both she and Susan Miller are mysterious people, so little is known about either of them. I think the Gunnerthwaite house might yet yield some kind of clue. If not, I may decide to visit her other home near Wakefield.'

'The fact we know next to nothing about her does suggest a range of hidden motives – secrecy can do that. If Susan Miller did kill her, there could be some kind of professional rivalry or misappropriation of funds, something to do with thwarted love, jealousy, rivalry for the same lover, all sorts of things can cause women to kill.'

'Whatever lies behind all this, let us hope my visit to Rowan Cottage will throw more light on it. Now, you said we have Scenes of Crime experts on hand?'

'Yes, we've a couple examining a car that was broken into over the weekend, although we've no reason to think the car crime is connected with our enquiry. It's a case of elimination, double-checking to be absolutely sure, but they should be finished with that job soon.'

'What was stolen from the car?'

'The radio. It was an old banger with an equally old radio set, so why on earth the thief would want to steal that is open to anyone's guess, especially as there are much more sophisticated sets on the market – or waiting to be stolen from other cars.'

'I'd guess the thief also has an old car whose radio set has broken beyond repair,' smiled Pluke. 'But yes, send them to Rowan Cottage when they're free, I want them to seek clues to the murder. And where is Detective Sergeant Wain?'

'He's gone out with the house-to-house teams, Montague, he asked me to tell you, you can raise him on his mobile if you need him.'

'Not just yet. Well, I must go, I shall walk down to Rowan Cottage, my mobile will be switched on and you know where you can reach me,' and Pluke plonked his panama on his mountain of bushy hair and sailed across the room, calling as he went, 'And this evening, we shall need to make sure the cottage is secure. A guard will be needed, Mr Horsley.'

'Already taken care of,' smiled Horsley. 'The uniform branch will be doing that.'

'Good,' and Pluke vanished through the front door.

He warmed to his brisk walk through the village, raising his panama to local ladies as he passed by and greeting them all with 'Good afternoon,' in the true manner of a gentleman. By this stage, of course, he was known to most of them, if only by reputation, and he did notice the fluttering of some curtains as he progressed; Miss Pyke was rearranging her shop window, it being a Monday afternoon, and he also noticed Sally Hall of Throstle Nest, with an empty egg basket, leaving a house half-way down Beckside Hill. Also, a large lady on a bike sailed imperiously past. The village was behaving quite normally in spite of the police activity in its midst, he realized, and then Rowan Cottage lay ahead.

In its splendid setting not far from the banks of the lower reaches of Thordale Gill, it now looked remote and perhaps a little sad. Deserted houses could look sad, he knew, and suddenly its plight reminded him of Trough House. The remaining stones of Trough House looked sad and neglected, and now those which had been removed and reused here, also looked sad and neglected. If only those stones – all of them – could tell a story, he sighed. Then he was at the small garden gate and pushing it open; the whole garden lay before him and he could not resist another look at the glorious trough which stood guard before the building, overlooking the dale across the ha-ha and the fields beyond.

He approached it and stood awhile, gazing at the splendid stonework and modern plumbing by which this handsome edifice accepted and then dispensed with its supply of water. He realized that this trough, in its domestic garden setting, would never again serve any horse let alone a regular procession of draught horses and pack-horses as they headed for those remote moors; now, it was merely decorative but, to the credit of those who had placed it here, it was intact and it was functioning. It had been saved from ruin and protected from a dismal existence in some dull part of suburbia. It was a very lucky trough.

He toured the garden, peeping again into the garage with its single occupant – which would be removed for scientific examination – then turned towards the house. As he did so, he thought he saw someone passing an upstairs window. A fleeting glimpse of a person, someone in a grey blouse or shirt, someone with just a hint of greying hair . . . He hurried to the back door. That should be open, it was the front door which had been locked during his earlier visit. With coat tails flapping and all senses alert, Detective Inspector Montague Pluke hurtled towards his quarry. The front door was secure, he was able to check that as he passed, and then, rushing around the house to the kitchen door, he found it standing open. Had the intruder escaped? There was no sign of anyone fleeing but then he noticed a bicycle standing against the garage wall. A lady's model, black and quite ancient, judging by its appearance. Not a modern bike by any means, not a mountain bike or a lightweight racer but a good old-fashioned solid bike with a basket on the front and a carrier over the back wheel. The basket contained some groceries, he noted, hardly the sort of thing a trespasser or burglar would take with them on a criminal foray. Nonetheless, he crept into the kitchen, listening, all senses on full alert and the hair at the back of his neck standing up like prickles on a hedgehog as he slowly entered the cottage.

'Hello, it's Mr Pluke, isn't it?' shouted a female voice from upstairs. 'I thought I recognized you in the garden just now. No need to come up, I'm coming down.'

As he moved into the hall below the stairs, a large woman appeared on the landing. With an apron over her navy blue skirt and grey blouse, a vacuum cleaner clutched in one hand and a fistful of dusters in the other, she began her descent. It was the woman on the bike he'd just noticed.

'I've just got here, I'm getting ready for Miss Feather-stone coming back,' she said. 'A bit of dusting and polish-ing, tidying up here and there. Not that it was very dirty, with her being away, but dust can settle in the funniest places, Mr Pluke.'

'I'm sorry, but I don't think I have had the pleasure . . .' He had no idea who she was even though she knew his name.

'Sylvia, Sylvia Livingstone,' she smiled. She had now reached the bottom of the stairs and he saw that she was a lady of considerable size, nearly six feet tall and broadly built; she handled the vacuum cleaner as if it was no heavier than a wooden spoon. In her late fifties with greying black hair, she looked a formidable woman.

'Ah.' He recognized the name. 'Livingstone. Winston's mother perhaps?'

'Yes, I am, Mr Pluke, I recognize you from Miss Pyke's description. I have had your officers in, asking about that poor woman in Devil's Dump.'

'And you are Miss Featherstone's daily?'

'Not daily, Mr Pluke, I only come once a while, not daily. I do other places, like the shop, the church, the village hall and a few houses and farms here in Gunnerthwaite and Thordale, it keeps me going and I need the money, Winston doesn't bring in much and I've no husband, so I have to earn my keep. I've never objected to a spot of cleaning. I do Miss Featherstone when she's in the village, and get ready for her coming back, clean up and get a few groceries in ready.'

'Ah, I see,' he nodded. 'So she is expected back? Has she been in touch?'

'Oh, no, she's not like that. Off she goes and you never hear another word from her. When she went away, though, she said she'd be back this coming weekend and would I pop in and do my usual, lay the fire, turn up the central heating, put the water back on, make sure milk and papers were started, get some groceries in, frozen meals, that sort of thing, all from the shop. So here I am.'

200

'Ah, well . . .' He now had to break some bad news to her. 'Mrs Livingstone –'

'Miss,' she said. 'As I said, I've no husband. Never have had.'

'Oh, well, er, I may have some bad news for you.'

'Has my Winston been up to something? He was a little terror as a kid and all the thrashing in the world wouldn't stop him, but since he got that job with Reuben, he's been as good as gold.'

'No, we've no complaints about Winston,' Pluke said. 'It's about Miss Featherstone. You said you hadn't heard from her recently . . .'

'No, not a word, not since she went off up to Wensley-dale, Hawes or wherever she was going, weeks ago, that was.'

'Well, you know about the lady in Devil's Dump.' Pluke spoke slowly and with as much feeling as he could muster, not knowing the exact relationship between these women. 'We have reason to believe that the dead lady is Miss Featherstone.'

'You can't be serious, Mr Pluke, oh, you can't!' and there were signs of tears in Sylvia's eyes. 'She was so good to us, such a nice woman . . . but surely, you can't mean this?'

'At the moment,' he admitted to her, 'we have only circumstantial evidence, fingerprints obtained from objects in this house and her home in Wakefield match those of the lady in Devil's Dump. We are 99.9% sure that the victim is Miss Featherstone, but we do need a positive identification.'

'You've really upset me, Mr Pluke, I don't know what to say . . . I was looking forward to her coming back and telling me about her trip . . .'

'Can you describe her? You know her well enough to provide me with an image of her?'

'Well, yes, I do. She's a smart lady, Mr Pluke, a real lady if you understand, from a good background. With money. Always well dressed and smart.'

'And her hair? Age? Build?'

'Age? Early thirties, I'd guess. Well preserved, I'd say, you could mistake her for being younger. She's very slim

201

and tall, taller than you maybe. Tall for a woman. Nice face, brown eyes and jet black hair, always smart. A striking woman to look at, I always wondered why she never turned up with a man, Mr Pluke.'

'What about her family, Miss Livingstone? Did she ever talk about family? Relations? Her background?'

'Nothing, Mr Pluke. So far as I know, she's all alone, her parents died some time ago and left her with this house. She has no need to work, I do know that, but I think she likes to be kept busy.'

Pluke had pondered whether to ask this woman to inspect the bodily remains of the victim, but with the deceased's eyes missing and her head of light brown hair, not to mention the state of the body, he decided to reject that idea. Miss Livingstone's description did not correspond to the woman in the gill; she'd never be able to say it was definitely Susan Featherstone.

'All I can say,' he proffered, 'is that the victim in the gill does not completely agree with your description, but we do have fingerprint evidence which indicates she may be Susan Featherstone. I stress the word may.'

'Oh, I see. Well, I don't what to say, Mr Pluke. I mean, it might not be her, might it? If she doesn't look like Miss Featherstone?'

'That is always a possibility, the prints we have managed to obtain might have come from some other person who has been in Susan Featherstone's house. But I thought you, due to your association with Miss Featherstone, should be aware of our current thoughts.'

'You've really upset me now, Mr Pluke, I don't know what to do . . .'

'I have to secure this house, Miss Livingstone, I have to prevent unauthorized access until we have established the truth about our victim and Miss Featherstone, and my officers are already en route to undertake a thorough investigation.'

'Oh dear, it's awful, people going through her belongings and she not here to stop them . . .'

'If she is the victim, Miss Livingstone, we must do all in our power to find the killer, and I am sure that if Miss

Featherstone was aware of that, she would readily give her consent to our search.'

'I'll go then,' she said. 'I haven't finished, in fact I'd hardly got started and haven't done the lounge or dining room . . .'

'I'm sure that is not important any more. But thank you for your help. We know where you are if we need to talk again, and if you do hear anything about Miss Featherstone's whereabouts, please let us know.'

'Yes, I will, Mr Pluke. If she has come to some harm, I'll do all I can to help you catch the person who did it.'

'One small thing before you go,' he said. 'When I called earlier, the kitchen door was open – unlocked, I mean.'

'She was like that, Mr Pluke, rushing off and forgetting to lock up. She was dreadful with keys, always losing them. I've often come here and found the door standing open, she'd leave it like that to make sure she could get back in the house, if she arrived late at night. She let me keep my key so I could come in whenever I had to. Luckily, the people are trustworthy round here, lots of us leave our doors unlocked.'

'I must ask you to hand over your key, Miss Livingstone, until we have finished our examination of the house.'

She dug into her apron pocket and produced it. He took it from her, then she replaced the vacuum cleaner in a cupboard under the stairs, took the dusters away to wash at home, and left. Pluke watched her wheel her cycle along the garden path and out of the gate, but she did not mount it because the hill back to the village was too steep. He watched until she was out of sight, thoughtful about some of her comments. It was as he turned back into the house that he realized she had probably obliterated a lot of important evidence – for a start, the two mugs had vanished from the kitchen table, the old milk had been disposed of and, when he checked the post in the entrance hall, she had also cleared that away. It might be in the dustbin, of course, but, he realized, she might have been in the house on a very recent previous occasion or occasions.

Then the two Scenes of Crime detectives arrived.

Chapter Fifteen

Before attending Rowan Cottage, the detectives had been fully briefed by Inspector Horsley – their job was to find evidence relating to Miss Featherstone's life and a possible motive for her death. Pluke added his own comments, however, relating the events of his earlier visit and Miss Livingstone's recent presence, hoping that her dusting and cleaning operations had not destroyed all Susan's fingerprints or any other material evidence. Pluke hoped they might find indications of the presence of other people, explaining about the mugs, now washed and tidied away. If the prints of unknown people were discovered, then it may be necessary for the entire village to be fingerprinted or tested for DNA so that genuine visitors could be eliminated from suspicion.

Due to Miss Livingstone's unexpected presence, Pluke had not undertaken his intended peramble of the house and grounds, a walk in which he'd hoped to find some inspiration or enlightenment about this mystery. Not wishing to interfere with or delay the specialized and scientific search, he handed the key to the detectives. He left the house in the knowledge that if these officers properly performed their duties, they might unearth that mysterious unknown clue which would serve as the key to the entire investigation. He walked away with another lingering glance at the wonderful horse trough and passed the rowan tree which had clearly been planted especially near the house. Its position near the front door suggested it had not planted itself.

Beautiful in its autumn colours, it was a young tree,

probably not more than twenty or twenty-five years old judging by its height, and he wondered if its purpose was purely decorative or if it was there to protect the inhabitants – if that was its purpose, then it did not appear to have been too successful! Susan Featherstone had not enjoyed much protection from it and neither had her parents. Even so, rowan wood had long enjoyed a reputation for being a wonderful form of protection against evil – cradles were made from the wood of the rowan to protect their infant inhabitants, tethering pegs were made from rowan to protect cows, so important for the supply of milk, meat and calves, and some people hung a garland of rowan around a pig's neck so that it would fatten rapidly – and, of course, a piece of rowan wood in one's pocket served as a protection against rheumatism and the forces of evil. As he examined the tree with its rich crop of red berries he recalled the old verse:

Many rains, many rowans.
Many rowans, many yawns.

What this meant, of course, was that a lot of rain produced a good crop of rowan berries but, conversely, that indicated a poor crop of wheat, yawns being the name for underdeveloped grains. And there was a good crop of rowan berries this year, he noted, probably due to the heavy rains of the recent summer . . . there had been rowans outside Trough House too and on the moor near the grave . . . and then he appreciated just where the gap in his knowledge lay. It was this flash of enlightenment that made his visit worthwhile – he had found what he had sought!

As he walked slowly away to begin the climb back to the village, he knew he must find out more about the links between Trough House and Rowan Cottage. That was where the answer to his riddles might lie. There was also the question of the complicated series of links between the Featherstones, the Livingstones and the Pymans. Those links, dating back many decades or even centuries, had resurfaced during this enquiry. From the little he knew, he was aware that the Pymans had owned Trough House when it was a thriving inn, but at some stage the Featherstones had acquired it. Now, both the Pymans and the Featherstones were involved in this enquiry. The Pyman link arose because Cragside was host to the mystery artist Susan Miller through her studio on Reuben's land. And surely her shepherd trademark was a reminder of some past links between those families? And, he reminded himself, her original painting of Trough House was now hanging on the wall of Rowan Cottage. Furthermore, a real shepherd called Featherstone had also been a murder victim – or so it had been suspected.

Was it relevant, he wondered, that stones from Trough House had been used to build Rowan Cottage, the home of Susan Featherstone? And likewise, could he place any relevance upon the removal of that famous trough? How was the modern Livingstone family associated with all these connections? Winston worked for Reuben Pyman as a farmhand, and his mother cleaned for Susan Featherstone . . .

As he approached the village with his confused thoughts buzzing through his panama-hatted head, he thought of Sylvia Livingstone and her silent son. Sylvia had never married, so who was Winston's father? Reuben? There was a likeness.

It was an intriguing thought – but even if that was the case, could such a thing conceal a motive for murder? Something to do with an inheritance? With such a tiny parcel of remote moorland to concern him, and with only three families interwoven into this complex affair, Pluke must now delve into the past of each family, and each surviving personality – and who better to help than the all-knowing Miss Pyke? He decided to pay her a visit without delay.

'Ah, Mr Pluke.' She smiled a warm welcome. 'How can I help you?'

'Among all the books you sell in the shop,' he said, 'are

there any giving a very detailed local history of the village, and especially Thordale?'

'There is this one, Mr Pluke,' and from a stand of several small volumes of local interest, she produced *Thordale – Past and Present*, a small book with a blue paper cover selling at £1.95 per copy – and signed by the author. 'If I may be so modest, Mr Pluke,' she said, 'it is the product of my own labours, a distillation of many years' research. I am the author, you see.' She flicked open the cover and there, on the introductory page, was the black ink signature 'Miss Pyke'.

'Oh, well, in that case I shall buy a copy.' He dug deep into his commodious pocket and produced the exact change.

'Well, I am very flattered, Mr Pluke, it has been selling steadily for the past thirty years – well over a hundred copies already – but I am sure it is not in the same league as your own very specialized and well-written volumes about horse troughs. But I am flattered you should wish to buy my humble efforts. Is there something of particular interest to you?' She took his money and passed the book to him.

'Well, yes, there is,' he told her. 'Clearly, I am fascinated by the history of Trough House but from a professional point of view, and with this murder enquiry in mind, I am also keen to know the backgrounds of the families who lived both there and in the nearby dale. I find it of immense value to secure a knowledge of past events when investigating serious crime in the more remote corners of the county.'

'Well, Mr Pluke, why don't I make you a nice cup of tea and find you a tasty bun, and then you can come through to my private quarters and I will explain the history to you. I do have all my original notes, you know, and family trees. Recording local history is a continuing process and I do need to keep thoroughly up to date. If you think my efforts will be of any help at all, then you may study them at your leisure.'

'I don't want to inconvenience you . . .'

'Not at all, Mr Pluke. Monday afternoons are very quiet, especially at this particular time when the ladies will be starting to prepare tea for their home-coming husbands. And as I have no home-coming husband to worry about, I would be delighted to entertain you to tea. If anyone comes into the post office while I am talking to you, the bell will ring. So follow me, Mr Pluke,' and she lifted up the flap of her counter.

Slipping the book into his coat pocket and removing his panama, Pluke followed Miss Pyke through the conglomeration of shelves and display islands into the domestic quarters.

They entered a cosy room with a coal fire burning and lace curtains against the windows; furnished with ancient but comfortable armchairs, clip rugs and an aspidistra on a polished mahogany table, the place bore a distinct air of the Victorian era, Miss Pyke probably having inherited these furnishings from her parents or even grandparents. She bade Pluke sit down in one of the armchairs, placed his hat on a sideboard and eased a small coffee table towards him.

'You be looking through my book to see if you can find what you're looking for, Mr Pluke, I won't be a moment. The kettle has boiled.'

As she busied herself in the kitchen, he opened the book and glanced at the chapter headings and found one entitled 'Thordale'. Miss Pyke had done her research very well indeed. The first pages dealt with the geographical and geological features of Thordale, followed by its ancient and medieval history, and it did not take him long to find the first reference to the Pyman Inn, as it was known around the mid-1700s. He skimmed through references to its role and rapid development as a roadside inn, being more interested in the personalities associated with it. It seemed it had been founded by a Pyman, growing from an ordinary farmhouse which they owned as yeoman farmers to become a thriving inn and then to fade as an inn and revert to a farmstead. Its name changed sometime between 1870 and 1910. In 1820 it had been the focus of the mysterious death of Joshua Featherstone. Born in 1795, he'd been found dead, presumed drowned, in Devil's Dump, a young man of twenty-six, recently married to Hilda Marshall. The story was well documented.

Even though no one had been prosecuted for the crime – it had never been possible to prove Joshua had been murdered – local talk had always blamed Henry Livingstone. In 1832, Hilda Featherstone had given birth to a son called Reuben who'd married Lizzie Scales to produce a son called Jacob who was born in 1868 – and it was this Jacob who had bought Trough House from the Pyman family. Since then, the site had belonged to the Featherstones.

Miss Pyke had managed to unearth a clause in the sale which had imposed a condition on the purchaser – that if Trough House was ever put on the market again, then the Pyman family must be given first option of repurchase, whatever its prevailing state of repair. Pluke wondered what would happen now that Susan was dead – were there any more Featherstones, or had she been the last of the line? Or would the Pymans – and there was only Reuben left – now have first claim to the old inn? The Pymans had moved to Cragside Farm where they had farmed ever since, and although the modern Featherstones, living in Wakefield, had contemplated a refurbishment of Trough House, that had never happened. Pluke could now see that Joshua Featherstone, probably murdered and the source of a haunting legend, was an ancestor of Susan Featherstone – and if she was also Susan Miller, then his portrayal by her was a means of perpetuating his name, the family name.

'Here we are, Mr Pluke.' He had not heard Miss Pyke's return as she entered with a tray of tea things. 'Help yourself, tea and sugar on the tray, and I made those rock buns myself.'

Making sure he had a full cup and a rock bun on his plate, she settled opposite and said, 'Well, have you found what you want?'

'I've just been refreshing my knowledge of Trough House,' he said. 'I know you told me about the Featherstone family rebuilding Rowan Cottage with stones from Trough House, and the fact that the trough itself had been transferred there.'

'Yes, Susan once told me that her father had wanted to rebuild Trough House, to restore it to its former glory, but the cost was prohibitive, there were planning difficulties and problems with the services like water and power, so they used the stone for Rowan Cottage. Even so, they never wanted to part with the site. Susan did once tell me, though, that as she had never married and there were no other family members, Trough House could revert to Reuben Pyman. But he has no family either, Mr Pluke. Such a waste of property. What on earth will happen to it all?'

It was then that Pluke realized that Miss Pyke had no idea that the dead woman was Susan Featherstone.

'Er, Miss Pyke . . .' He now adopted a very solemn tone. 'Perhaps this is the time to add another factor to the equation. The lady in Devil's Dump – well, our investigations reveal that she is almost certainly Susan Featherstone.'

'Susan? No, Mr Pluke, it can't be! She said she was going away somewhere on business and besides, you said the dead lady had light brown hair . . . well, Susan was jet black, Mr Pluke . . . no, you must be wrong. It can't be her.'

'We have conducted tests, Miss Pyke, and all point to Susan Featherstone. I might add we have yet to make a formal identification.'

'This is dreadful, Mr Pluke, she was such a lovely woman, so nice to us all, she loved the village and the dale . . . Dear me, you have shocked me . . . I don't know what to say, really I don't.'

'I have to ask if you know why anyone would want to kill her?'

'No, I do not, Mr Pluke! No one in this village would ever contemplate that and if you're wondering whether Reuben Pyman would stoop to such a thing to get his hands on Trough House, then I'd say no. He's getting on himself, he's into his fifties and he has no sons to pass his farm on to and, I might add, he's often said he wouldn't want Trough House back. There's nothing he can do with it. That old clause wasn't put in by him, Mr Pluke, it was done by his great-grandfather when he sold it to the Featherstones.'

'I must consider that a motive for murder might lie buried deep in the ruins of that old house.'

'Not nowadays, Mr Pluke, not since that shepherd murder all those years ago. It's all forgotten now, I do hope this doesn't resurrect any hard feelings in the dale.'

'That shepherd was a Featherstone,' noted Pluke.

'Yes, he was. A young man about to start married life . . . and you'll know his reputed killer was called Livingstone. The rumour persisted in the dale for years and years, right down to modern times. They always said Henry Livingstone killed Joshua the shepherd because Henry wanted Joshua's wife. Hilda, she was. Hilda Marshall.'

'And those same Livingstones still live in Thordale?' Pluke asked.

'Oh, yes, Sylvia's from that family and that lad of hers, Winston. But they've never been landowners, Mr Pluke, they've always worked on the land, farmhands, labourers, hinds, daytal men, that sort of thing.'

'You said you have family trees? Of these families?'

'Oh, yes, I was meticulous in my research for that book, Mr Pluke, one has to be so careful when dealing with local families and long memories. Do you want to see them?'

'I would like to study them at length,' he said. 'These things are so complex and a cursory glance can so often produce a misleading result.'

'I have them all in a file, one file per family, and they are up to date as of this month, Mr Pluke – except for poor Susan of course, but I must await confirmation of that. It will be in the *Gazette*, won't it? A notice of her death?'

'That can be done once we have got her formally identified.'

'I'll get the files,' she said. 'You can take them away, Mr Pluke, I know I can trust you to let me have them back when they have served your purpose. But you have shocked me terribly, to think that poor Susan has been lying there without any of us realizing . . . It is dreadful, Mr Pluke. I do hope you find the man . . . What sort of man can do this to another human being, Mr Pluke?'

'If I could answer that, Miss Pyke, it might help us find peace and security through the world. But it is the evil people of society who are the most puzzling, one can rarely enter their minds. Rest assured we will do all in our power to trace the killer of Miss Featherstone – but we do need help.'

'I will help all I can, Mr Pluke, you know that, for Susan's sake,' and she went off to find the necessary files of family trees so that he could take them away for study.

Half an hour later, Pluke was sitting in his office in the ante-room of the church hall, wading through the pile of papers loaned by Miss Pyke. For an amateur historian, she had revealed a talent for detailed organization and he had little trouble finding his way around her collection; along with almost every family living in Gunnerthwaite and Thordale, the families of Pyman, Featherstone and Livingstone were all neatly arranged with details of births, deaths, marriages, along with the full names of female spouses, sometimes with their home of origin, if known. The sad drowning of six-year-old Cissie (Cecily) Featherstone was recorded; her funeral had been the last occasion a maiden's garland had been used. Miss Pyke had also uncovered lots of little asides, such as the fact that Nora Watling, b.1870, the wife of Jacob Featherstone, had come to Gunnerthwaite from the Lake District as a young girl, there being a hint that she was the illegitimate daughter of a member of the aristocracy, or that Reuben Pyman's grandmother, Hannah, b.1871, wife of Thomas Pyman, was an expert on rare breeds of poultry, while Henry Livingstone, b.1795, had joined the merchant navy for ten years, visiting the Mediterranean countries and India to return with amazing stories, and an ancestor of Lizzie Scales, who married into the Featherstone family in the 1850s, was reputed to be a witch. She was Cissie's mother. One of the

Livingstone women was reputed to be a witch too – Jemima, born in 1800 and the wife of Henry. While Pluke was ploughing through this information, someone knocked on his office door.

'Come in,' he called, and looked up to see Anna Waring standing before him. 'Ah, Detective Constable Waring,' he smiled.

'Sorry to disturb you, sir, but I'm just back from Cragside and thought you'd better hear what I have to say.' She strode forward and stood at his side. 'I've talked to Reuben Pyman about that dress.'

'Good. And?'

'He recognized it, sir. From photographs, though, but he said there is no doubt it used to belong to his grandmother. Hannah was her name, wife of his grandfather, Thomas. She made it herself, Reuben's mother often talked about her skills as a dressmaker. If you think it is necessary, I could take him to see the actual dress in the forensic lab, although he did check his wardrobes to confirm it was missing.'

'We'll decide that later. So what explanation did he offer? How did that dress come to be upon the deceased?'

'He has no idea, sir. He said it is one of dozens of dresses in the wardrobes around the house, his mother never threw any clothes out, sir, she always said they'd come in useful for something, even rug-making, and she did like to hang on to anything considered a bit special. He showed me the wardrobes, sir – it's a huge house is Cragside, there's eight bedrooms all containing three or four wardrobes full of clothes. My theatrical friend would have a wonderful time among that lot, sir, there's loads of authentic pieces. Anyway, sir, I asked if he could account for its presence on the body of the deceased and he couldn't. He'd not missed the dress, he said, he never goes to the wardrobes unless somebody asks especially, apparently his collection is quite well known, but he had no idea it was missing. He can't tell me when it went missing, nor can he say when he last noticed it in the wardrobe or even which

213

wardrobe it was in. He never locks the doors of the house, he says, but he's always around the place although he does go up to the moors every day to see to his sheep.'

'And leaves the place unoccupied while he does so?' smiled Pluke.

'Yes, I pointed that out to him, and I also mentioned that if Susan Miller had her studio in his grounds, that might attract people to the premises and, well, you never know who might take it into their heads to wander around an open house.'

'But to steal an old-fashioned woollen dress is rather an odd thing to do, is it not?'

'It is, sir, unless you want to use it to bury someone.'

'But why do that? Why was it selected when there was surely lots of other material around the farm which would have served the same purpose? A white sheet, for example.'

'I wondered the same, sir, but it was Reuben who said that if the murderer had taken something like a sheet off a bed or an eiderdown, it would have been missed – he'd have missed it – or if they'd used a piece of tarpaulin from the hayshed it wouldn't have rotted down in the ground . . . He thought whoever had taken it wanted something that wouldn't be missed and which, if it had been there some time, would have rotted away.'

'And,' said Pluke, 'imagine someone finding that grave in years to come . . . the remnants of an old dress would make the finders believe the corpse was very old and thus it would not be subjected to an enquiry. The use of that dress suggests several possibilities.'

'Yes, sir, it does. I find it very puzzling.'

'But done for a reason. Now, what about Winston? Did you manage to get anything out of him?'

'Just a lot of head shaking, sir. Reuben interpreted it as Winston knowing nothing about it. I'm not even sure Winston has ever been upstairs, sir, I think his knowledge of the farm is restricted to the kitchen and the outbuildings. Wherever Reuben goes, Winston follows, and Reuben is not in the habit of going upstairs during his working day.'

'Thank you, you've done a very good job. Now, your next task is to find out, if you can, just how many local people knew about that collection of historic clothes. Your theatrical friend might throw a little light on that. Who, among those people, is capable of dressing a corpse?'

'You mean like people who prepare bodies for the undertakers, sir?'

'Now that is a good beginning. Yes, off you go and well done.'

As he watched the young detective leave his room, he wondered if she would remain in the force long enough to make it her career and, if so, whether she would rise through the ranks to replace him. One day, he reflected, he would have to retire to make way for a younger person. In all probability, that would be Wayne Wain but his succession was by no means certain. And then he turned back to the family trees spread out before him. The first thing he noticed was that Sylvia Livingstone had given birth to twins – and that meant Winston had a sister.

So where was she?

Chapter Sixteen

Ramming his panama firmly on to his head, Pluke rushed out of the incident room and hurried along to the post office. Miss Pyke smiled and recognized his haste.

'Mr Pluke, you look flustered –'

'Winston has a sister,' he gasped. 'I've just discovered this . . . Where is she? Do you know?'

'Oh, yes, Mr Pluke, Winifred. She's in Australia. She's a very bright young woman, she saw the wisdom of leaving this dale. There was nothing here for her, she went to university, got a good law degree and moved to Australia. She's there now, married with a young family, they run a sheep farm there, she gave up law. Sylvia writes once a week and often rings up, they're very close.'

'Oh.' He sounded deflated. 'Oh, I thought there was some mystery here . . .'

'Mystery? Good heavens no, Mr Pluke, there's nothing mysterious about it. You didn't think she was dead, did you? Winifred's a real nice young woman and she's always said she'll care for Winston when her mother dies or becomes incapable, they intend coming back to England, they never did intend settling out there. They've even said they'll take Winston to Australia if anything happens to Sylvia before then but she's hale and hearty, she'll live awhile, I reckon. Winifred's husband is English, he's from Stokesley, name of Atkinson, and they just fancied seeing a bit more of the world before they settle down.'

'She's not in England now, is she? Winifred, I mean.'

'Oh, no, Mr Pluke. She was here about two years ago, she spent time with her mother and Winston. She's a large girl, Mr Pluke, the image of her mother. In looks, I mean, and I know I shouldn't say this, but Winifred's a good deal brighter than Sylvia. Sylvia's nice but she's no Einstein.'

'Ah, I see. Well, thank you. Sorry for the intrusion.'

'Not at all, Mr Pluke, glad to be of help.'

And so he trudged back to the incident room, this new information having punctured one of his secret theories. Until now, he'd thought, deep in the recesses of his mind, that the tangled web of relationships between the Livingstones, Featherstones and Pymans had produced a modern desire in Sylvia Livingstone to rectify past wrongs. On top of that, from all the people likely to have committed this crime, Sylvia was the only one with all the opportunities. She worked at Cragside several days a week, including Tuesdays – and it was a Tuesday when Reuben had been away at the All-Yorkshire Agricultural Show, a Tuesday just one week before Susan's body had been resurrected in that flood. A Tuesday when she could have killed Susan, taken that dress from Reuben's bedroom and removed Susan's body, probably with Winston's help. He could drive, Pluke had seen him at the wheel of a tractor. Sylvia had the time and opportunity to take the body from the studio and up to the moor, unseen by anyone, and then bury it. And she was a church cleaner – with access to those garlands on Wednesdays – so she could have obtained the garland without anyone suspecting her; that meant she'd had Tuesday and Wednesday to dispose of the body before Reuben's return from Harrogate.

And if Susan, in either of her guises, was in the custom of going away without explanation, and staying away for a time, then her absence would not appear unusual or alarming. And who, now, was there to raise the alarm if she was missed? The gardener at Calderton was not concerned, Reuben had no idea of her movements and the other people of Gunnerthwaite had no idea where she was or when she was expected back. Except for Sylvia Livingstone; she seemed to be more in touch with Susan (as Susan Featherstone) than anyone else.

Furthermore, it was important to Pluke that Sylvia

knew that Susan Miller was the same person as Susan Featherstone – his recent chat with her had confirmed that. She had spoken of Susan Featherstone in the past tense and had also referred to her trip to the dales in the same way that Reuben had spoken of Susan Miller's . . . and she could have cleared away any evidence from both the studio and Rowan Cottage – wigs, clothes, food . . . But what about Susan Miller's car? Where was that? And why had Susan adopted this twin personality? It did sound feasible that Sylvia, now in her fifties, would want Winston's future to be secure and if her family, through the convoluted relationships with the Featherstones and Pymans, were to inherit Rowan Cottage, Trough House and even Cragside, then that provided a real motive. But it was by no means certain – Pluke had no idea how the Featherstone wealth and property would be distributed. Maybe she'd made a will, leaving it to some other person?

Nonetheless, if there was no such specific will, and with Susan out of the way, the path could be clear for Winifred and Winston.

With that in mind, Pluke wondered if Susan had recently found herself a man. Did she intend to marry? If so, had Sylvia learned of this development, something which might represent a threat to her family's future, the loss of what she regarded as her rightful inheritance? But was Sylvia sufficiently intelligent to work out such a plan and then execute it? She had come from a family of labourers and farmhands while the others in the story had been landowners, yeomen farmers of the moors with property and status. Unmarried herself, she had produced a son who would need constant care, particularly when she died, or when Reuben either died or retired. It was all very well Winifred making promises to look after him, but all manner of things could go wrong with such a long-term plan. Pluke wondered if Sylvia had felt she, or her family, should have owned Trough House and other Featherstone properties, Rowan House included. Even from his own limited knowledge of the family histories, it was clear that the Livingstones and Featherstones were, due to past indiscretions, intertwined to a remarkable degree. When the shepherd, Joshua Featherstone, had died as a possible murder victim, Henry Livingstone was chief suspect and thus there had developed an everlasting antagonism between the two families. A recipe for revenge perhaps?

He'd considered the death of Joshua Featherstone, an ancestor of Susan who'd died in 1821, drowned in Devil's Dump. The prevailing theory was that his supposed murderer, Henry Livingstone, had coveted Joshua's young wife, Hilda. They had married only a year earlier. It was a feasible theory, Pluke felt, but even his own modest enquiries had revealed that Hilda had later given birth to a son, Reuben Featherstone, in 1832. That Reuben was Susan's great-great-grandfather. But the date of that birth meant that the shepherd, Joshua, could not have been Reuben's father. Even if the child had borne the Featherstone name, it was likely his father was really Henry Livingstone. He was the man who had allegedly killed to win Hilda. After the drowning, Henry had gone away but had later returned to the dale, and Pluke felt he might have then become the father of Hilda's son, either by love or by force. Such a union was highly probable in this dale of so few people and at such a time. Assuming that had happened, then it meant the modern Featherstones and Livingstones were related by blood; Susan Featherstone's great-great-grandfather, although bearing the Featherstone name, may in fact have been the son of a suspected killer, and a Livingstone into the bargain.

Thus the Featherstones and Livingstones were really of one blood. Pluke's brain began to reel as he tried to disentangle these relationships, realizing that the once-powerful Pyman family were on the sidelines of this saga, albeit the former owners of Trough House. Unless Reuben was the father of Winston and Winifred? That would bring him back into play. The Featherstones had worked for Pymans at Trough House when it was an inn and their ownership had endured until 1910 when Jacob Featherstone bought the property from the Pyman family. By that time, Trough

219

House was already a ruin and it had never been occupied since, but the Pymans had expressly stated they wanted first option to repurchase the premises if the old house was ever sold or otherwise disposed of.

With Susan Featherstone dead, a lot of property was now at stake – Rowan Cottage, Thordale House in Calderton, Trough House and even Cragside, that's if Winston and Winifred were Reuben's offspring.

As Pluke pondered, he become more convinced that Sylvia, a big and powerful woman, was a prime suspect for Susan's murder. The tangled inheritance question was a possible motive, the precise nature of which had to be unravelled, and she had had the opportunies – she must be interviewed. In his opinion, it became increasingly possible that Sylvia had murdered Susan Miller alias Featherstone, in the studio barn, and disposed of her body on the moors during Reuben's absence. She had done so in such a way that if it was discovered, people might think it was the remains of a woman from a bygone time. Winston could have helped her bury Susan . . . Reuben's tractor and trailer would have been available – Winston could drive it. Could he also drive a Fiat? If anyone had seen Winston and Sylvia chugging up to the moors with a load, who would have guessed what they were carrying?

And Winston could never reveal what he had witnessed – how would he know he was doing wrong if his mother had persuaded him to go ahead with the project? She was domineering and protective so far as he was concerned – that had emerged during interviews with the other youngsters in the dale. And later, she had been able to remove some of the evidence . . . Had she also disposed of the wigs? The Fiat? And pretended that Susan Featherstone was still alive by preparing for her homecoming? She had all the hallmarks of a guilty person.

And yet, Pluke had doubts.

If Winston was Reuben's natural son, surely Cragside would go to him, and to his sister? That being so, there was no need for Sylvia to kill Susan to ensure Winston's future . . . Then there was the maiden's garland. If Sylvia had murdered Susan, why place that garland with her coffin? Wasn't it a sign of love and respect? Hardly the sort of thing a killer would do. And then those flowers had appeared on the grave. But what about Susan's belongings – the little red Fiat and her wigs among others . . . where were they? And why had Sylvia taken such care to pretend Miss Featherstone was alive and returning soon; she'd acted out that scenario by cleaning her house and preparing it in readiness for her return. Were all these the actions of a normal guilty person? Or a very clever guilty person?

He walked beyond the incident room, wrapped in thought, anxious to clarify his own suspicions. Sylvia Livingstone had been his chief suspect, a fact he'd not mentioned to anyone, and if it had been her, then she'd been very clever, using the old dress, burying Susan in peat, hiding her car, wigs and other belongings, cleaning the house to remove evidence once she realized the police were investigating . . . but why? How relevant was the tangle of relationships surrounding Trough House, the dead shepherd and the relationship between Winston and Reuben? He knew he could not untangle the threads without speaking to Sylvia Livingstone and Reuben Pyman. He would interview Sylvia Livingstone as a matter of priority but he'd better talk to Reuben first – about Winston and Winifred. He turned on his heel and hurried back to the incident room. As he entered, he sought Wayne Wain because he required transport to Cragside, but Horsley hailed him.

'Ah, Montague, glad I caught you. We've had word from Headquarters. That glass from Susan Miller's studio. The prints are the same as those we obtained from Wakefield, and they match those of the dead woman. You were right, Susan Miller is Susan Featherstone – and she is the dead woman. We can get further proof through DNA, but our boffins are not in doubt. And they've got the results of the nail varnish on her nails – it's an expensive brand, made in the last three years.'

'Good, that's just the proof we need. Now, we must have

her studio searched as a scene of crime – and Rowan Cottage too, as a possible scene of crime. We need to seek bloodstains, Mr Horsley, we must find the object which cause the head wound to Susan Miller alias Featherstone. She was alive at the time so there should be some blood. Have a look at the video of her injury, the object we seek might be among the clutter in that studio – your men should play close attention to the stone troughs at the foot of the ladder to the sleeping quarters. One of them bears what I believe to be bloodstains and evidence of an attempt to remove those stains. Have that trough taken to the lab, Mr Horsley; if it is blood, have it compared with that of Miss Miller alias Featherstone, and search the floor area too, and the walls, or anything else that might have been spattered with blood. And I would like confirmation that the trough is too heavy for someone to wield as a weapon. I am sure that two people could lift it but I doubt if they could jointly use it as a weapon – even if they did drop it from a great height. But those troughs are big enough and solid enough to do a lot of damage to anyone striking their head against them.'

'I understand. Our SOCO team is still at Rowan Cottage and we'll treat that as a scene of crime as well, until the contrary is proved. We can seal the studio until they've finished at Rowan Cottage, we have the key. So, you were right, Montague – but if Susan Miller did not kill Susan Featherstone or vice versa, then who did?'

Pluke paused. 'For some time, I have suspected Sylvia Livingstone –'

'A female murderer? You mean that cleaner at Rowan Cottage?'

'Yes, but that was in the past, the recent past I must admit. Now, I have modified my suspicions –'

'About time! We all know it's that farmer, so bring him in, and that farmhand of his. We need to question them here or down at the nick.'

'Before we start upsetting the dales people by arresting suspects, we need to examine the studio with infinite care with particular emphasis upon identifying the object which caused the death of Susan Miller, alias Featherstone. That trough, I suspect. And we need to find the Fiat and the wigs and any other missing belongings of Susan Miller.'

'You're not suggesting she fell down the ladder, banged her head, died and then buried herself, are you?' scorned Horsley.

'I am merely considering alternatives.'

'So while we're searching Rowan Cottage and the studio, what will you do?'

'I want another chat with Reuben Pyman, and then I shall talk to Sylvia Livingstone.'

Fifteen minutes later, Pluke was sitting beside Wayne Wain as their little car drove away through the village. Wayne said, 'So we're off to pick up Reuben, are we? This business has all the hallmarks of a vicious death and secret burial, exactly the sort of things we'd expect in this neck of the woods.'

'No, we are not going to pick up Reuben Pyman, we are going to talk to him. And to Miss Livingstone. Consider the garland, Wayne, and the fact that Winston has a sister who'll care for him if necessary.'

'I know all that, but I don't understand your reasoning. So who's first? The lady or the gentleman?'

'In this case, the gentleman is first,' smiled Pluke. 'When we've seen Mr Pyman, we'll come back to Gunnerthwaite for a chat with Miss Livingstone.'

Chapter Seventeen

They found Reuben and Winston feeding the pigs and the farmer broke off his work to speak to them, indicating with his hands that Winston should continue.

'What is it this time?' Now he looked rather more indignant than hitherto. 'It's getting a bit regular, all this questioning. How many times is this?'

'I'll be brief,' Pluke told him as Winston set about his lone task, his eyes never leaving the policemen. 'First, the dead lady. She is Susan Miller, also known as Susan Featherstone. I promised to tell you.'

'Never!' he spluttered. 'Never in a thousand years, Mr Pluke.'

'Fingerprints confirm it,' Pluke told him. 'Her red hair was a wig.'

'But who would do that to her? I hope you don't think I had anything to do with that, Mr Pluke. Is that why you're here?'

'No,' said Pluke. 'I don't think you are guilty, but we need to establish the truth. Now I must ask you a personal question about Winston.'

'Winston?' Reuben glanced across at the youngster, who had halted his work to watch them. 'He'd never do a thing like that, he's as gentle as a kitten, you should see him with my lambs and piglets.'

'He's a gentle giant, Mr Pyman, I've seen him in action,' said Pluke. 'But I must ask you this – and I apologize in advance for being so personal. But who is his father? Is it you?'

The dour farmer looked at Pluke for a long time without

speaking and then said, 'Well, I can't see what this has to do with Susan Miller being dead, but yes, Winston's my son. A fling, years ago. And there's Winifred, she's his twin. You know about Winifred? I should think you'll have found out most things by now. I didn't mention it before, when you asked about Winston, I don't go about admitting things like that to strangers.'

'I understand, and I do know about Winifred.'

'When Sylvia got pregnant, we talked about marriage, just to make things right, you understand, it was the done thing in those days, but we didn't love each other so we decided to go our own ways. I said I'd help Sylvia all I could, accept my responsibilities and see the twins were all right – this farm's theirs when I go. It's in my will. Down the years, I've given Sylvia a home, Winston work and I even helped set up Winifred and her husband in Australia. They've promised to come back and take over this place when I'm too old or dead. So there you are, Mr Pluke. A bit of family scandal but it means Cragside will stay in my family for another generation or two. Winifred has bairns, you see, my grandchildren by blood if nowt else. For me, blood counts, not bits of legal paperwork.'

'And what about Trough House?' asked Pluke.

'Well, that's not mine, not since my ancestors sold it to the Featherstones.'

'Susan Featherstone, whom you knew as Miller –'

'I never met the Featherstone woman, Mr Pluke. Are you saying Susan had two names? I've allus known her as Susan Miller, the artist. I never knew she was a Featherstone. Not that it would have made any difference, not these days. What's past is past.'

'It's a long story but yes, she was really called Susan Featherstone. Her family own Trough House, or what's left of it. She wore a wig for when she was behaving as Featherstone too, when she worked at selling the paintings or came to the village.'

'Well, I'll be damned . . . I knew the Featherstones had Rowan Cottage and that the Featherstone woman sold

Susan's work, but I never set eyes on any of them, mister or missus or Susan.'

'You didn't know Susan Miller by her real name, then?'

'Nay, Mr Pluke, I did not. So far as I was concerned, she was an artist I was helping out, a lass who liked to be alone. Susan Miller. But dressing up like that . . . the things folks get up to. Why would she do that?'

'I have yet to find out, Mr Pyman, we have a lot more work to do. But Susan – and I will avoid her surname due to the confusion – Susan seems to be the last of her line, although we are trying to trace any of her relatives. I understand that the Pyman family have first option on Trough House if it is sold or comes on the market for any reason, an option to buy it back, that is.'

'Aye, we have that option, it goes back years, but who'd want it? There's nowt there, Mr Pluke, it's a poor site, nowt worth salvaging, not now the stone's all gone. I won't put a bid in for it.'

'But now Susan's dead, there could be more property. Rowan Cottage in Gunnerthwaite and Thordale House in Calderton near Wakefield, they're both Featherstone family homes.'

'Well, so far as I know, the arrangement only affected Trough House and nowt else. I've no claim on those other places, Mr Pluke, even if Rowan Cottage is built of Trough House stone. It's the site that counts.'

'And even if the blood lines of the Featherstones and Livingstones are so intermingled as to provide a possible line of inheritance? It seems Winifred's children could have the Livingstone blood as well as Pyman's, they could be the true inheritors. Having said all that, of course, properly drawn up wills can ignore any blood lines.'

'Mr Pluke, I've enough on my plate, running this set-up, and I don't want any other houses or farms or ruins or owt else. I shan't bid for Trough House if it does come up for bids and I don't need anywhere else, not at my time of life. I've no interest in the Featherstone estate. What Winifred does is up to her and her husband, he's mebbe more ambitious than me, but I reckon she'll be happy with Cragside. She liked it as a bairn. I shan't be long before I retire, Mr Pluke, I don't intend staying here till I die. I just want to see Winston looked after, that's all, he's a good lad and deserves a helping hand, nature hasn't been kind to him.'

'Thanks for talking to me. So who do you think killed Susan?'

'Not me, not Winston and not Sylvia, if that's what's in your mind. She wouldn't, would she? You can't benefit from murder, can you? Even if those houses did go to the Livingstones, through the blood line, they'd have to go to Sylvia, she's head of that family right now. And she can't benefit from a murder, so if she killed Susan and got found out, she'd lose everything. She'd not risk owt as daft as that, Mr Pluke, not Sylvia. She's not daft, you know. You'll have to look somewhere else.'

'We'll consider all the alternatives. Thank you for your co-operation, Mr Pyman.'

'Well, if it helps catch whoever did it to Susan, I'll help all I can.'

Minutes later, with Winston and Reuben standing like two sentinels to watch them leave, they were heading back down the dale towards Sylvia Livingstone's home at Mountain Ash Cottage.

'So you think Reuben's not our man, sir? Or Winston?' said Wayne Wain. 'I must admit I think that Winston could have done it . . . he's very capable, I'd say. Did he do something to make her fall heavily? It's a pity we can't communicate with him. But if it's neither of them, it only leaves Sylvia. You think she's done it, don't you?'

'No, Wayne, I don't. But I do think she is covering up the truth, I think she knows what happened and is trying to conceal the truth from us. Both Rowan Cottage and the studio have been thoroughly cleaned. Several times, I would imagine. Sylvia's had the time and opportunity to do both – and she's had time to bury Susan.'

'So it's back to Winston, you mean? She might be protecting him?'

'Yes. If Winston killed Susan, isn't that what she'd do? She'd do anything to protect him as she has done all these years. She's had ample time to remove evidence of his guilt, especially when Reuben was away. We must talk to her.'

'She was interviewed during house-to-house enquiries, sir, by one of my teams, not by me, and she couldn't help. She denied knowing the identity of the dead woman. You're being very guarded about this, sir.'

'I am, but I want to hear Miss Livingstone's story, Wayne, without having my mind cluttered with other factors. I need to know if what she tells us is feasible and true, so I must let her tell me what happened, then I can make a judgement about the veracity of her story. I am sure she knows everything.'

'So what makes you think she'll talk to us now? She's kept things to herself so far.'

'The difference is that *we* now know who the dead person is, Wayne, and we know of Susan's deception. With that in the open, what else is there to hide?'

'A murder and a murderer, sir?'

'Or a very unfortunate accidental death, Wayne.'

'Accidental? You mean this might not be murder?'

'The garland would indicate that. And those chrysanthemums. But come along, let's see what Miss Livingstone can tell us.'

When they arrived at her delightful stone cottage, Sylvia was in the garden, tending borders rich with chrysanthemums and Michaelmas daisies. She looked slightly nervous as Pluke opened her garden gate, but invited them to join her on some seats in the garden. The garden, bathed in autumn sunshine, enjoyed panoramic views along the banks of the gill which ran behind the cottage.

'A nice place,' commented Wayne Wain as he closed the gate.

'I like it here,' she said. 'It's not mine, it belongs to Reuben Pyman, it used to be the hind's cottage for Cragside, but he lets me use it, it's mine for life.'

'He seems a nice man,' said Pluke. 'Generous and kind, solid and dependable.'

'He is,' she nodded. 'He's been wonderful to Winston . . .'

The expression on her face told them she was wondering why they had arrived but that same expression revealed something of her concern. She knows why we are here, thought Pluke as he settled on the garden seat.

'We'd like to talk to you about the lady in Devil's Dump,' Pluke began.

'You think it's Susan,' she whispered. 'From Rowan Cottage.'

'Yes, but there is an artist who rents a barn from Mr Pyman . . .'

'I know the barn, yes, Susan Miller, I've seen her there. I go there, you know, to Cragside, helping Reuben, washing and cooking and cleaning and things.'

'Susan Miller and Susan Featherstone are the same person, Miss Livingstone.' Pluke spoke quietly while observing every reaction on her face. 'But from our earlier conversation, I am led to suppose you already know that.'

She did not reply immediately, but hung her head and allowed a huge sigh to issue from her ample body. 'Yes, I've known a long time but I promised Susan I'd never tell anyone, never reveal her secret. She regarded me as a friend, Mr Pluke, she told me all sorts. She loved Rowan Cottage and came whenever she could. I would spend hours with her, talking, just being friendly. She had no one else, no family. I was her best friend, she often said that. And now she's dead . . . It's dreadful, Mr Pluke, really dreadful. Such a waste of a good and lovely woman.'

'Can you tell us why she dressed up like that? Two names, two different personalities?' asked Wayne, speaking with surprising gentleness. 'The wigs, the two lifestyles, the deception . . .'

'She had a very unhappy life, as a child and young woman.' Sylvia's eyes were moist. 'Her father ruled her rigidly, he was terrible. She always wanted to be an artist

229

and he refused to let her, he wouldn't let her go to art college or night classes . . . He wanted her to enter the professions, to be a solicitor or doctor or something a bit classy. She worked in a gallery for a time and that's how she got the idea of working with paintings, she knew how artists got their work into exhibitions and displayed for sale. Unknown to her parents, though, she was working as an artist and selling her work – she used the name Susan Miller and dressed up to look different. She deceived them, Mr Pluke, all those years. They never knew she was a popular artist. She continued with the deception after they died, she was already well established and just kept up the pretence. She saw no reason to change. She was so happy doing that, just dressed in old clothes and sitting on the moors, painting . . . She hated her father, Mr Pluke. Maybe I don't have to spell out the reason but she always said she'd never have anything to do with men. She never did. And she had researched her family background, Mr Pluke, she had no wish to perpetuate the Featherstone dynasty. Marriage was not for her. She knew all about the tangled relationships between our two families, she'd done a lot of research into family trees and once said me and her were practically cousins – and the last in our lines – except for Winston and Winifred, my twins. I have a clever daughter, you know.'

'I know,' said Pluke, adding, 'And I know the identity of their father.'

'I guessed you wouldn't be long finding things out, there's not many secrets in this dale even if Susan managed to keep her own secrets. And I should tell you that Susan left her houses and estate to Winifred and Winston, to share if they want, to sell the houses if they don't want them. She said she was going to leave it all to me but I said no, I didn't want it, not at my stage of life. I have everything I need. I thought you should know this, Mr Pluke, in view of what's happened.'

'It is an aspect I would have researched, Miss Livingstone, so thank you for telling me. I did guess so, I ought to say, and I do know about the relationship between your

230

families. But after all, this was Susan's secret retreat, this area along with her studio at Cragside. And it is the home of her ancestors.'

'Yes, but her parents never knew about the studio, or her Miller name, although she did let them know she was an agent for artists, selling their work. I think they approved of that, perhaps not entirely. When they died, she had a new lease of life, Mr Pluke, she was so happy, she had money and freedom . . . and now this.'

Pluke did not speak for a long time, allowing Miss Livingstone to breathe heavily and deeply as she struggled with whatever was going through her mind. Then he said, 'Miss Livingstone. I must ask you this. Do you know what happened to Susan Featherstone?'

She did not respond but sat on the bench, gazing at the ground at her feet, and Pluke saw she was weeping silently. He waited patiently; Wayne looked at him for guidance but Pluke shook his head, as if to say, 'Wait.'

For what seemed an eternity, no one spoke, then Pluke said, 'Miss Livingstone, I think you put the maiden's garland in her grave. Would you like to tell us about it?'

'She was fascinated by those garlands, Mr Pluke, she wanted to paint them and always said that if she died, she would qualify for one. She used to laugh about that, saying she was an old spinster, a true maiden, and said she'd love to be buried with one of those garlands. One of her ancestors was the last person to have a maiden's garland, you know. Cissie, the girl who was drowned in Devil's Dump. She wanted to maintain the tradition. She was very romantic, Mr Pluke, Susan I mean, she loved all the lore and mystery of these moors.'

'So you placed one in her grave?'

She nodded, the tears coursing down her cheeks.

'Tell me what happened.' Pluke spoke with surprising gentleness. 'You must tell me, Miss Livingstone.'

'Winston didn't kill her, you must believe me, Mr Pluke. I was just trying to protect him . . .'

Speaking through her tears she told them that when Reuben had gone to the All-Yorkshire Agricultural Show, she had stayed at Cragside overnight on Monday night, for an early start next day, and overnight on Tuesday, to look after the livestock with Winston's help. It was something she did every year, it let Reuben have a short holiday – and by staying at Cragside, it allowed Winston to work as normal, albeit under her guidance.

It was something they both enjoyed. It had been a Tuesday, the day she would normally have been there, and sometime during the mid-morning Winston had come rushing to her, crying. It was about eleven and she was in the house, preparing their midday meal. She'd set him on clearing out ditches between the farm and Susan's studio. Whenever Susan saw Winston working near the barn, she'd invite him in for a drink of tea or coffee or something cool in summer. She liked Winston and he liked her, they were friends, and Reuben was content to leave them alone together. Susan could understand Winston and, in turn, he regarded her as his friend – perhaps his only real friend. He could walk into the studio at any time, she welcomed that. On that morning, though, because he couldn't speak, Sylvia had no idea what he was trying to tell her but realized it was something dramatic and serious, so she had hurried to the barn with him. The door was unlocked as it always was when she was living there and she found Susan lying at the foot of the ladder which led down from her bedspace. She was naked and her head had been bleeding where it had crashed on to the edge of a stone trough.

'She was dead, Mr Pluke, she was cold and stiff . . . I didn't know what to do . . . I panicked, I locked the barn and took Winston back to the farmhouse to think it over. He was crying all the time and I could not understand what he was trying to tell me, he just waved his arms a lot and shook his head. Poor Winston.'

'Did you call a doctor? Or the police?'

'No, I didn't tell anybody. I must admit I wondered if Winston had done something to her and I didn't want him blamed, especially as he can't speak up for himself . . . I thought he might get taken away or put in prison or something. Then as I thought about it, I remembered Susan had always said she wanted to be buried on the moor, under the rowans, it was her favourite place. You get a view of the whole dale from there, it's so wild and beautiful, she wasn't a Christian, she didn't want a funeral in the local church, nothing like that. She wanted to lie on her favourite moors . . . So that's what we did. Me and Winston. We had to go up to the moor to see to Reuben's sheep that day so I took a couple of spades – garden spades – and we dug the grave, under the rowans. Winston was good at it, he'd dug lots of graves for the pigs. He cried a lot, he knew it was for Susan.'

'And you buried her there?'

'Yes, later that night, in the dark. We took her up on the tractor and trailer, she was naked so I got a dress from Reuben's bedroom, I knew they were there, and we dressed her in it and buried her, decent and proper. As she would have wanted.'

'Did you revisit the grave? At any time? After the flood perhaps?'

'No, never, Mr Pluke. I had no cause, Susan wouldn't have wanted that, she didn't believe in the afterlife and all that stuff. It was all over. But I never thought the water would do what it did . . . It was dreadful . . . If I had thought it had done all that, I would have gone for a look . . .'

'So when did you place the garland on the grave?'

'Well, yes, I went back for that, nothing more. It was the next night, Wednesday. I cycled down to Gunnerthwaite from the farm, Winston came with me on his bike and went home, I daren't leave him alone on the farm. I clean the church on Wednesdays, you see, Mr Pluke, and I hooked down one of the garlands. It was the best and I popped it in my pocket, then that night, when it was dark, I cycled up to the moor and put the garland on the grave. I thought it might blow away so I broke a twig of rowan from one of the trees, scratched a deep hole and put the garland inside, then covered it up. I went back to the

233

farm and finished some work, then decided to go home. I didn't stay overnight on Wednesday.'

'And the next day, Thursday, Reuben came back?'

'Yes, he came back very early on Thursday morning, he'd gone out with some friends on the Wednesday night, at Harrogate after the show, but I never saw him. I didn't go to Cragside on Thursday, and I never told him about Susan. I made Winston understand he must not let anyone know what had happened, not even by going to visit her grave. Winston's good like that, I can tell him things, with hand signals, and he'll obey. Susan had said she was going away, up to the Yorkshire Dales to look for scenes to paint, and when she does that, she's often away for a long time and we never see her from one month end to the next. I thought Reuben would just think that she was away as usual. She'd prepared for that, emptying the fridge and so on. So I just said nothing about it, and I knew Winston couldn't. Those who knew Susan would think she'd just gone off on one of her jaunts. I knew nobody would find her up there . . .'

'So the authorities were never informed?'

'No, I didn't want anyone to know, because of Winston. I don't know anything about the rules and regulations, I didn't know what to do, except I knew she needed burying. I wanted it to be a secret so I buried her as she wanted, Mr Pluke, nothing more than that. I did tidy things away afterwards, at the studio and the house, just as I would have done anyway. Tidied up and cleared things away, cleaned up the mess as best I could. She'd already left Rowan Cottage, of course, that was empty, I had a coffee with her, then she rushed off like she does, leaving the mugs and things, and she took me with her, up to the studio, to help her pack ready for her trip to the dales. I meant to come back and finish off at Rowan Cottage but never got round to it . . . To be honest, I couldn't face the idea of going back there, not after putting her to rest like that . . .'

'And when you tidied the house and her studio, you removed her wigs and things?'

'I put them in the dustbin, Mr Pluke, along with some of her clothes. All the things she might have taken with her. I cleared up as best I could, to make it look as if she'd gone away for a long time. I made Rowan Cottage look as if she was not expected back for a time . . . the dust cart took everything away weeks ago, it was all in black plastic bin bags.'

'And her little car? The Fiat?'

'I sold it. I saw an advert in the *Gazette* from a man who wanted a little car and sold it to him, for cash. I gave him the documents, Susan kept them at the barn. I told him I was acting for Susan and put the cash into a charity she supported, for artists in need of care. She often put money there. I have the receipt if you want it.'

'I don't doubt you, Miss Livingstone, although we shall need sight of it, for our official report. But first tell me this. When I saw you at Rowan Cottage, you pretended Susan was alive and that you were preparing for her to come home.'

'I was very very frightened by then, Mr Pluke, with all those policemen about and stories of her being murdered. They said you were looking for a murderer . . . I'm no killer, Mr Pluke, and neither is Winston. I was just trying to protect him, to stop you arresting him. I had to pretend I knew nothing. Even when she'd been found in Devil's Dump and your officers came asking questions, I never thought you'd discover it was Susan, not without her wigs and clothes . . . not after being buried . . . It was dreadful, though, that floodwater doing that to her . . . it really was. If that flood hadn't happened . . .'

'So the old dress was not a ploy to make the body look as if it was from a bygone time?'

'No, Mr Pluke, not at all. I just had to find something to make her decent, especially with Winston being around . . .'

'Now, this dual identity. She must have had somewhere to change from one outfit to another, somewhere to keep her wigs and clothes. And hide her car.'

'At Rowan Cottage, Mr Pluke. It's far enough away from

people and neighbours not to be overlooked and she could keep both cars in the garage there, it's large enough. After her parents died, she got quite bold. In recent weeks she'd even walk through Gunnerthwaite in her Miller outfit, and I know she once went into the church to look at the maidens' garlands. I don't think anyone recognized her. She enjoyed that, being anonymous.'

'In some ways, a very sad story. So if neither you nor Winston killed her, how did she die?'

'That's the trouble, Mr Pluke. I don't really know. There was a point when I thought Winston might have been responsible in some way – he found her, you see, naked and I did wonder if he'd done something wrong – but she was lying face down, at the bottom of the ladder, with her head broken on that trough and she was quite dead by that time . . . Thinking about it later, I realized she'd been there a while before Winston found her, she was cold and stiff, you see. I think she fell, Mr Pluke. I think she slipped on the ladder . . . I tried to get Winston to explain, but all I got was his way of saying he'd found her like that. It is a very steep ladder, Mr Pluke, anyone could miss a step and go crashing down.'

'I agree,' he said. 'I have seen it and climbed it.'

'I know now I should have told you right away, but I thought you would think Winston had done it. As time went by, I got more and more frightened but I didn't kill her, Mr Pluke. I wouldn't, not Susan. I buried her because I thought that was the right thing to do, it was what she wanted . . . You do believe me, don't you, Mr Pluke?'

'If you had not placed that garland in the grave, Miss Livingstone, I might not have believed you. That was a sign of love and affection and knowledge of her maidenly state. Without it, we would have believed Susan had been murdered.'

She said nothing but sat and cried and cried and cried.

'We'll need a statement,' Wayne Wain whispered to Pluke.

'Later,' said Pluke, rising to his feet.

Chapter Eighteen

'So that's it,' Wayne said as they drove down the dale towards Gunnerthwaite. 'Accidental death with a somewhat unusual form of burial. Some minor breach of the burial laws or the registration of deaths? I'll get to work on a report for the coroner. But you didn't seem too happy about things, wanting to take her statement later. Normally, we strike while the iron's hot, sir.'

'I cannot see any reason to doubt Miss Livingstone's account, Wayne. It all seems perfectly logical and it fits with the scene . . . I am sure forensic evidence will support her account.'

'But you are not entirely happy?'

'I must confess I feel it all happened at a most opportune time. Susan died and was buried on the only two days in the year when Reuben Pyman would be away from the premises. She also died precisely at the time she was about to leave for an extended period, when her absence would not have caused comment or worry. And Miss Livingstone did appear very anxious to explain the business of the will, about her children being beneficiaries.'

'Rather like some killers pretending to find the body, in the hope it will make them appear innocent?'

'That kind of logic, yes, Wayne.'

'So you think there has been a very clever murder here, sir? But surely, no one could benefit from Susan's will until she had been officially declared dead, and in the event of her body not being found, that could take up to seven years.'

'Yes, there might have been a murder – but there might

not. There is no evidence either way, certainly not enough for a court of law or even the Crown Prosecution Service. Nonetheless, Wayne, there are inconsistencies in Sylvia Livingstone's story. On the one hand, she said she'd had coffee with Susan Featherstone prior to her leaving Rowan Cottage and in another account, she said Susan had rushed off and left the door unlocked. And she spoke of knowing when Susan was returning to Rowan Cottage, while at other times stressing she had no idea when Susan was going to return. Small inconsistencies, I know, but perhaps important. And don't forget Sylvia slept at Cragside overnight on the Monday before Susan was found dead by Winston – an opportunity perhaps? To do something unlawful so that Winston would find it next morning? And perhaps get the blame? Remember Sylvia did say that when Winston found the body, it was cold and stiff, clearly having been dead for some time. At least six hours, I would guess. So had Susan fallen in the dark? Been sleepwalking? Had a dizzy spell and crashed over the landing and down the ladder? And on top of all this, there is the question of the blood line . . . Don't forget that in 1821, the shepherd Joshua Featherstone was murdered – we think – by a Livingstone but that it is distinctly likely that Livingstone blood has come down the Featherstone family tree ever since. The Livingstones never had money or wealth, Wayne; now they have, thanks to Susan's death. Is there some kind of ancient justice here? Or will this convoluted story become just another in the long folklore history of Thordale?'

'So if Sylvia killed Susan, sir, she's effectively got rid of that shepherd for the second time? He'll be forgotten if there are no more pictures of him.'

'That's one way of looking at it. Perhaps she has tried to prevent more pictures that might have resurrected the whole sorry family history once more.'

'So if the flood had not occurred, sir, Sylvia Livingstone would have benefited to a great extent?'

'And the fact it has occurred also means she has benefited to a great extent,' said Pluke. 'Either a dreadful accident occurred as she said, or she is a very skilled operator. We have suspicion of both, but we have no evidence of either, Wayne. No evidence at all. So has Sylvia got away with murder? Is this another mystery death which will enter the folklore of Thordale? Only time will tell.'

As Millicent had been involved from the outset, Pluke explained it all to her over dinner that evening, concluding with, 'Out of it all, my dear, there came forth some goodness. I did find the trough of Trough House, thanks to your help, and in view of the circumstances it might be possible to restore it to its former setting but I am left with a nagging suspicion about the new mystery of Devil's Dump. I may just pay a return visit for another chat with Sylvia Livingstone. She may decide to tell me more.'

'No, Montague, you can't. You're thinking like a police officer!'

'But I *am* a police officer!'

'Yes, but throughout all this, Sylvia has been thinking like a mother, being very protective towards her vulnerable son. She's not clever like you, Montague, the moment she found Susan dead, discovered in that dreadful state by Winston, she'd wonder whether Winston had harmed her, wouldn't she? Anyone would have thought that, it's natural in a parent, more so with a young man like Winston. She's been protecting him all through this, Montague, even if she did tell a few minor untruths. From what you've told me, it's pretty obvious that Susan fell down her ladder during the night, in the darkness, and broke her skull on that trough. Doesn't it take up to six hours for rigor mortis to set in? She was stiff and cold when Sylvia reached her. Maybe her lights fused, Montague, or perhaps a bulb blew at a most critical moment. Did you test the lights in her studio?'

'Er, no, I must admit I did not . . . I overlooked that . . .'

'Shame on you, Montague Pluke, that's the first thing I would have done.'

'The power was off, but I'll ring the incident room now . . .'

He rang immediately. The duty officer checked the computer records detailing the painstaking examination of the barn and said, 'Yes, sir, the lights fused at 3.12 a.m., the oven-timer stopped at that point. It was a faulty switch, sir, at the top of the ladder she used to go up to bed. A spot of rather too amateurish workmanship, it seems.'

'Thank you,' said Pluke.

When he told Millicent, she smiled. 'Well, there you are. Now you can relax, Montague, I'm sure it was an accident and I am sure you're not letting a murderer evade justice.'

'I am sure you are right, my dear, I will take a statement from Miss Livingstone in due course, after she has had time to think things over. If this was nothing more than an accident, it does make me wonder whether the shepherd's death was an accident too, even if murder was suspected at the time. But we shall never know.' However, he did wonder whether Winston had paid an unwelcome nocturnal visit to Susan and terrified her . . . If he had, Sylvia would never say so. He sighed and said, 'Now, sadly, there is a downside to these events – one other dreadful matter to consider.'

'And what is that, Montague?'

'That old coat of mine, the heirloom, the coaching coat handed down from generation to generation of worthy Plukes. It might be a fake, Millicent. I must begin immediate enquiries into its provenance.'